THE DARKEST WALK OF CRIME

Malcolm Archibald

For Cathy

Published by Fledgling Press 2011
www.fledglingpress.co.uk
Printed and bound by:
Martins The Printers, Berwick Upon Tweed, TD15 1RS
ISBN: 9781905916313

Contents

PRELUDE

Lancashire, England: August 1847

Sir Robert Trafford pulled at his cheroot and allowed the tip to glow bright red before slowly exhaling blue smoke above the heads of his companions. They watched him carefully, their expressionless faces hiding the rapacity of hunting hounds. Eventually one spoke.

"Are you going to play?"

"I will play when I am ready." Sir Robert eyed the pile of money and promissory notes occupying the centre of the table. He smiled, lifted the glass of brandy that stood at his elbow and drained it in a single swallow.

Standing at his shoulder, a slender woman pressed against him as she glanced at his cards. When he ignored her, she pouted and walked to the fireplace, emphasising the swing of her hips so the rustle of her dress competed with the low crackle of the fire in an otherwise hushed room.

"Play then, damn you!" The speaker leaned across the table, his face florid with tension and drink.

"As you wish." Sir Robert flicked the ash from his cheroot into the fireplace, then placed his cards on the table, one at a time. Every man in the room counted the numbers. Only the woman appeared unconcerned. He held the last card for an agonising moment before displaying it with a sneer.

The woman smiled as the florid man threw down his hand. The cards splayed across the smooth green baize.

"Damn you! Damn you Trafford! You've ruined me!"

The woman's laugh mocked him. "You ruin yourselves, I think, chancing all your possessions on the turn of a card." She brushed past each of the four players in turn, stopping opposite Sir Robert.

He looked up, smoothing a hand over his unfashionably long hair.

"What is life without adventure? The fun of the game is being prepared to risk everything, or gain nothing." Scooping up the pile of money and documents from the centre of the table, he lifted his eyebrows. "These are all mine, I believe?" He rose from his seat and paced the length of the room, stopping only to pour himself another glass of brandy from the crystal decanter on the sideboard.

"Without adventure, Sir Robert, there is no life." The woman did not conceal her interest as she allowed her hand to momentarily rest on his arm while her eyes roamed slowly from his face to his feet.

"Will you at least give us the chance to win something back?" the florid man asked. He followed Sir Robert to the sideboard, sloshing brandy into an empty glass.

"No." He was dismissed with a shrug. "What can you possibly have that I should want? I already own everything you ever had."

The third man looked up and spoke slowly, "I believe you may be mistaken, Sir Robert. I have something you desire."

Sir Robert halted under the great chandelier so the light played on the glossy mane of his hair. "And what might that be, Sir Henry?"

"He has me," the woman said simply.

"I can have any number of women," Sir Robert told her.

"You can have any number of bobtails, bunters and hell-cats," the woman corrected his statement, "but not a high flier like me."

Sir Henry laughed then, the sound harsh in the warm room, until Sir Robert fixed him with a venomous stare.

"She has you there, Sir Robert," the florid man said. "You're a ladies' man of note, but your reputation precedes you. No lady of *quality* would touch you, by God!"

"Oh, I would do more than touch him," the woman said, "but only if he proves himself worthy."

She stroked his arm with a gloved hand. Sir Henry smiled while the fourth man, tall, whiskered, and erect as a guardsman, merely looked bored.

"Sir Robert has already won this evening," he said. "There is no need for him to gamble further." He looked over to the woman and smiled coldly. "Besides which, perhaps he is not quite as willing to risk all as he says he is."

Sir Robert might have ignored the challenge, had the florid man not laughed. The sound was short and ugly.

"Not willing?" Sir Robert banged the decanter down on the polished walnut, his voice a whisper. "By God, I'm always willing. Make your wager, Sir Henry. What must I chance to gain your daughter?"

Sir Henry looked at the woman and smiled. "What should we say, my dear? What are you worth?"

"The question is not what I am worth, Father, but rather what value does Sir Robert put on his word?" She swayed over to Sir Robert and leaned against him. "Would you risk everything, as you said?"

The atmosphere in the room changed as everybody looked at Sir Robert. While the florid man was openly triumphant, Sir Henry appeared merely curious, and the whiskered man swirled brandy around his glass.

"Well, Sir Robert?" The woman stepped back, smiling. "*I'm* sure that you are man enough to keep your word," she hesitated coyly, "but some of these gentlemen are less certain."

"Damn it!" Sir Robert's laugh was explosive. "Shall we have another hand, gentlemen?"

"Let's make it simpler," Sir Henry suggested. "Let us have a straight cut of the cards; if you win, my daughter is yours. If you lose, I have all your winnings and the value of your property in hard currency."

"You drive a hard bargain, Sir Henry," Sir Robert said.

"Am I not worth it?" Widening her eyes, the woman allowed her hand to drift across Sir Robert's shoulder.

Sir Robert drained and refilled his glass. "I will have to find out," he said, handing the cards over to the tall, whiskered figure of the Duke of Maldon. "The game's the thing . . ." "The game's the thing. Shuffle the cards, Your Grace, and let fate decide."

They sat around the table, with the chandelier casting wavering shadows and the woman watching over her father's shoulder. The Duke shuffled slowly, building up the tension before he handed the pack over to Sir Henry.

"I would be obliged, sir, if you would care to cut first?"

There was a second's pause as Sir Henry accepted the cards. "My dear, your future is in my hands." He winked at his daughter and cut quickly, placing the top card face down in front of him before sliding the pack over to Sir Robert.

"And it soon will be in mine." Sir Robert divided the cards and selected one.

"Turn over your cards on the count of three, gentlemen," His Grace said, and slowly counted. "One . . . two . . . three."

The hiss of a piece of coal shifting in the fireplace was the only sound until Sir Robert flicked over his card. The hooded eyes of a king stared sightlessly upward as he breathed out slowly and looked up in triumph.

"King of spades, by God," he gloated and extended a hand to the woman. "Come here, my dear. I believe you are now my property."

"Not so fast with my daughter, sir." Sir Henry paused, still holding his card. He turned it slowly, grunted, and looked to His Grace. "Well now, there's a pickle. What the devil do we do now?"

The card was the king of hearts; there was no winner.

The Duke decided for them: "You have both won, so the solution is obvious. Sir Henry gains the value of Trafford's property and his previous winnings, and Sir Robert gets Sir Henry's daughter."

"You'll give me time to raise the readies, of course?" Sir Robert accepted the decision with equanimity.

"You may have three months," Sir Henry told him, rising from the table. "I leave you with my daughter, sir. Good day to you." He left the room without a backward glance, followed by the florid man.

Sir Robert was quiet for a long moment, and then he looked up at the woman.

"Winning you has impoverished me," he said quietly and poured out more brandy. He emptied the glass in a single swallow and refilled it quickly before making an ironic salute to the closed door. "I hope you are worth the price, my dear."

"You'll find that I am worth every penny," she told him evenly. "I have a rich uncle, you see, and he would hate to see his niece live in penury."

"Indeed?" Sir Robert passed a glass toward her as the Duke silently watched.

"Of course, he will require a favour in return." The woman took his arm, smiling. "I fear that we must walk a darker path for a while, Sir Robert."

CHAPTER ONE

London: November 1847

"Ready?" Sergeant Restiaux blinked the drizzle from his eyes and looked upwards to where drab dawn cracked open the terrible dark of a London night. 'Pray to God that we don't get lost today, lads.'

"I thought you knew this place like the back of your hand?" Constable Mendick nodded towards the ugly morass of the Holy Land, whose foul stenches only enhanced the feral reputation of the inhabitants.

"As well as any man on this side of the law," Restiaux agreed and quickly qualified his statement, "Well enough to have no desire to linger." He lifted a black-gloved hand. "Listen."

Mendick heard the chimes of St Giles, an oxymoron of hope beside the seething slum that crowded its walls. Unconsciously, he counted out loud, feeling the familiar hollowness in his stomach, "Four, five . . ."

Restiaux nodded and slowly intoned the old words, "Lord, I shall be very busy this day; I may forget thee, but do not forget me." He exaggerated his wink. "These are good words to remember at times like these." He turned to the silent man who stood at the back. "What do you think, Foster?"

Foster nodded. "Anything that helps is worthwhile."

The only man among them who did not wear the blue uniform of the police; he straightened his arm and brandished the blackjack he carried in lieu of a truncheon. The foot-long sausage of reinforced linen was weighted with sand and tipped with solid lead.

"Now, I've chased this man to Manchester and back, so let's make sure that he doesn't escape this time."

"We'll do our best." Restiaux lifted his head as St Giles clattered its final message. "Seven o'clock. And in we go!"

Raising his voice to a yell, he rose from the shelter of the scarred brick wall. For a second he was silhouetted against a candlelit window, his prominent nose verifying the French ancestry his name suggested, and then he was moving forward, head up, booted feet splashing through the unthinkable filth on the ground.

The two constables followed, checking that their long staffs were secure in their pockets and directing the beam of their bull's-eye lanterns to illuminate Restiaux's path. The lights jinked over walls weeping tears of dirt, passed windows blank with despair and settled on a repellent door.

"God knows what depravity is hiding behind that," Restiaux muttered. Mendick sighed. Was this what his life was reduced to? Crawling about in the dark chasing insignificant criminals through the back slums? Surely all those hours poring over books as he painfully learned to read and write must have had more purpose.

"Keep the light steady there!" Constable Williamson slammed himself against the wall beside the door, waiting for Restiaux to take the lead and Foster, the Scotland Yard detective, to follow.

Restiaux lifted his foot. “No point in knocking politely,” he explained, “not in the Holy Land.” He smashed his massive boot against the bottom panel, which shook but held so he kicked again, putting his entire weight behind the blow. Candles began to flicker in the adjoining windows.

“The Holy Land is awakening,” Mendick warned.

Dogs began to bark, their racket echoing in the crooked street.

“For Christ’s sake, boot that bloody door in!” Foster looked around in some apprehension; nobody wanted to linger in the Holy Ground.

Taking a step back, Restiaux tried again, this time grunting with satisfaction as the wood splintered. “That’s it! Light!”

Mendick’s lantern illuminated the panel, and in a series of short, savage kicks, Restiaux created a jagged hole. Kneeling, he thrust his arm through and withdrew an iron bolt.

“Stand aside, sergeant!” Williamson pushed past, staff in hand.

“Be careful, you young blockhead!” Restiaux warned, but Williamson clattered ahead, his boots echoing on a flight of stone steps that led downward to a black abyss. The stench of dampness and human waste rose to greet them. Restiaux shook his head.

“Shine that light just ahead of me, Mendick, and don’t stray. God alone knows what’s down here.” He produced a pistol from his pocket. With its four inch barrel and wide muzzle, the weapon would be deadly at close range. “This barker has a three quarter inch bore, so it can stop an elephant dead, but let’s hope we don’t need it.” With the pistol held in his right hand, he began the descent.

"Blake's the most efficient forger you'll never want to meet," Foster said quietly, "but I need him alive, not face up in a coffin." He glowered at Restiaux. "He's far too valuable."

"So are my men," Restiaux said bluntly. "So if he is a threat to any of us, I won't hesitate to shoot him." Turning his back on the detective, he nodded to Mendick. "Ready?"

"Aye." Mendick looked into the darkness ahead. He did not feel ready, but did it really matter?

The lantern light picked out crumbling stone steps descending through darkness into a stink that seemed so tangible it could be cut up and packaged. There was a loud cry ahead, a hollow shout that echoed for agonisingly long seconds.

"Williamson!" Restiaux yelled, but there was only the sound of scurrying footsteps, followed by solid silence.

"What the hell's happening?" Foster sounded alarmed as he tapped the blackjack against the wall. He peered narrow-eyed down the steps.

"Williamson!" Restiaux called again, but the empty echo mocked him. He lowered his voice. "It looks like there's trouble ahead; have you anything more lethal than your staff?"

"Yes, Sergeant." Mendick patted his shoulder holster, where his pistol nestled uncomfortably but reassuringly against his breast. Emma had never been happy with his choice of profession, but she had insisted that he should at least be prepared for trouble.

Restiaux nodded. "After me then, and don't worry about taking Blake alive." He ignored Foster's savage glare.

Testing each step, they negotiated the remaining twenty stairs with the light flickering and bouncing from chipped stone and crumbling mortar.

"What's that?" Foster pointed to a darker shadow ahead.

"It's Williamson."

The constable lay crumpled across the bottom step, blood oozing from a ragged wound in his scalp. Beyond him, faint light flickered and coarse voices grumbled from behind a closed door.

"I told him to wait!" Kneeling at Williamson's side, Restiaux checked his pulse. "He's alive, thank God." He glanced at the door, and grunted. "Spring your rattle."

Hauling the rattle from his inside pocket, Mendick swung it around his head. The spring pressed a wooden tongue against a ratchet wheel, creating a distinctive sound that would immediately summon all available police constables.

"Christ, man, that noise will warn anybody for half a mile." Foster looked behind him to the cruelly crowding dark.

"That's the idea. Now, follow closely and mind your backs!" Restiaux poised himself then kicked open the door and rushed through, his pistol levelled in front of him.

From the darkness of the stairway they rushed into a scene of which Dante would have been proud. Lit by the guttering remains of three candles, a mass of human bodies covered the floor of a low room and piled onto a grease-darkened bench. There were men and women of all ages from twelve to sixty, some whitely naked, others clad in itching rags and one in the remains of a clerical suit. Some were stirring, rising from torpidity to suspicion as they struggled to see who had entered, but others merely glanced up and returned to the anonymity of the mass.

"He's not here," Foster said at once and prepared to move on, but Restiaux placed a heavy hand on his shoulder.

"Wait. Somebody will know," he advised, and raised his voice: "We're looking for Thomas Blake!"

Mendick flashed the lantern across the chaos, catching a poisonous eye, a scarred back, a tangled mess of lousy hair or the slender curve of breast or buttock.

"Who?" the man in the suit asked, blinking as the light focussed on his face.

"Flash Tom," Restiaux said. "You know him."

When the man shook his head, Restiaux sighed. "Remind him, Constable."

"Yes, Sergeant." Pulling his staff from its pocket, Mendick stepped forward, ignoring the squeal as his nailed boot thumped on the leg of a teenage draggletail.

"No!" The clerk cowered backward, seeking sanctuary from companions who seemed only too eager to allow him all the attention of the police. "I don't know him at all!"

"I'm afraid I don't believe you." Mendick pressed the rounded edge of his staff, with the VR lettering in faded gold, hard against the clerk's chin. "Where is Thomas Blake?"

"I don't know," the clerk said, but for a second his eyes flickered toward a door at the far end of the room.

"Thank you," Mendick kept his voice dry as he stepped over the cleric. "This way, Sergeant. You too, Sergeant Foster, if you will." He treated the Scotland Yard detective with cautious respect.

"I hope Flash Tom kills you both." Covering herself with what looked like a handful of rags, a woman pointed a long-nailed finger at Mendick. "I hope you die squealing, you Peeler bastard."

"If there is any trouble from you or anybody else in this room," Restiaux told her quietly, "you'll be in the Bower before this day's finished."

The woman closed her mouth and sat down with a thump, her eyes screaming hatred.

"Right, Constable, lead on." Foster glanced over his shoulder as a cacophony of curses came from the room behind them. "Christ but I hate this job."

They plunged through the door into a short passage, scented with sewage and punctured with three dark openings.

"Which one?" Mendick allowed the beam of the lantern to linger over each doorway in turn.

"The nearest," Restiaux said and barged in the door. They thundered into another room reeking of human misery as huddled children stared up from their rags. One boy, his eyes ancient and evil as Hades, spat at them. The next room held more filth, more destitute people, more sorrow, but no Thomas Blake.

"We're wasting time." Foster sounded worried.

Restiaux shoved the last door. "Locked," he said laconically, and again resorted to his boot. The door shuddered once, twice, and finally gave with a mighty crash. The lantern probed ahead, revealing more steps, spiralling upward.

Foster swore foully. "This place is a maze."

"Tom! Tom Blake!" Restiaux's shout echoed endlessly in the dark. Feeling his way with care, he began the ascent, pistol held ready to fire. Mendick followed, aware of the clinging dankness and the sudden alteration in atmosphere. The foetid stench had metamorphosed into something much worse. He could sense danger, as if unformed evil was hovering above.

"He's up there," he whispered, touching the butt of his pistol. Years of experience in the back slums of London had heightened him to the importance of instinct. If he felt that something was wrong, then something *was* wrong.

Restiaux nodded. "I know."

Restiaux was the expert on the Holy Land. He knew every slithering alley, every crumbling building, every half-human denizen of the ten rat-run acres that huddled between the soaring spire of St Giles and the bulk of St George's church in Bloomsbury. The name Holy Land was a mockery, taken from the proximity of the churches, but although there were worse rookeries in London, there were few that gave such easy access to the more privileged areas of Leicester Square, Regent Street and the Haymarket. For that reason, the Holy Land was a thieves' paradise, a devil's playground of the downtrodden and the vicious, a Satan's sanctuary for the pickpockets and cockchafers, the coves, cracksmen and queer dealers who scraped a dishonest living by robbing their betters.

"Jesus!" Foster glanced over his shoulder as somebody unleashed a laugh fit for bedlam. "Please God I live to see my retirement and a pension."

The steps ended at a brick wall pierced by a ragged hole through which a man might just be able to squeeze. A draught edged aside a fraction of the stench.

"Bastard's escaped again!" Foster kicked the wall with his iron-studded boot.

"Lantern," Restiaux ordered, and Mendick bent forward, one hand holding his pot hat in place. The light probed the hole and vanished into the unknown beyond.

"After me, I think; this is my parish." Pushing him gently aside, Restiaux took a deep breath and thrust his head and shoulders through the hole.

The sound of the shot was very loud in the confined space, and he yelled and fell back cursing.

"Sergeant!" Mendick saw blood on Restiaux's face. "Are you all right?"

Restiaux nodded but suddenly paled and slid downward until he was sitting with his back to the wall.

"Douse the glim," he said, and Mendick pulled the metal shutter across the lantern. The sudden darkness pressed down on them, thick with menace.

Another shot cracked out, the bullet bouncing from the brick wall behind them and ricocheting dangerously around their ears. Mendick swore, ducking down, as Restiaux flinched and covered his head with his arm.

"Tom!" Foster shouted, keeping back from the hole in the wall. "It's me, Foster of the Yard. I have other police officers with me. Better come out quiet now."

"Bugger you, bluebottle bastards! Did I kill Restie?" The voice was surprisingly high-pitched.

"No," Mendick said. "It's not the rope yet, Tom. You'll just get a spell in limbo or maybe a free voyage across the pond."

"Twenty-one years I'll get, Peeler, twenty-one years of transportation, slaving under the lash in Van Diemen's Land. Better the rope than that." He fired again; the shot splintered the bricks opposite the hole. Dust drifted over Restiaux, who coughed and wiped away the blood that trickled down the line of his jaw.

Keeping his head back from the hole, Mendick eased open the shutter of his lantern to examine the residue left by the bullet. “Half-inch calibre lead ball,” he said, “and judging by the gap between the shots, he probably has a single-barrelled pistol.” He raised his voice, taunting. “You’re trapped, Tom, there’s no escape.”

“Then I’ll die game, Peeler!”

The pistol cracked again; the ball ripped past Mendick's face. Choking white smoke surged through the hole. Mendick cocked his pistol and raised his eyebrows toward Restiaux.

Standing flat against the wall, Foster shook his head. “I want him alive,” he reminded. “I have a particular task for Flash Tom, so a corpse is no use to me.”

“We’ll try to keep Blake alive,” Restiaux assured him. “There are forty seconds between each shot, Mendick, and you’re about the most active officer in the force.” He jerked a thumb toward the hole. “Could you do it?”

Mendick’s shrug was genuine. “I can try,” he said, “but not in this hat. Do I have your permission to discard it, Sergeant?”

Restiaux smiled weakly. “Just make sure you protect your head.” He put a hand to his head. The blood now covered the left side of his face and dripped onto his broad leather stock.

The rabbit skin hat weighed eighteen ounces and was intended as protection against an assailant’s cosh, but in this confined space it was only an encumbrance. As an afterthought Mendick shrugged off his swallowtail coat which would catch on every jagged brick. Taking deep breaths, he crouched at the side of the hole as Foster hugged the wall. The detective swore softly.

“Are you Peeler bastards still there?” Tom fired on the last word. As soon as the pistol sounded, Mendick threw himself into the hole, kicking madly in an attempt to gain momentum. The wall was thicker than he had expected, and rough brick scraped the flesh from his outstretched hands as he frantically hauled himself through. He had forty seconds to reach the screever before Flash Tom finished reloading. Forty seconds between life and possible death: how long had he already been?

Did it really matter? He hesitated, embracing death for a fraction of a second, but duty forced him onwards. Peering into the darkness, he glimpsed a bearded white face and the blurred hands of somebody urgently working the ramrod of a pistol. The man looked up, his eyes vicious above a rainbow waistcoat. Mendick scrabbled with his feet, seeking purchase, as Flash Tom withdrew the ramrod and stepped backward into the dark. There was a solid click as he cocked the hammer.

"Peeler bastard!" The words were followed by a torrent of foul vituperation that echoed repulsively around the dark chamber.

Mendick flinched; with his head and upper body protruding from the hole, he was hideously vulnerable. "It won't do, Tom. If you shoot me, it will be the gallows. Think, man."

"Gallows or not, bluebottle, you're a dead man." Extending his arm to aim, Tom pressed the trigger just as Restiaux gave Mendick a final push that propelled him through the hole. He gasped as burning powder from the muzzle of the pistol filled the air, but the ball screamed wide and smashed into crumbling brick. Coughing with the reek of shrouding smoke, he instinctively rolled away, but Flash Tom did not attack.

Jerking upright, he glanced around, grateful for the beam of light that Restiaux directed through the hole.

He was in a small chamber with an arched brick roof and walls smeared with flaking white plaster. A small stove emitted residual warmth, while the pot on top still contained the congealed metal that was the raw material of the coining trade. Half a dozen spoons lay scattered on the ground, together with a number of tools, a pile of documents and a variety of pens and bottles of ink. It was obvious that a master forger worked here. There was no sign of Blake, but there was a small opening in the far corner.

"Sergeant," Mendick called through, "the bird's flown. I'm going to follow."

"Don't be a fool, man," Restiaux ordered, but there was no strength in his voice. "You can't wander around the Holy Land on your own."

"There's no choice, Sergeant. We can't let him escape now."

Before Restiaux adjusted his advice into an order, Mendick crouched at the opening through which Flash Tom had escaped. Taking a deep breath, he plunged in, to find himself at the top of half-rotted wooden steps descending to a square courtyard piled high with human filth. There was a single exit between two buildings, so narrow he had to squeeze through sideways, emerging into a crooked street of misshapen houses. The dirty light of dawn did nothing to alleviate the dismal appearance of soot-smeared walls, stagnant filth-spilling gutters and shuffling, dull-eyed people. Mendick did not hesitate.

"Police!" he roared. "Stand aside!"

One or two edged aside as he splashed through the street, but others made to block his path. He barged them aside, their underfed bodies fragile before his weight. There was movement ahead, a glimpse of a rainbow waistcoat as Flash Tom briefly turned, eyes bright with malice, before sliding into another narrow alley.

"Blake! Tom! It's no good, man!"

Slithering on human filth, he eased into the alley, slipped sideways and tottered for a second, swearing as he realised he had walked into a trap.

"Badgered, by God!"

He stood at the edge of a deep cesspit, straddled only by a single greasy plank. Beyond the pit, Blake stood with his arm extended and his pistol levelled directly at his face.

"Bye, bye, bluebottle."

As Blake pulled the trigger, Mendick ducked, put his boot under the edge of the plank and heaved upward. Heavy with moisture, the timber did not travel far, but it made enough contact with Blake's shin to distract him so his hand jerked aside.

"Jesus!"

The crack of the pistol echoed around the alley, but the bullet flew wide, flattening harmlessly against the wall.

It was a four-foot standing jump over the cesspit, but with no other choice Mendick leapt, pushing himself onwards with sideways pressure on the wall, and landed just as Blake threw his pistol and turned to run.

"It's a dead end, Tom!"

Without looking back, Blake scrabbled up the broken brickwork of the wall, finding purchase on the ledges of windows and swearing frantically as rotted wood crumbled under his feet.

"Bye, Peeler!"

Ignoring the crowd that had gathered to roar Blake on, Mendick searched for handholds to follow the forger. His fingers slithered across damp bricks, but his childhood as a climbing-boy, a chimney-sweep's apprentice, stood him in good stead, and he followed quickly as Blake raced upwards and sideways.

"Nobody climbs that fast," he muttered until he realised there was a series of iron spikes cunningly set in the brickwork. He grunted; anywhere a screever could climb, he could follow.

The spikes were old and partly rusted through, but he had to trust them, pulling himself across the wall only a few yards behind Blake.

Pausing at an upper window, Blake glanced back, his breath clouding around his head like smoke from some infernal demon. Spitting contemptuously downwards, he hauled himself onto the roof.

"Here! Catch this!" The first of the slates missed Mendick by an inch, the second bounced from a window ledge to splinter on the ground below, and the third crashed onto his right shoulder.

He flinched at the shock, and his right hand slipped so he hung one-handed with that appalling drop sucking at him. Below, the crowd was baying for his life.

"Die, you Peeler bastard!" Another slate hurtled down, turning edge over edge before it splashed into the dung heap below.

With his entire weight dragging agonisingly on his left shoulder, Mendick swung himself against the wall, scrabbling for purchase. He gasped with relief when he found the spike and clung motionless for a second. He sensed the disappointment from the crowd as he dragged himself up and over the gutter onto the roof.

Dawn's early grey had changed to an arterial red that highlighted the skyline of spires and towers marking the greatest city in the world. Mendick surveyed the litter of uneven rooftops that lay before him. Blake skidded on damp slates before ducking behind a crazy chimney-breast twenty yards ahead. He followed, balancing his feet either side of the cracked ridge of the roof. When Blake glanced back, the slanting sun caught him, momentarily glittering on narrow eyes in an anxious face.

"You're a persistent bugger, peeler, whatever else you are."

Gathering his strength, Mendick leapt the gap between two buildings, felt his boots scrape down the slates and reached down for balance just as Blake turned to descend another ladder of spikes. Mendick followed Blake through an open window into a small room where semi-naked women howled abuse. The building smelled of damp and human excreta, but Blake was only a few yards ahead, thrusting at a door that led outside.

"Hold the bluebottle, girls!" Blake roared, and the human detritus swarmed to obey.

"Police!"

Mendick tried to defend himself from a score of filthy hands. The room seemed full of women, all talons and bile as they raked at his face and grabbed hungrily for his genitals. One was screaming, her voice rising to a maniacal screech.

Reaching for his pistol, he pointed it upward and fired. The shot reverberated around the room and brought down a shower of plaster from the ceiling.

"He's got a gun! The bastard will kill us all!"

The women backed off, some howling in vitriolic frustration, others gesticulating and promising obscene revenge. Mendick pushed through the door just as Blake disappeared over a stone wall into a neighbouring timber yard.

The wall was easy to scale, but as Mendick dropped down, Blake was twenty yards ahead and easing through the yard gate; outside waited a dark four-wheeler. Cursing, Mendick stumbled past piles of neatly stacked timber. As he reached the gate, Restiaux nodded calmly to him through the open window of the coach. Blood stained the bandage that swathed his head.

"Glad to see you kept up; you drove Blake to me very adequately."

"You have him?" Mendick leaned against the wheel of the coach, only now aware that his breath grated in his chest and that his legs and shoulder throbbed with pain.

Restiaux nodded. "I knew he would run and that you would not give up. Over the roof and through the brothel is a recognised escape from the Holy Land, so it did not take much to have the four-wheeler waiting." His grin faded slightly. "In you come. You'll have to pay for the damage to your uniform, of course."

"Of course," Mendick agreed, replacing the pistol in its holster and clambering inside the cab.

His wrists secured by handcuffs, Blake glowered at him from behind the beard. "If I get the chance, Peeler, I'll kill you. That I swear." His eyes were acidic.

Sitting at Blake's side, Foster thumped a meaty hand on his shoulder. "That will not be for a very long time, Tommy Flash. You and I have work to do."

CHAPTER TWO

London: November 1847

Although the single window was closed, the grumble of carriage wheels from Whitehall intruded into the room, combating the crackle of the fire. Above the heads of the people present, the brass chandelier swung slowly, sending shadows across the portly man behind the desk.

"So, Constable," the portly man leaned back in his leather chair, small eyes shrewd as he slid them over Mendick. "I heard that you did well in the Blake case." He tapped his fingers on the desk.

"Thank you, sir." Mendick remained at attention, his top hat under his arm and his face immobile. He was well aware that Inspector Field headed the small group of plain-clothes detectives at Scotland Yard but was unsure of the identity of the man who sat silently against the far wall.

"Sergeant Restiaux informed me that you followed Blake even after he fired at you, through one of the worst rookeries in London." Field shook a shaggy head. "Why, even Detective Foster praised you, and he's not the most enthusiastic of officers."

Mendick said nothing. Foster was the first Scotland Yard detective he had met, and he had been vaguely disappointed. Rather than a dashing man capable of instant decisions, Foster had seemed hesitant, cynical and unenthusiastic.

"Sergeant Restiaux was quick to inform me that you are a constantly persistent constable," Field said, "and I am also aware that you have twice applied for a transfer to the detective division at Scotland Yard."

"Indeed, sir." There was no need to remind the inspector that both his applications had been curtly rejected.

"It was considered that you lacked the necessary experience," Field explained. He looked up suddenly and leaned forward. "Are you still interested in such a position?" There was steel behind the apparent benignity of his eyes.

"I am, sir." Mendick fought to control his enthusiasm, reminding himself he was a disciplined constable, not some flighty youth.

"I see." Field leaned back again, pressing his forefinger against the arm of his chair, a gesture familiar to all who knew him. "You are aware that the detective branch is the most unpopular in London?"

"I am, sir." Many of the population still resented the uniformed police and were even more suspicious of plain-clothes detectives. To the British public, there was something almost continental about having such spies creeping around the streets.

"And yet you are willing to court such unpopularity?"

"Yes, sir. I have some experience as an active officer." Each division of the London police deployed a small number of men in civilian clothes, known as active officers. Mendick had enjoyed two spells on such a duty.

"I am aware of that, constable." The podgy forefinger stabbed again. "As I am aware of your five years experience in police uniform and the ten years you spent in the army before that."

Again Mendick lapsed into silence. There was probably very little of which Inspector Field was unaware.

Having established the superiority of his knowledge, Field was prepared to be magnanimous. He leaned back again. "I remain unsure if you are quite suitable to be a detective, although I know of your many fine qualities. However, a situation has arisen in the North and Detective Sergeant Foster has persuaded me you might be useful after all."

"Yes, sir." Mendick could hardly believe what Field had just said. He was about to be transferred to Scotland Yard; his opinion of Detective Foster rose tremendously. He kept any emotion hidden; ten years in the army had taught him that every silver lining concealed a dark grey cloud.

"Well now, Constable, I trust that you are pleased with your good fortune?" Inspector Field waited until Mendick assented. "But you will no doubt be wondering to what special circumstances I am referring and who this gentleman is?" He indicated the silent man at the end of the room. "Let me bring enlightenment to the darkness within your mind. Pray join us, Mr Smith, if you would be so kind?"

At first Mendick thought there was something familiar about the man who eased into the circle of warmth by the fire and placed his leather valise at the side of the desk, but a second glance assured him that he was mistaken. He would never have forgotten a face such as that. The eyes alone were memorable, calm as a summer sea, yet with an indefinable quality of intelligence that bored like a drill, probing, questioning, seeing everything. For some reason Mendick flinched, but nevertheless he felt his jaw thrust out in bloody-minded defiance.

"No, you do not know me." Mr Smith seemed to have read his mind. "But you may have seen me. Inspector Field told me about you a while ago, and I have been watching you. The man in the corner of the Black Bull, remember? And do you recall the face at the hansom cab window three days ago? Aye, that was me."

"My apologies, Mr Smith, but I am still unaware of your position." If Inspector Field treated him with respect, the man obviously had influence, but Mendick was not used to deferring to anonymous authority, and he refused to be cowed.

"My name is John Smith."

It was such an obvious lie that even Inspector Field smiled.

"And I represent Her Majesty's government."

"Of course," Mendick agreed. He should have realised that there was something supremely official about this man: he carried himself with the utter confidence of an aristocrat or a member of the government.

"Sit yourself down, and let's talk." Smith dragged over two hard-backed chairs from the far wall.

"Sir?" Mendick glanced toward Inspector Field, who nodded his assent. He sat cautiously, placing his hat on his knee, unused to such informality in the presence of his superiors.

"Drink?" Smith gestured toward the closed cabinet that stood in the corner of the room. "Are you a drinking man? I am sure that Mr Field has a bottle of medicinal brandy somewhere on hand." The grin was so sudden and so conspiratorial that Mendick could not help but respond, and Field was on his feet in a second, returning with a decanter and a silver tray on which stood three balloon brandy glasses.

Mendick eyed the decanter guiltily before he shook his head. "Thank you sir, but no." He was unsure what was happening, but he knew that he should retain as clear a head as possible.

"As you wish. You don't mind if we indulge?" Smith sloshed generous amounts of Field's brandy into two of the glasses. "Now," he said as he sipped quietly, "no doubt you are wondering why I am here?"

Mendick nodded slowly, watching as Smith swirled the brandy.

"Good, you'd be less than human if you were not. Tell me," his eyes pierced Mendick's impassive mask, "in your opinion, what is the function of the police?"

The question was so unexpected that for a moment Mendick could only stare. He recovered with a start, trying to recall Peel's nine principles of policing that he had learned when he first started tramping the beat.

"To prevent crime and disorder, sir, as an alternative to their repression by military force; to maintain a relationship with the public . . ."

Smith pursed his lips and flapped his hands in the air. "That's the official line, but not what I wanted to hear. Now, Inspector Field, what would you say to the same question?"

Field had not touched his brandy. "We patrol a volatile border, protecting the rich from the desperate and preventing anarchy from overwhelming respectability." He mused for a second. "However, I would say that the primary function of the police is to protect the seclusion of respectable neighbourhoods."

"That may be more accurate," Smith agreed. "A touch cynical, but not far off the mark. So would you both agree, then, that one purpose of the police force is to guard the respectable and propertied classes from the effluvia of society, the residuum, if you will?" He waited only a second for the answer before continuing. "Or would you say that the police have the task of ensuring that society retains its natural shape and should remain unaffected by those who would wish it otherwise?" Although he addressed the question to both, it was to Mendick that Smith looked for an answer.

"I would say so, sir, but I see my principal duty as a defender of the law, more than as a protector of any particular class of person . . ."

"Ah!" When Smith held up his hand, calloused ridges showed across the base of his fingers. Whatever position he presently held, at one time Smith had known hard manual labour. "Define that word; define that word, *law*."

Mendick found he was unable to look away from Smith's quizzical stare. He struggled for clarity. "Law is the rules by which we live, a collection of regulations that maintain the balance and fairness of society . . ."

"And there you have it precisely, sir." Smith rose from his chair, jabbing a long forefinger at Mendick. "Well done, Constable; you hit it when you said the *balance* of society. We must all do our utmost to *preserve* that balance, or we may see this nation crumble. That is our duty, sir, and that is *your* duty."

"I understand, Mr Smith." Mendick would have liked to look toward Field, but Smith's near mesmeric gaze held him securely.

"Good, then we are in agreement." Smith sat back down, seemingly content that he had made his point. "Now, Constable, you will be attuned to the present unrest in the country? You will know of the repeated demands for the

People's Charter and other subversive nonsense?" Smith had assumed his previous air of chilling detachment, but Mendick was aware of the passion beneath. He nodded. "Nobody in Britain can be unaware of the underlying unease among some of the lower classes, sir."

"So tell me what you know, Constable."

"Yes, sir. The People's Charter was born after the 1832 Reform Act when the middle orders obtained the vote but the aspirations of the workers to achieve the same were discarded. The Charter demands six electoral reforms, including secret ballots, payment for MPs and the franchise for all males over the age of twenty-one. Those who support the Charter are known as Chartists, and in 1839 they presented their demands to parliament in the form of a petition."

"All correct so far, Constable." Smith's eyes never strayed from Mendick's face. "Pray continue."

"Parliament rejected the petition out of hand, but Chartists are persistent, and whenever the economy dips and there is unemployment and distress in the country, there is more support for them."

"That's accurate enough, Constable, as far as it goes." Smith looked toward Field, who gave a brief nod. Mendick realised that Smith was unsure exactly how much information he could safely impart to a lowly police constable.

Helping himself to Field's brandy decanter, Smith recharged their glasses and poured a third, which he pushed toward Mendick. "You may need this before I am finished, Constable." The glass sat on the silver tray, its contents an amber temptation as Smith continued, "There are new developments among the Chartists. You are obviously unaware of the militancy that is increasingly gripping these people. There is something extremely nasty brewing up north, Constable, something that they term Physical Force Chartism."

Mendick nodded. He knew of the split in the Chartist ranks. While most of the Radicals believed in Moral Force Chartism and hoped to persuade the government to accept their demands by peaceful protests and great petitioning, others were more militant. Led by Feargus O'Connor, the only Chartist Member of Parliament, the Physical Force Chartists spoke of armed revolution unless the government accepted the six points of the Charter.

Smith sipped at his brandy and continued, "We are unsure exactly what these people contemplate, perhaps a worker's strike or a *national holiday* as they term it. Perhaps they plan a series of such strikes that may well cripple the economy of the country, or perhaps something even worse, but we would like you to find out."

Mendick curled a hand around the crystal balloon and swirled the liquid inside. The smell of the brandy was sharp and inviting, but still he desisted. He knew that even a single drink could induce him down the sweet descent to stupidity.

"Me, sir?"

"You, sir."

Once again Smith was ice-cool. "Mr Field speaks most highly of your resourcefulness and I have witnessed your dedication and courage myself. We need somebody to enter the ranks of the Chartists, pose as one of them and relate their intentions to us."

"I see, sir."

Mendick had expected a Scotland Yard detective would investigate murders and serious theft, but he was being asked to act as a spy, the very thing that British people hated most about the plain-clothes police service. The brandy exploded reassuringly inside his stomach, and he paused for an instant, relishing the sensation even as he assessed Smith's proposal.

"But why me? There must be many other officers with more experience."

"There are," Smith agreed. He glanced at Field again. "Look, Constable, this matter is more delicate than you yet realise. Inspector Field did not select you at random. Firstly, we require an officer who would be at ease in the north, and you are no Londoner."

"No, sir, I am from further north." Mendick could feel the brandy weakening his normal reticence, as he had feared it would. "But there are many established Scotland Yard officers from outwith London." The brandy pushed him into continuing, "There is more to this case than you are revealing."

"Much more," Smith agreed. Sighing, he reached for the valise, placed it on his knee and snapped it open. He looked up, and Mendick chilled at the force of his eyes. "What you are about to see must remain strictly within these four walls, Constable. Is that clear?"

"It is sir." Mendick took another sip of the brandy, closing his eyes as the spirit warmed the inside of his mouth and eased into his system. Strangely, now that he knew what he was being asked to do, he felt neither apprehension nor excitement. He had desired a transfer to the detective branch of the service since his first day of duty, but obtaining it had been an anticlimax. Unconsciously, he placed two fingers beneath his leather stock; he would certainly not miss the constant chafing at the tender skin of his throat.

"Right then, Constable. What do you think of these?" Reaching into the valise, Smith produced a bound notebook and placed it carefully on Field's desk.

Mendick bent closer. Each page held a pen-and-ink sketch of the head and shoulders of a man, with two paragraphs of detailed description. "These are well executed." He read the first paragraph.

Mr James Tyler, born 16th January 1810 in Maidstone, Kent. Ten years' service in G or King's Cross Division, transferred to the Criminal Investigation Department, Scotland Yard, on its conception in 1844.

He skipped to the next:

Mr William Gilbert, born 3rd June 1809 in Peckham, London Eleven years' service in H or Stepney Division, transferred to the Criminal Investigation Department, Scotland Yard in 1845.

The third face stared at him, the features familiar.

Mr George Foster, born 13th February 1810 in Carlisle. Fifteen years' service in A or Westminster Division, transferred to the Criminal Investigation Department, Scotland Yard on its conception in 1844.

Mendick looked up. "These appear to be details and pictures of Scotland Yard officers, sir."

"That's exactly what they are, Constable. Each page gives a picture and a written description of one plain-clothes man." Smith leaned closer. "But more important is from where this information originated."

Mendick was already used to Smith's use of a dramatic pause to highlight anything he considered of importance. He waited and wondered about the significance of the notebook while balancing his mounting desire for the brandy against the knowledge of its subsequent effect.

"A man died to secure this book, Constable. It was recovered from these so-called Physical Force Chartists." Smith leaned back, watching Mendick's reaction.

Mendick drew a quick breath. "I understand, sir. How did they get the information about our detectives?"

"We do not yet know that, Constable, but we suppose that they have somebody working within Scotland Yard, perhaps a clerk or similar. Pray stop for an instant and consider the ramifications."

Mendick nodded. "If we presume that the Chartists have other copies of this book, then they would recognise any established Scotland Yard officer who is sent to them, which means that an unknown man must be used."

"Precisely," Smith agreed. "And that is where you come in." He leaned back once more. "One of our people found this notebook in Manchester and brought it to a local police sergeant named Ogden. Unfortunately, our man died doing his duty."

"I see, sir."

"The Chartists butchered him, Constable. He may still have been alive when they tore him to pieces." Smith waited to allow the information to sink in before he continued.

"Sergeant Ogden seems to be a good officer, but we do not consider him suitable material for this type of undercover work, and we need more information. We require somebody on the inside, somebody the Chartists will trust." He raised his eyebrows, his eyes intense.

"I see, sir. You want me to take the place of the officer the Chartists killed."

"There is more." Inspector Field had been listening, his eyes fixed on Mr Smith. "And it may be the most important point of all."

Mendick fortified himself with more brandy, waiting for whatever horror Field unleashed on him. He could feel the spirits working on his mind, muddling his thoughts yet simultaneously pressing him to drink more.

"You see, Constable, we think that there is a new mind directing the activities of the Physical Force Chartists. Feargus O'Connor, who, as you know, has led them for years, has advocated force but has never backed his rhetoric with action. Indeed, we believe that the great O'Connor is a spent volcano. We suspect that someone more formidable has taken his place, and Constable, this person seems to have money."

"But I thought that the Chartists were impoverished workers, sir."

"That is precisely my point, Constable. Most can barely afford to live, let alone contribute money to their cause, but the Chartists are buying land. So somebody with more resources must be backing them."

"I see, sir." Mendick nodded. "And you wish me to find out whom?"

"I do. And more than that." Field glanced at Smith before continuing, "The death of our officer is unprecedented and, given the horrendous circumstances, extremely disturbing. We think that he came across something else the Chartists wished to keep hidden, and that is why they killed him. I fear . . . *we* fear there may be an Irish dimension, Constable, so you may be embarking on a very perilous investigation."

Mendick nodded. He had seen death enough before, but to willingly enter an operation where a police officer had been savagely murdered was not pleasant. He sighed, reviewing the facts: the Irish connection with the Chartists was no secret, but years of famine had created a new desperation in that island, and desperate men were capable of terrible acts. This combination of unemployed English workers and starving Irish immigrants may have added a new dimension to the Chartists, but news of a wealthy patron was perhaps even more alarming.

Field rose from his chair to pace the room, stopping to stare out of the window at the bustle of Whitehall.

"You do not have to take the job, Mendick. We know that it will be dangerous. If you are discovered, the Chartists will probably try to kill you too, and we may not be able to help; we may not even be able to admit that you are one of ours. If you decide to refuse, you may replace your hat and return to your duties without anybody ever knowing that this interview took place."

Mendick hid his smile; the choice could not be more obvious. Either he accepted this perilous position, in which case he would retain his new status as Scotland Yard detective, or he refused and remained a uniformed officer for the remainder of his career. He did not consider for long; he had nothing much to lose anyway. He lifted the brandy glass and took a last loving swallow.

"When do I start, sir?"

"Very shortly." Smith did not offer to recharge his glass, although he was not loath to help himself. "First you must lose some of your police bearing and tone; you *do* look a typical police officer, you know." He nodded to Field. "Give him a few days, maybe a week or so, at ease in London, Inspector. And you, Constable, allow your hair to grow longer, forget to shave for a while, strengthen that uncouth northern accent of yours, and then we will contact you again with further details." He leaned forward in his chair and scribbled on a scrap of paper. "Here is the address of Sergeant Ogden. You will see that he lives in White Rose Lane, just outside Manchester, where the mainspring of this Chartist nonsense appears to be based."

Now that the decision had been made, Mendick realised that he still did not feel anything. Inveigling himself into the Chartist network was just another job, something to fill the emptiness of his life.

Smith was talking again. "We have supplied Sergeant Ogden with various items that could be of use to you. Contact him as soon as you can."

"You have already supplied him?" The brandy made Mendick too loquacious. "I might have refused the position."

"No, Constable." Smith was nearly smiling. "You would not refuse. Now memorise and destroy Ogden's address," he ordered. "We cannot leave anything to chance." He nodded at the door. "That will be all, Constable, except for one thing. I would be obliged if you did not tell anybody about this meeting. Best for the nation, don't you know?"

"I won't tell anybody," Mendick promised.

*

As always when he was alone in his home in Bethnal Green, brooding over the dying embers of his fire, Mendick felt utter loneliness seeping over him. His promise to tell nobody had been genuine, for outwith his colleagues in the force, there was nobody else to tell. He lifted the poker and stirred the ashes, watching as the dim redness flared into life again before immediately beginning to fade. Once, not long ago, he would have enjoyed the evening, basking in the intimacy of his wife's company, creating fanciful images from the flames, planning for a shared future.

Not now.

He looked across to the empty rocking chair at the opposite side of the fire.

"Well, Emma, I'm going away again."

He had spent many hours making that chair, carefully carving the curved rockers on which the framework rested, smoothing the seat with a piece of glass, adding the fixed cushions on which she would rest when nursing their child.

"I would wish that you were coming with me."

The memories were never far beneath the surface, ready to overcome him if he relaxed. When he closed his eyes, he could see her, smiling away her fear as she lay back on their marriage bed, pretty as a picture, plump and pregnant. There had been no warning of any problems: her waters had broken on time, her birth pangs had been normal, and then came the tormented agonies, the moans that would remain with him for the rest of his life. The midwife had shaken her head hopelessly.

"We'll need a doctor," she had said as the sweat streaked her flushed face. "This is beyond me."

Emma had writhed, fighting her screams until the doctor came, and his examination had been thorough. He had taken Mendick aside, speaking in a quiet, serious voice,

"I am afraid your wife is in a critical condition. You might be best to prepare yourself for the worst."

Mendick had blinked away the tears, searching for strength that he no longer believed he had.

"Can you save her, doctor?"

The doctor did not answer for a long minute. "I cannot save them both." He had waited for the reply.

"Then save my wife," Mendick pleaded. "For God's sake, save Emma."

"It will not be easy," the doctor told him, "and it will not be painless."

"Dear God," he looked to Emma, writhing on the stained bed. "Save my wife."

"And the cost?" The doctor looked around the room. He knew that a police constable earned a bare guinea a week and few had any savings.

"I'll meet any expenses."

The next few hours were the worst he had ever experienced, or, he imagined, ever would. He had watched, holding Emma whenever he could, suffering with her pain, and ignoring the tears that scalded his face as the doctor did his terrible but necessary procedures.

The baby came forth in a gush of bright blood, and for a second Mendick touched his son before he returned all his attention to his wife. Pain had aged her in the last few hours, but there was still a faint light of recognition in her eyes as she looked at him. Her hand reached for his one last time, then the agony twisted her away and she slipped into a screaming white void that no amount of laudanum could subdue.

He had watched Emma die, tortured by her agony and his helplessness. At the end, amidst the blood and the writhing, twisting horror, he had felt great sobs breaking over him but knew that he was not a lesser man for revealing his emotion. When her final spasm came, he was aware only of relief that her suffering had ended, and he hated himself for his own callousness as much as he hated himself for having caused Emma so much pain.

Now he spoke to the empty chair he had fashioned for her.

"I'm going away again, Emma, up north this time."

He could sense her presence, faintly disapproving of his choice of career but supportive of his endeavours. Emma had always been there for him, ready to encourage while still attempting to guide him to a less hazardous path. Now the danger did not matter; if he lived, he would help keep the country stable, and if he died, why, then Emma would be waiting to welcome him home. That would not be a bad day.

He stared into the dead embers, contemplating his immediate future. He was to infiltrate an organisation of obviously violent men, which would be difficult enough, but then he was to discover who their patron was and what they planned, and relate the intelligence to Inspector Field. At least the latter part would be easy, with the telegraph now covering every city in the country.

Mendick glanced up for inspiration, but the chair remained unoccupied, a void echoing the emptiness within him. He could not look for help from Emma, so he had to work out his problems himself. It was obvious that the Chartists had somebody working within Scotland Yard, but who and why, he could not imagine. To an extent, that situation had worked to his advantage, for it had led to his selection as an unknown face, an officer who had never walked the corridors of Whitehall. It seemed a poor qualification for a man set to take on a position of such responsibility, but he knew that he was only one strand in a tangled web.

With Emma gone, only duty gave him a purpose in life. The rocking chair remained empty, an accusation of his failure. He sighed; he knew that Emma was not blaming him. She would never do that. Only his Calvinistic conscience pointed the poisoned finger, but the sensation of guilt remained strong. Ultimately, it had been his lust that had killed Emma, and that was something for which he would spend the remainder of his life in atonement. By concentrating on his work he could forget his loss, at least for a time. He knew his position would be precarious; the murder of the last man who infiltrated the Chartist ranks was a stark warning, but he had lived with danger most of his life; it was the least of the demons that crouched on his shoulder.

The knock at the door broke his train of thought. Foster entered, nodding dourly beneath his low-crowned hat. He carried a large canvas bag in his hand.

"Mendick."

"Foster." Mendick ushered him to the chair by the fireplace.

"I won't stay long." Foster examined Mendick's furniture with a long stare, lingering over the silhouetted picture of Emma that decorated the far wall. "Your wife?"

"I'm a widower." He tried to keep all emotion from his voice.

"I see." Foster nodded without sympathy. "Nice picture." He lifted the bag high. "There are clothes and documents in here, and a train ticket for Manchester."

Mendick frowned. "Clothes? What am I supposed to do with them?"

"Wear them." Foster sounded weary, as if he were instructing an infant. "And use the documents." He sighed, opened the bag and produced a large packet. "These will come in very useful."

Breaking the official seal, Mendick unfolded the top piece of stiff paper. It identified him as delegate for the East Indian Branch of the Chartist Federation.

"The East Indian branch does not exist," Foster explained, "so there is no chance of the genuine delegate arriving. You will say that you helped found the branch when you were in the army." He stepped back. "You were out East with the army, were you not?"

"I was."

"Don't tell me which regiment," Foster said, "I don't care; one's much the same as another to me, but your military experience might come in useful."

He did not explain further, watching as Mendick pulled out a rectangular piece of pasteboard headed *The National Charter Association of Great Britain* and decorated with beehives and the twin figures of a working man and woman. It again claimed that James Mendick was a member of the East Indies Branch, and Peter McDouall, one of the Physical Force Chartists, had accredited his membership.

"Are you impressed?" Foster had been watching intently. "You should be; I employed a master forger to create that card – none other than Flash Tom Blake."

"Blake?"

"That's why I wanted him; he's the best in the business, and now he's working for us." Foster sounded extremely smug. "I've been after him for months. This Chartist business has been planned for some time, Constable, so you had better not let anybody down."

"I'll try not to," Mendick assured him. There was a single sheet of instructions, with an illustrated copy of the Charter and a dozen leaflets of Chartist speeches.

"Crib up on the Chartists," Foster advised. "If you're meant to be a delegate, you'll have to know what you're talking about." He stood up, placing the bag on Emma's rocking chair. "The change of clothes will help you look the part." Reaching inside his jacket, he produced a rolled-up newspaper. "Read this too. It's the *Northern Star*, the most significant of the Chartists' own publications. I'd advise you to keep up with the latest copies and memorise everything."

He stepped away and opened the door, stopping just outside to add casually, "Whatever you do, don't let them find out that you're a bobby. Remember what happened to the last fellow."

Mendick nodded grimly. "I remember."

"They're still finding bits of him."

Mendick waited until Foster walked away before he inspected the clothing that was supposed to transform him into a Chartist.

There was a fustian jacket with the nap worn through at one elbow and two buttons missing, a pair of moleskin trousers with a patch on the left knee, a linen shirt with no collar, and a pair of well-worn boots, beautifully oiled as befitted a one-time soldier of the Queen. Once he donned them, he would appear a northern workman to the life. All he lacked, he told himself bitterly, was the itch.

He had spent years dragging himself out of the mire of poverty, from the utter degradation of unemployment to the routine tedium punctuated with moments of terrible fear that was life in the queen's army, to his eventual position as a police constable. Now, he reflected as he lifted the fustian jacket, he was reverting to a type he hoped he had condemned to the past. He also wondered whether a delegate of the

Charter would appear so threadbare; surely he should have at least a modicum of respectability?

He looked around the room, wondering what would happen before he returned. Once, this had been a comfortable home, warm with Emma's smile and filled with the promise of a family future, but when she died all that mattered to him had also died. He kept the house as tidy as ever, but the heart had gone. It was stale, nothing more than a place in which to eat and sleep.

He had survived the dismal funeral, the lonely mourning period that the shy sympathy of his colleagues had made more acute, and now he could only face the future if he kept both eyes firmly fixed on his duty. He was a police officer, nothing else.

Lifting his eyes, he examined the silhouette of Emma that hung proudly on the far wall. He was even less of an artist than he was a carpenter, but on their first anniversary he had traced her outline as accurately as his clumsy fingers would allow.

"When I get the promotion to sergeant," he had promised as she made a paper frame for the picture, "I will take you to a real artist and have a proper portrait painted."

She had laughed, telling him that she was quite satisfied with his attempt, but he could tell that she was secretly pleased with the thought of being an artist's model. That dream had died along with her, and now he was left only with the silhouette, which, although imperfect, was the best likeness he had. He smiled across the room to her.

"Say goodbye to your man in uniform," he told her, for the rules stated that a police officer must wear his uniform at all times, on and off duty, and he could never break a rule.

He stripped slowly, removing the issue shirt and the heavy trousers and watching himself in the oval mirror that had been Emma's pride and joy. He remembered her standing there in her favourite cream dress, twirling slowly to admire herself and smiling at him over her shoulder. He remembered the echo of her laughter and the way her eyes had crinkled at the corners whenever she saw him coming.

He remembered . . . no. He must not; it was time for duty, not self-gratification. Mendick blocked the images and instead saw himself in the glass. He watched as the policeman, the very guardian of respectability, slowly disappeared and somebody else took his place. For an instant he saw a naked man standing there, just tall enough to edge into the police force, too slim to be muscular, with a scar to remind him of the wound that had nearly cost him his life and hair as black as Lucifer, and then he hauled on the moleskin trousers and the image altered.

"God save us, Emma, for nobody else ever will."

The shirt was next, surprisingly soft against his skin, and finally he pulled the fustian jacket over his shoulders. An impoverished working man stared back at him. He eased on the boots, working his feet against the harsh leather, knowing that the heels would rub his skin and the soles would raise blisters, but not caring. And there he was, a budding Chartist, eager to wage political war on the British state and already hating the image he presented.

Lifting the packet of documents, Mendick removed a single foolscap sheet. It had the name *Kersall Moor, Manchester*, the date *2nd December 1847* and the words *Chartist Rally: infiltrate and join the cause*. Just that: simple instructions that could put him in as much danger as his military service ever had. Sighing, he crushed up the paper and threw it on the dead embers of the fire. He swore softly and took a last look into the room and its poignant memories.

He shrugged; what did it matter if he was wearing a fustian jacket, a police uniform or the scarlet jacket of the queen? Physical Force Chartists? They did not even count beside the loss of his wife.

"Good bye, Emma," he said to the silhouette, "I'll be back to see you as soon as I can."

He softly closed the door behind him then strode to the railway train that would take him north.

CHAPTER THREE

Kersall Moor, Manchester: December 1847

"Brothers and sisters! Signatories of the People's Charter!" Standing in the back of the open wagon, the speaker lifted his hands to encompass every member of the multitude that spread across Kersall Moor. "I thank you all for coming here at this time of desperation."

The crowd applauded, drumming their feet in rising excitement, and the speaker waited until the noise subsided. He was obviously an experienced orator, able to judge the temper of any crowd and manipulate them to follow his lead.

"However," he said, and his altered tone alerted his audience that he was about to impart some serious information. "However, does Her Majesty's government know about our lives in the north? Does Her Majesty's government know about the sufferings of the people that they fail to represent? Does Her Majesty know about the mothers and children who exist in conditions worse than those of slaves in America?" The speaker paused, allowing the tension to grow as his audience waited for a reply. He lowered his voice so that they had to strain to listen. "More importantly, does she care?"

The crowd roared again, some shaking their fists in the air as they yelled, "No! No!" and added their own opinions to those of William Monaghan, the speaker.

“It’s the first time that I’ve heard him speak.” The woman standing next to Mendick leaned closer, raising her mouth to his ear. “He’s very good.” She was about medium height, but in the half-light he could not make out her features.

“He’s all that and more,” Mendick agreed. “He’s just the man to lead the fight.” He raised his voice in strong support, damning Queen Victoria and all that she stood for until the woman hushed him into quiet.

“There’s no need for such strong language,” she reproved, softening the barb by adding with a small smile, “however much I agree with your sentiments.”

“But, brothers and sisters.” Monaghan held up his hand for silence as he spoke again. “Brothers and sisters, is it the fault of the Queen? Is Her Majesty to blame for her ignorance?” He waited, smiling at the buzz of confusion that rose from the crowd. Above them, the bright skies offered an illusion of hope, while below, sprawling along the banks of the Irwell River, sat the dark mass of Manchester, cotton capital of the world.

Mendick thrust a stubby pipe into his mouth and scanned the city. Save for the impressive commercial centre at its heart and the arterial roads that reached to the middle class suburbs, Manchester and its attendant towns seemed to be entirely composed of squalid terraces of red-brick buildings; tall factory chimneys vied with the occasional church spire or steeple to thrust their mingled message of commerce and Christianity to the Lord.

“Is Her Majesty to blame?” Monaghan repeated. “I tell you that she is not.” Monaghan spoke the words softly, but repeated them louder, “I tell you that Her Majesty is led astray by those who should be her most truthful advisors. By whom?

By the nobility, by the gentry, by the clergy, by the factory masters, by all those who have the vote and the power to elect representatives who sit in Parliament and decide our future for us while we languish in poverty and suffer under oppression!" He raised his voice with every word, so by the end of his speech he was shouting, raising the ferocity of the crowd.

Mendick cheered with the rest, raising his hat, clapping one hand against the latest edition of the *Northern Star* and glancing at the woman who remained by his side. She seemed to share his enthusiasm, holding on to her hat with her right hand while she held up her left.

"In short," Monaghan lowered his voice again, and the crowd quietened to listen, "in short, Her Majesty is led astray by the very people who deny us the rights *they* enjoy, even as they press us ever further into the mire of degradation!" He shook his head in obvious despair. "We ask for the franchise and what do they offer us? They offer us a repeal of the Corn Laws. Why?"

There was no reply as the crowd waited for the answer they already knew.

"Why?" Monaghan repeated, "I'll tell you why! Is it so we can afford to eat bread? No! No, and a hundred times no! The Whigs did not repeal the Corn Laws to make our lives easier; they repealed the Corn Laws so they could keep our wages down! If bread is cheaper, they can pay us less for more work!"

This time the howls were deafening, ringing around the gathering. Mendick gauged the crowd to be in the hundreds, composed mainly of undersized working people who stared desperately at Monaghan as if his words would generate jobs to transport them from their present dreadful poverty to a place of warmth and security.

"Quite right!" The woman clapped her hands vigorously, removing her threadbare but carefully washed gloves to be better heard. "Is he not quite right? Isn't he just speaking the truth that we all know?" She looked earnestly into Mendick's face.

"He is," he agreed.

"The more we protest," Monaghan continued, "the more the government will fear us, and the more they will seek to grind us down. What can they do?" He waited for a response, and smiled when one or two of the more foolish gave him the required answer.

"Nothing!" they yelled, "they can do nothing against the people!"

"Oh yes, they can," Monaghan retorted, sobering the crowd he had so successfully stirred. "They can use the army, as they did at St Peter's Field, not so very far from here, as they did with the Scottish Radicals at Bonnybridge, as they did at Newport in Wales only eight years since and in the Potteries but five years back. But I tell you this . . ." he held up a finger to command the silence that descended upon the gathering. "I tell you this. When they do so, and they will, they will; when they do, that moment will *live in history*. The moment when the first gun is fired among the working men of England will be succeeded by a short but awful pause, and the future history of this country will be written in characters red with human gore!"

From the height of their anger, the crowd subsided. While many of the men and women were dressed in their ragged best, others were bare-footed or wore wooden clogs with threadbare trousers and collarless shirts. Many of the men sported the fustian jacket that was the mark of the respectable worker, people proud of their contribution to society, willing to work and hoping for work. These men were no raging revolutionaries but unfortunates suffering from unemployment and the hopeless frustration that came from enforced idleness and the inability to even voice their anger through the ballot box.

There were men who had given their last scrap of bread to their family days before, women whose babies sucked on breasts empty of milk, seventh-year apprentices who stared at a jobless future, desperate wives and broken husbands. Most people in the crowd looked to Monaghan for hope. In return he had offered them defiance and a target for their anger while warning them of the possible consequence of their actions.

"He's clever," Mendick said. "He's treating us like adults, not leading us like children."

"We have the choice," the woman sounded eager, "to remain mute and suffer, or fight for a better life and chance the swinging sabres of the yeomanry."

Mendick looked at her; she was obviously intelligent and calmly accepted that the government would use the army to put down any dissent. "And does that not concern you?"

"It should concern us all," the woman told him, "being subject to a power that treats its own people with such contempt."

"I cannot argue with that," he said, trying to hide his surprise at finding such an articulate woman at a Chartist rally.

"So," Monaghan was speaking again, "only by making ourselves heard will our concerns be addressed. We demand the six points of the Charter. Suffrage for all men over twenty-one; equal constituencies; payment for MPs . . ."

The woman stiffened and raised her voice,

"Pray excuse me, Mr Monaghan, but why should the Charter be only for *men* over twenty-one? It should be for universal suffrage." As she stepped forward to be more easily seen, those nearest turned towards her, while those further back tried to hush her into silence. "Have you not listened to the words of Reginald Richardson and Ernest Jones? Male suffrage would still deny large numbers of adults full participation in the country; why should women not have the vote?"

Momentarily taken aback, Monaghan stared as the woman continued:

"Why should women not have the vote? I can read and write as well as you, if not better. And I can work with my hands, when there is work available. I can reason as well as any man yet born." When she smiled, raising her eyes to Monaghan, Mendick realised that she was a truly attractive woman, although he could not pinpoint why. "So is there a reason that I cannot have the vote? Am I so inferior?"

Raising both hands to still the clamorous curiosity of the crowd, Monaghan leaned forward to address the woman.

"I do not believe that there is anything inferior about you," he told her seriously. "And I do not believe there is anything inferior about any woman. You are the equal to any man; if a woman can be queen, if a woman has to pay taxes, if a woman is subject to the same laws and penalties, if a woman adds to the wealth of the nation by her labour, then yes, she is well worthy of the vote." He waited until the renewed hubbub subsided. "However, we may persuade the government to grant men suffrage, but they will not yet agree to women."

"So let us make them agree!"

The woman raised her voice and accepted Monaghan's hand to haul herself onto the back of the wagon that acted as a platform for his speech.

"We have tried reason; we have tried petitions; we have tried patience, surely now we can use stronger methods? Surely it is time for physical force?"

It had been neatly done, Mendick grudgingly acknowledged. The woman's interruption had strengthened Monaghan's position. Now the appeal of the Charter had been widened to include women as well as men, and it was the woman, the supposedly gentler of the two sexes, who was appealing for force. Women might follow her simply because she was female, and men would be ashamed to hold back where women were not afraid to tread.

"May I be so bold as to address your audience, Mr Monaghan?" The woman gave a half curtsey.

Now she was in full view, Mendick saw the patches on her immaculately clean dress and the odd button on her boot which had been replaced with an imperfect match, yet these details did not detract from her undeniable magnetism. It was not the curve of her mouth or the attraction of her disproportionately large eyes, but something indefinable, as if she were greater than the sum of all her parts.

Monaghan gave her his hand. "Madam, of course you may speak. We should all be entitled to the free expression of our beliefs."

"Thank you, Mr Monaghan." Turning to the audience, the woman introduced herself. "My name is Rachel Scott, and I have been an operator in a cotton mill for many years." It seemed obvious that years of working in a dusty environment had given her voice that appealing huskiness, but her choice of words revealed a level of education above anything Mendick would normally expect from a mill hand.

"I have experienced, as have we all, the long hours and short wages of our present system, and as Mr Monaghan so rightly says, it is time to do something about it." Turning to the crowd, she pointed directly at Mendick. "You, sir! A minute past I saw you cheering the words of Mr Monaghan. Are you willing to go beyond words? Are you willing to take a step towards real freedom?"

Mendick felt the eyes of the gathering upon him. He took a deep breath and stepped forward, feeling inside his pocket for the membership card that Blake had forged.

"Aye, I am," he said, "willing and more than willing."

"How willing?" Rachel Scott spoke the words quietly, but those huge eyes were sharply quizzical. "Tell me, sir, how willing is more than willing?"

Those nearest to him were silent, waiting for an answer, while those at the back were craning forward, demanding to know what was happening.

He produced his membership card. "As willing as that," he said.

Scott turned away, her smile fading. "So you are a member of a Chartist branch." She sounded disdainful. "So are many thousands of others." She looked at him over her shoulder. "That means nothing, Mr . . ." leaning closer, she read the name, "Mr Mendick."

"This may mean more," he said, producing the document that proclaimed him a delegate for the East Indian Branch of the confederation.

"East Indian branch?" Scott read the address aloud, her tone mildly mocking. "I had not realised that there was such a thing. Pray tell, Mr Delegate, which part of this nation is in the East Indies?"

"The military part." Mendick had his answer ready. He felt the sudden surge of interest from Scott but did not expect her swift intake of breath and short, explosive laugh.

"Military? So you are one of these men who wore the uniform of the oppressors, one of those who are ready to kill or maim your fellow workers."

Mendick was aware of the silence around him, and the slow murmur of disapproval from those at the back of the gathering.

"I am one of the many who donned the scarlet jacket rather than starve in the streets." He held her eyes, unsure if he was already failing in his first task as a detective officer.

"And now you want to atone for that decision." Scott did not disguise the contempt in her voice, but Monaghan put his hand on her shoulder.

"Life is about decisions and mistakes," he said quietly. "I am sure that our colleague is as sincere in his beliefs as you or I in ours." He nodded to Mendick. "Is that not so, my friend?" Close to, the Chartist speaker was not so tall and had a distinctly lined face and an accent more Liverpool than Ireland.

"It is, and I am very willing to take a step towards real freedom."

"Real freedom? You would not understand the concept." Again Scott gave that distinctive indrawn laugh. Turning, she whispered something to Monaghan, who glanced at Mendick and nodded.

"Perhaps," Monaghan said cryptically.

The crowd were growing restless at this private conversation, and some began to ease away. Monaghan lifted his voice again.

"It is time to close this meeting, brothers and sisters, fellow Chartists all, so unless we have already done so, let us now sign the Charter." Stooping, he produced a long roll of paper from the body of the wagon and stood ready with a quill pen and a pot of ink as a number of people came to add their names.

"This petition will go to the House of Commons," he reminded them. "It is both a token of our loyalty to the cause and a demand from the ordinary people of Britain for a fairer and more just society."

Mendick was surprised that most people could actually sign their own name; he remembered the number of illiterates in his regiment. When the last man and woman had signed, Monaghan continued:

"I thank you all for your support and loyalty. And now let us end with something to cheer us; let us sing a paean of praise." As he roared out a Chartist song the crowd joined in, the desperate voices merging in aspiration to a future of which they could only dream:

"Truth is growing – hearts are glowing
With the flame of Liberty:
Light is breaking – Thrones are quaking –
Hark! The trumpet of the Free
Long in lowly whispers breathing
Freedom wandered drearily
Still, in faith, her laurel wreathing,
For the day when there should be Freemen shouting
Victory!"

They shouted the last word in a triumphant peal, and then some subsided in sobs, as if their singing could soften the heart of the pitiless Whigs who controlled the factories and dribbled their wages like blood through an impermeable stone.

As they began to drift away, Monaghan beckoned Mendick closer and spoke in low, urgent tones,

"You say that you are willing to step towards real freedom. Is that a genuine desire, or are you just hoping to impress Miss Scott?"

Mendick seized the opening. "I could not be more sincere," he said.

"I don't mean just shouting acclaim and waving your hat in the air," Monaghan warned. "The charter needs *men* to advance its cause, not rowdy mice."

"Your friend was sneering at me for my army service." Mendick did not look at Scott, who was listening closely. "But my time in uniform could be useful, Mr Monaghan. Like you, I have had enough of singing songs and listening to rousing speeches that avail nothing; perhaps I can offer more than that." He took a deep breath, and continued, "Will the ability to drill and shoot and fight help your cause, Mr Monaghan? Or the ability to kill?" For a second he thought he had overplayed his part as Monaghan appeared to flinch, but Scott stepped forward.

"The fellow talks a good deal, Mr Monaghan," she said, "but some of his words may be of interest."

"Maybe, if they are correct." Monaghan glowered at him and came to a sudden decision. "There is a beer shop named the Beehive; meet me there at eight tomorrow morning."

For a second he scrutinised Mendick, and then he climbed back into the wagon. Scott looked over her shoulder just long enough to flick her eyes from his face down the length of his body and back, before following the last of the straggling crowd. Mendick watched for only a moment, barely noticing the provocative swing of her hips as he murmured the words of the Chartist song that reverberated around in his head,

"Truth is growing – hearts are glowing
With the flame of Liberty"

Shaking his head removed neither the words nor the image.

*

The name of the Beehive may have been chosen for the impression of industry and organisation, but the interior provided nothing but a confirmation of the misery outside. Even at that hour of the morning, groups of haggard men and women crouched around battered deal tables while others slouched against the bar, attempting to make their beer last as long as possible. Tousle-haired children sat on the floor, but when Mendick winked at them they looked up listlessly, no animation in their ancient eyes.

The barman was a nondescript individual with thinning brown hair under a peaked railway cap. He grunted when Mendick asked for Monaghan.

"Is he expecting you?"

"He asked me to come."

"Did he indeed." The barman looked him up and down. "What's your name?"

"James Mendick; I'm a . . ."

"I don't care what you are." The barman consulted a small list before indicating a door in the corner of the room.

“Through there.” He rapped his knuckles on the top panel before ushering Mendick inside.

The door led into a smaller room with an oval table around which sat a dozen men, all seemingly intent on puffing as much tobacco smoke as possible into the atmosphere. Monaghan dominated the room, sitting erect in the only heavy carved chair with Rachel Scott proud at his side. When Mendick entered, Monaghan nodded and Scott allotted him a long, languid look before rising to greet him.

“Mr Mendick.” She responded to his bow with a slow smile. “I did not really think that you would come. Find a place at the table, if you please.”

Even as they shuffled to make room for him on the bench, the seated men stared at him suspiciously. Mendick scanned them quickly, noting eyes embittered by poverty, gaunt faces with skin pulled tight over sharp cheekbones and thin, compressed lips. One cadaverous man wore the red cap of liberty pulled far down over his forehead and carried an ugly scar that twisted his lips into a permanently cynical smile. None offered a greeting until Monaghan spoke again.

“Mr Mendick is a delegate from the East Indian branch, which means he has army experience.” He waited for the silent men to complete their examination before continuing, “Peter McDouall approved his membership.”

There were a few murmurs then, and the man with the liberty cap raised a face so worn and leathery that Mendick thought he must have spent time under some foreign sun himself.

“I know McDouall. He hasn’t mentioned you.”

“And you are?” Mendick faced the man; his eyes were like pits of pure poison.

"Josiah Armstrong." The mouth twisted further into what may have been a smile, or a deeper sneer. The scar across his lips seemed to extend right round his face and continue to the back of his neck. "You may have heard of me?"

Josiah Armstrong was a Chartist lecturer who had been transported to Van Diemen's Land back in 1842. He had been one of the most vociferous of the early Chartists, renowned for his acrimonious attacks on the Whigs. Well aware that every word he said would be weighed and scrutinised, Mendick spoke slowly,

"I've heard of you, Mr Armstrong, but wee Peter did not mention you. Maybe he's too intelligent a man to name names, for all his bad temper." Mendick knew McDouall was a medical doctor from the west of Scotland, noted both for his irascibility and his vehement support of the Charter.

"He's got you there, Josiah," another of the men said with the first touch of humour Mendick had heard since his arrival in Manchester.

Armstrong did not appear amused. "I've never heard of you, and I've never heard of the East Indies branch." Shifting restlessly on the bench, he produced a short clay pipe, stuffed coarse tobacco into the bowl and glowered venomously at Mendick. "Tell me about it."

Hoping to appear nonchalant, Mendick shrugged. He knew his future depended not only on his answers, but also on how he delivered them. If he hoped to infiltrate this band of Radicals, he must make them trust him, as well as offer them something they desired.

"There were not many of us, because the *officers* did not approve." It was not difficult to inject a sneer into his voice, for the gulf between officers and rankers was so immense it was virtually unbridgeable. “But we were as dedicated to the Charter as any Lancashire machine operator, or Liverpool-born Irishman,” he looked directly at Monaghan, who gave a cold nod of acknowledgement.

Armstrong pulled on his pipe until the tobacco glowed red, then puffed foul smoke toward Mendick.

“You say the officers did not approve. How did they voice this disapproval?”

“Extra duties, mainly, and the occasional unpopular posting.” Mendick had to think quickly. “Do you remember Uriah the Hittite, sent to the forefront of the battle?”

“Of course.” Armstrong’s face darkened at the suggestion that he would not know his Bible.

“Well, change the name and the campaign, and there you have us.” He heard the uncomfortable shifting of men in chairs as the delegates in the room considered his words.

“So they made you suffer for the Charter.” Armstrong nodded. “Aye, they do that, don’t they? And in which battle were *you* at the forefront?”

“The capture of Amoy.” Mendick had no need to lie. He remembered the heavy, humid air and the strange sights, the Manchu soldiers and the two hundred pieces of artillery, the thousand-yard long granite wall and the sound of the gongs and firecrackers. The memories were so vivid he knew they would stay with him forever.

Armstrong grunted and sank back down, his eyes as narrow as before.

“The Chinese war,” he spat, “a war of exploitation!”

“It was,” Mendick agreed. “It was a war to force opium on the Chinese people, against the will of their mandarin masters.” He sat back and let them think of that type of exploitation. He felt Rachel Scott's eyes on him and wondered if he had said too much.

"So you played your part in this opium traders' war?" Armstrong's accusation sliced venomously through the smoke.

"I did," Mendick admitted. He remembered the comradeship on campaign and the friendships forged by shared suffering which no civilian could ever understand. For a second he recalled singing the old Covenanting psalms while waiting for the order to advance against the Chinese city, the strange lanterns bobbing on the defended walls, the painted banners and the bravery of the Tartar and Mongol soldiers. He remembered also the hundreds of British soldiers lying sick in the stinking mud. That memory was still powerful.

"Which regiment were you with?" Again there was that sneer as Armstrong indicated that one regiment was much alike another. "Were you a Guardsman? Were you one of those tin soldiers who stand outside the palace to intimidate the people if they dare to approach Her Majesty?"

"I was in the 26th Foot." Mendick told the truth. He felt his fists clench as he prepared to defend his regiment. He knew that to do so was to forsake his duty to the police force, but he refused to desert an older and fiercer loyalty.

"Why did you join?" Monaghan's milder tones oiled what could have developed into very troubled waters. He remained seated at the head of the table, while Scott watched, her head tilted to one side, eyes musing.

"Like most soldiers, it was a choice between the army and starvation."

"Of course," Monaghan nodded his understanding. "So you were as much a victim as any of us, forced to defend a system that had betrayed you, and all for a shilling a day."

"Less stoppages," Mendick reminded him, trying to win sympathy through humour.

"Less stoppages," Monaghan agreed.

"However –" Hardening his tone, Mendick put the flat of his hands on the top of the table, "I thought I was asked here to help further the Chartist cause, not to entertain you with my military past."

"Perhaps the two are not so far apart," Monaghan told him, and the others gave nods of approval. "What rank did you hold in the 26th Foot, Mr Mendick?"

Mendick had never risen higher than corporal and had been broken back to a private soldier within two months. "I was a sergeant," he said.

"And you are still as committed to the Charter as you appear to have been when you were a soldier?"

"I am, sir," Mendick said. "Mr Monaghan, I am not by nature a patient man. The working men were cheated back in '32 and ignored in '42; I think it is about time we pushed harder for our rights. If that means using physical force, then so be it." Warming to his task he rose, addressing the assembled men as if he were lecturing to a bunch of Johnny Raw recruits who had just assembled, all mouth and wonder.

"I presume that everybody present has signed the Charter, so I can speak plainly. I do not like the idea of revolution, and I do not like the idea of bloodshed; few soldiers do, once we have seen the real thing. However, sometimes a lesser evil is necessary in order to defeat a greater, and I believe that the present situation is . . ." He halted and searched for the right word. "Indefensible. As we know, the Whigs' *so-called* Great Reform Act of 1832 only made matters worse by giving the vote to the middling classes and leaving us, the real workers of Britain, out in the cold."

Mendick stopped for breath, realising that the men at the table were agreeing with every word, while Scott was still standing with her head to one side, smiling softly.

"So yes, I am committed to the Charter; tell me how I can further the cause and I will strain every muscle and sinew I possess to that aim."

Monaghan had been listening carefully, and now he looked around the room, his eyebrows raised. One by one the men grunted or nodded, answering an unspoken question. Armstrong was the last to give even such grudging approval, and he continued to stare at Mendick, slowly puffing at his pipe.

"How can you further the cause?" Monaghan mused. "Well, Mr Mendick, at this very moment the master workmen of Birmingham are manufacturing pikes for the nail makers of Staffordshire to smuggle out to us in their aprons. We have people making hand grenades and others creating caltrops to slow down the cavalry."

Mendick listened, trying to mask his horror with a look of anticipation. So Mr Smith had been correct and the Chartists were going to attempt a revolution. He remembered similar rumours back in 1842, but this time there seemed to be more substance. The thought of armed men marching through Manchester, or dragoons deploying in Darlington, was terrifying.

"We have other plans," Monaghan told him. "If the magistrates try to Peterloo us, then we will Moscow England. We will burn Newcastle to the ground and destroy the house and factory of every Whig between Birmingham and Preston, aye, and more than that . . ."

"Enough, perhaps, for now." Rachel Scott seemed to be warning Monaghan. "Perhaps our colleague here would rather know how *he* could help." Her gaze did not leave Mendick's face.

"We want you to use your military experience to train an army of workers," Monaghan told him bluntly. "But if you are caught doing so, it will be the rope. Are you willing to help?"

Mendick nodded, surprised at how easy it had been. He had succeeded in inveigling himself into the Chartist ranks.

When he looked up, he felt the tension in the room, with every person present watching him. Some were clearly suspicious about him, others challenging and Scott plainly curious, but Armstrong's right hand was inside his jacket, as if he were holding some sort of weapon.

"Are you willing, Mendick?" Monaghan demanded a reply.

His shrug was genuine. As a policeman, he was in far more danger from these revolutionaries than from any government hangman, but if he was caught and killed, well then . . .

"What is the rope? What is one life when the happiness of millions is at stake?"

"Oh, very melodramatic," Armstrong said, "but let's hear you say that when the noose is tightening around your neck." He leaned closer, his voice lowering to a hiss and the scar raising the corner of his mouth. "Have you ever seen a man hanged, Mr Mendick? Have you seen the sweat start from his forehead as the rope is positioned and heard his grunting gasp as he realises he will never see another day?"

Mendick nodded. "I have."

“And you are not afraid?” Armstrong’s sneer was pronounced, but Mendick realised that others in the room were becoming uncomfortable at his persistent harassment.

“I did not say I was unafraid. I said that losing my life may be worthwhile.” Mendick felt the tension in the room ease slightly as most of the delegates approved his statement. They were working men, made hard by adversity, but beneath the inflexible shell they were prepared to be fair to those of whom they approved.

Armstrong grunted and raised his reptilian eyes.

“It’s easy to play with words when you are safe in this room. I’ve seen hangings enough to sicken the devil and other things that would make you squirm in horror. I’ve seen much worse than hangings; I’ve known men commit murder just so they could welcome the noose as a release from unendurable torment. If you join us, you might see the same. Are you willing to risk that?”

This time it was Mendick who grunted.

“I’ve said my piece. I am a man of my word so there is no need for me to repeat myself, but I do object to speaking to people who seem to doubt everything I say.” Straightening up, he looked directly at Armstrong. “Your commitment to the Charter is well known, sir, but that does not give you the right to bullyrag me in such a manner.”

Armstrong’s mouth tightened, making the scar gleam white across his lower lip.

“I believe that my commitment gives me every right, Mr Mendick. You turned up at our meeting with a piece of pasteboard and a paper that you might well have written yourself and with no known history of dedication to the cause. Have you ever been jailed for the charter?”

Mendick shook his head. “I have not,” he admitted. It was obvious Armstrong thought of himself as a martyr, someone who had suffered for the Charter in the same manner as Christ suffered on the cross.

“*I* was,” Armstrong said, “I was, and the bastards carried me through England in an open cart, chained hand and foot, and sent me to Van Diemen’s Land.” The bitterness increased as he recalled vivid memories.

The arrest and transportation of Armstrong had infuriated many of Mendick’s police colleagues, who had hoped for the death penalty. They had accused Armstrong of being responsible for some of the worst violence of the Chartist outbreak of 1842, when men had died and buildings had been torched in the name of an extended franchise.

“Well, you’re back now.” As Mendick focussed determinedly on those acidic eyes, he fought the chill which emanated from this man and wondered what else in Armstrong's life had contributed to such bitterness.

“Aye, I’m back,” Armstrong jabbed the stem of his pipe at Mendick, like some foul-fumed weapon from the Pit, “and I intend to ensure that no more Chartists are sent across the pond. Do you agree now that I have the right to query the commitment of others?”

“I think there has been enough querying,” Monaghan decided. “Mr Mendick has offered his services, and I believe we should accept them.”

“As you wish, Mr Monaghan, as you wish,” Armstrong capitulated immediately. He stood up, banging the embers of his pipe onto the floor. “You claim to have come from London to help us, Mr Mendick, and now is your chance. Come with me; we have much to do." On this last word Armstrong rose and limped towards the door.

"Where are we going?" Life in the army had taught Mendick to accept such abrupt changes in his life.

"We are going to show you why we so urgently need the Charter, and then we will put you to work." Walking with a peculiarly hunched gait, Armstrong led Mendick out of the public house and through the arched door of a stable. Daylight from the open door silhouetted something square and bulky in the gloom.

The sudden beam from a bull's-eye lantern blinded Mendick as a deep voice challenged. "Who's that?"

"It's all right, Peter," Armstrong said. "It's me, and I have an ally."

"Sorry, Mr Armstrong." There was a faint scrape as the man named Peter opened the shutter of the lantern. "I didn't know it was you." The light altered to a less direct and wider glow, illuminating the interior of the stable and revealing the bulky object to be a four-wheeled brougham.

Peter absently fondled the muzzle of the white horse delicately feeding beside the carriage. Well over six feet tall, his shoulders spread like the gable end of a house, yet he walked so lightly that the straw beneath his feet barely rustled. He stood quietly, eyes fixed on Armstrong and cradling the lantern as though it were his last hope of sanctuary.

"This is Mr Mendick," Armstrong spoke slowly. "He used to be a soldier, but now he has joined us, so we will show him exactly why the Charter is so important to the people of Manchester."

"Are we going on a trip, Mr Armstrong?" The idea seemed to please Peter.

"Drive, Peter. I'll tell you where." Armstrong jerked a thumb to the carriage. "Get in, Mr Mendick, and I'll educate you."

As Peter climbed on to the elevated driver's seat, Mendick ran his hand over the yellow stripe along the blue paintwork.

"Nice carriage." He remembered that some of the London criminals liked the brougham because of its tight turning circle and wondered if Armstrong had similar reasons for his choice of carriage. He slid inside, where fresh straw on the floor combined with the clean upholstery to create an impression of prosperity that contrasted with the general malaise that seemed to permeate Manchester.

Armstrong glared at him through these malicious eyes while his mouth retained the twisted sneer.

"You come from London, and you think you know deprivation." His voice had the hard edge of Newcastle, without the lifting twang.

"I have lived in London," Mendick agreed.

"Well, London may have pockets of poverty, but here we live with it every day and everywhere." Armstrong's tone was as challenging as his eyes, and Mendick wondered if he was adopting the pose of the experienced Chartist educating the man from the South. "We do not just toy with the idea of Chartism; it is not a theory for those blessed with some education; it is the only hope of escape for the majority of our people."

Mendick heard the sincerity in Armstrong's voice; the man was not posturing but attempting to convince him of what he believed was truth. He narrowed his eyes as his policeman's cynicism momentarily faltered.

"Perhaps you should show me," he suggested.

"That is my intention." Armstrong shifted restlessly on the padded seat.

It took Peter several minutes to back the single horse into position, and then they were moving out of the stables and growling through the streets of Manchester, passing groups of broken people standing in the streets, watching listlessly.

"They wonder who we are and why we are driving a carriage through their streets," Armstrong spoke quietly. "It's not something they see every day."

Pulling back the curtains from the gleaming window, Mendick looked outside. Brick terraced streets followed one another in row after squalid row, with the crowds becoming ever more tattered, ever more hopeless.

"Aye, that's what we're fighting for," Armstrong said. "Maybe our lives are worth losing, eh? We may die, but we give hope to the hopeless." Mendick was surprised to see compassion in the acidic eyes. "You gave a glib enough answer, but for some of us, this is more than just a pastime; it's a crusade."

Mendick listened as Armstrong spoke to him about Manchester.

"It is an amazing city: the phenomenon of the age, a microcosm of the new industrialism that has transformed the country. What happens in Manchester is copied elsewhere, and what we do here must be an example to others." Again Armstrong sounded intense. "We *must* succeed; we *must* make this government see that the present system is murdering the people of this country."

"I agree," Mendick said, and at that moment, with the images of appalling poverty grinding past, he was not insincere. "But how can we make them listen?"

"As you know, we are torn as to our methods." Armstrong was nearly in tears at the frustration of constant failure. "We have the Moral Force Chartists, who hope to use petitions to persuade the government, either Whig or Tory, and we have the Physical Force Chartists, who prefer sterner methods."

Mendick nodded; this was what he had hoped to hear.

"Physical force would appear to be the better method," he said. "We already tried the petitions in 1839 and 1842."

"And the beak handed me twenty-one years' transportation for my pains," Armstrong reminded him, easing himself into a more comfortable position. "So this time we have a combination of both methods. We have O'Connor's petition, which will be handed to Earl Russell after a great meeting in London, but that will be combined with the threat of physical force." He looked out of the window as the carriage turned off Oldham Road. "This is Angel Meadow; it is as bad as anything you have in London."

Mendick glanced outside. The brick streets were uniformly narrow with scarcely enough space for the brougham to pass between the smoke-blackened houses. Clad in rags that barely covered their decency, crowds of gaunt men and women watched them from the doorways. Many seemed to be nursing injuries or deformities.

"Pretty, isn't it?" Armstrong shook his head. "This is the result of Whig policies, of profit followed by higher profit and expecting the poor to fend for themselves. Do you know that a labourer in Manchester has an average lifespan of seventeen years? Seventeen years! Sweet God, Mendick, at that age he's hardly begun his life."

The venom was back in Armstrong's voice. "Aye, so we will offer the petition to Finality Jack Russell and his Whigs, and if he turns it down again, why, then we will have an army ready up here. Thanks to you and others like you."

So that was it, simple and direct, the iron fist of physical force hidden within the velvet glove of the petition.

"Have you seen enough?" Armstrong did not flinch when one of the watching destitute threw a stone which bounced off the carriage. "Do you want to see more poverty, more suffering, more dirt and disease, or shall we travel to our antidote for this disease?"

Mendick was used to the slums of London and had known the decaying Old Town of Edinburgh; he had seen the teeming morasses of cities in China and the Middle East, but he was still shocked by Manchester. This town was famed as one of the leading industrial centres of the world; if it treated its people in such a manner, then any future for the working majority seemed grim.

"I think we need an antidote," he said.

There was quite a crowd gathered now, with more missiles bouncing off the body of the coach. He heard Peter shout and saw his whip crack in front of the attackers.

"Peter! Leave them be!" Armstrong shouted. "They are not the enemy; they are just victims. But get us to the village, now." He leaned back. "You look surprised, Mr Mendick. Perhaps Manchester is not as you expected?"

"I am not exactly sure what I expected," Mendick admitted, "but I was surprised myself to see you had a carriage. I thought only the rich could afford such a thing."

The sudden sour grin took him off guard. "It's not mine," Armstrong said. "Let's just say that I borrowed it, horse, carriage and all. I only own the driver."

Mendick thought it best to appear impressed. "You borrowed an entire carriage? Does the owner not mind?"

"The owner has many carriages," Armstrong said, "he will not miss one." The grin widened, revealing stumps of teeth. "We have an arrangement."

"You stole it," Mendick accused, "from a gentleman." He looked at the sordid streets outside. "That was a daring act, Mr Armstrong."

"Oh, we are full of daring acts, Mr Mendick, as you will see."

Stealing something as expensive as a carriage would mean transportation at the very least, but as a returned Demonian, Armstrong was probably facing the death penalty anyway. Mendick settled back on the seat and shuffled his feet in the deep straw. He was quite used to travelling in an omnibus but had never been in a private carriage before; more amenable company might even have made this experience enjoyable.

"Jesus!" The brougham rocked as a barrage of missiles clattered off the coachwork, and it mounted the kerb. It crashed back on to the ground, jarring Mendick and knocking Armstrong from his seat.

"What the hell!" Armstrong lifted his voice into a hoarse roar. "Peter! What sort of driving is that? It's the black hole for you!"

"The what?" Mendick asked.

Armstrong pulled himself back onto the seat, rubbing one hand across his back and grimacing with obvious pain.

"The black hole; you'll see later. It's the only way to keep Peter under control. He doesn't understand anything else, the ignorant slubber."

Mendick nodded, mildly interested that a Chartist delegate should speak so callously of a fellow worker. He sat back; his next step was to find Sergeant Ogden and then telegraph Inspector Field to inform him of his progress. Closing his eyes, he wondered at the turn of events. Ten days ago he had been an ordinary constable in London, now he was sitting opposite a red-capped revolutionary on a mad careen through Manchester, bound for God knew where to do the devil knew what.

He sighed, wondering what Emma would think of him now.

"Where did you say we were going?"

"I didn't."

Armstrong was back to his old cagey self. His eyes challenged Mendick to ask another question. Instead, Mendick listened as the grinding of the wheels altered to a lighter rumble, and the drumming of the horse's hooves softened to a rhythmic throb. They had obviously left the town and were on a country road, with the horse thumping through mud and the carriage swaying on an uneven surface, and the occasional branch scraping alarmingly across the bodywork.

"Not long now," Armstrong broke a long silence, "and you can begin your work." He leaned forward. "You have an army to train, for we have a country to set to rights."

"An army? How big an army?"

"You'll see, by and by." Armstrong's smile twisted his mouth further, but his eyes were as cold as December sleet. "You boasted of your military experience and your commitment to the Chartist cause. Now you can prove it." He produced a percussion pistol from his coat. "Of course, if I find that you have been throwing the hatchet, then . . ." He pointed the pistol full at Mendick's face. "I will kill you stone dead."

CHAPTER FOUR

Lancashire: December 1847

Rain pattered rapidly on the exterior of the coach as Peter negotiated a series of increasingly jolting tracks. The coach rocked and rolled along the rutted country lanes, rattling between dripping trees and past well-cultivated fields until they eventually stopped at a brick stable.

"Straight in, Peter!" Armstrong yelled, and Peter, swathed in a box coat stretched to splitting point, hastily leaped down from the driver's perch, opened the stable door and then drove inside.

"It's only a small step from here," Armstrong said. "Peter, join us once you have dealt with the horse."

"Yes, Mr Armstrong." Peter had spoken over his shoulder, but there was a noticeable tremble in his voice.

"This way."

Walking with that awkwardly hunched gait, Armstrong followed a winding footpath to the summit of a heavily wooded knoll. Rain pelted through the bare branches above to cascade on to their heads and shoulders.

"I'll have to stop for a moment," Armstrong said, gasping as he leaned his hand against the trunk of a wind-twisted birch.

"Take your time."

A small but broad valley stretched ahead, dull under the hissing rain. Sad trees and small steadings sat stolidly amidst a patchwork of square fields, while a church stood in everlasting promise within its own grassy grounds.

"Take a good look," Armstrong advised. "This is your new home."

"I've seen worse," Mendick said. He was not sure about the implications.

"But few better." There was genuine pride in Armstrong's voice. "You'll know all about O'Connor's Land Plan."

Mendick nodded. "Of course."

It was an idea of the Chartists to fight the horrors of industrialisation by having people work on their own piece of land.

"Well, this is the end result: Chartertown. Just over a hundred acres divided into thirty-five smallholdings, each one between two and four acres, with a specially built comfortable cottage. O'Connor raised a subscription to purchase the land, and he is creating a Chartist settlement here in Lancashire."

Mendick nodded. After seeing the terrible conditions in which most Mancunians seemed to live, he had only respect for O'Connor's utopian ideas.

"It seems a fine place, Mr Armstrong, but I thought I was to train an army?"

"All in good time." Armstrong seemed pleased with Mendick's commitment. He began to walk down the hill, rotating his shoulders as if he were in pain. "First we have to attend to Peter."

The giant coachman had followed them, walking so quietly that Mendick had scarcely heard his feet flatten the sodden grass.

"Please . . ." Peter cowered as Armstrong took hold of his shoulder. "I could not help it; they were throwing stones at the horses."

"You knocked me from my seat," Armstrong pushed the huge man in front of him, "so it's the black hole for you."

"Please, Mr Armstrong, the horse was scared."

"And you'll be scared now, Peter, alone in the dark with the spiders and the slithering things." Armstrong said the words slowly, obviously ensuring that the giant man understood the full implications.

"Yes." Peter was crying, great tears rolling down his rough face. "Don't put me there, Mr Armstrong, please don't."

Mendick watched with some interest. He must have seen hundreds of miscreants being led to the cells, some defiant, others weeping or affecting mocking nonchalance, so one more made little difference to him. Nevertheless, Peter seemed capable of killing the much slighter Armstrong with just one swing of a mighty arm, so it was strange to see him obeying an obviously objectionable command so meekly.

"Come along, Peter, or it will be the worse for you." Armstrong showed neither remorse nor anger as he hurried Peter along to the first of the buildings in the valley.

The black hole was a stone structure with no windows and only a single small door, outside which Peter hesitated, holding on to the wall. He was whimpering pitifully,

"Please, Mr Armstrong, I was afraid they would hurt the horse. Please don't make me go in there."

"Get in," Armstrong ordered quietly, "or you'll be there for a week."

Squeezing under the low threshold, Peter immediately turned to face them. His eyes reminded Mendick of a terrified puppy.

"I'll allow you out when I think you've learned your lesson," Armstrong said, "and that might be a long time." He rubbed his back as if the minor fall inside the coach had caused him great pain.

"I'm sorry," Peter wailed, but Armstrong banged shut the heavy wooden door and dragged two iron bolts into position. Peter's whines rose in pitch.

"Ignore the shine," Armstrong advised. "He can't come to any harm in there, and it keeps him under control. I'll let him out tomorrow morning and not before."

Immediately dismissing his prisoner, he indicated the settlement with a sweep of his arm. "Welcome to Chartertown, Mr Mendick. What do you think of the new utopia?"

Turning his back on the lock-up, Mendick took a long look around the valley. The smallholdings looked comfortable under the rain, and each field was neat and carefully kept.

"I can see why people would want to live here," he said. "But don't the neighbours object to having a Chartist community in their midst?"

"Not in the least." Armstrong seemed to be almost choking with repressed satisfaction. "We are hard by Trafford land, and he has not the slightest objection."

"Trafford land? Sir Robert Trafford?"

"The very same."

The irony was unmistakable. Sir Robert Trafford was a dyed-in-the-wool Tory, a landowner of the old school, one of the regulars in the clubs of St James and Piccadilly and surely one of the worst enemies that the Chartists could have. When Trafford was not hunting with the Quorn, he was flicking cards across the green baize tables of London's gambling hells, while rumour insisted that he also made free play with society ladies or anyone else in a skirt.

"Let me show you around," Armstrong offered suddenly, surprisingly genial now that Peter was locked safely away.

Chartertown comprised a scatter of detached cottages, each set within its enclosed rectangular fields. At the head of the village stood the square church, with a simple tower from which rose a flagpole, but rather than flying the Union Flag or the Cross of St George, a green Chartist banner drooped in the rain. Backing on to the church was a swathe of meadow stretching to the skeletal trees of a regular plantation that marked the end of the enclave.

"We seem to have everything we need," Mendick said.

"It's a small beginning," Armstrong told him, "but we have over a thousand acres of land in England, and 70,000 people hoping to return to the land." He spat on the ground. "So much for the industrialists with their hellish working hours which tear families apart." There was fierce pride as he looked around him. "We don't have a total utopia, but it's worth fighting for, and that's where you come in. Walk with me."

As they moved through the settlement, a silent phalanx of men formed in their wake. Aged from their late teens to their early thirties, some wore fustian clothing, others moleskin trousers and smocks, but all looked painfully undernourished. Some were wide-eyed innocents; others had the solid maturity of married men while a few would certainly have cut their mother's throat for a shilling or a free drink. The only unifying factor seemed to be the universal determination with which they marched.

Armstrong led them to the meadow behind the church.

"This is our training ground," he announced with a short gesture of his arm, "and Trafford land begins inside that belt of trees." He grimaced, twisting his back. "Somebody once said that the Battle of Waterloo was won on the playing fields of Eton. Well, we have no Eton, but we do have this field, and in place of the Duke of Wellington, we have Mr Eccles here." He indicated a wiry, swarthy man who was looking penetratingly at Mendick. "And we now have you."

"I'm hardly Wellington," Mendick said.

"Maybe not, but you fight for a better cause. Wellington fought to maintain the status quo in Britain and to return the monarchical system to Europe. You will fight to create a fairer world. This will be *your* playing field, Mr Mendick, and *this* is the vanguard of the Chartist army." Once again there was pride in Armstrong's voice as he presented his collection of agricultural labourers and mill workers. "These are the men you are to train." He stepped back and watched Mendick survey his command.

More like a forlorn hope than a vanguard, they stood in ragged rows, fifty men in tattered clothes, looking at Mendick through patient eyes. Most carried broomsticks or tree branches, some carried blackthorn cudgels, a few carried pikes, and a handful, a desperately pathetic handful, held a musket.

"Good God in heaven." Mendick shook his head. He remembered the recruits trickling into the 26th: young men, old men, men in need of food, men who only desired drink, men who lacked the mental capacity to load and fire a musket and men who had slithered down the social scale to the ranks, and he shivered. Whereas there had always been an organisation to care for the Johnny Raws - a hierarchy of veteran soldiers who had grown old and wise in the ways of the British Army - he had only himself.

Armstrong grunted and touched the breast of his coat, where the bulge was a reminder of the threat he had made.

"Have you been throwing the hatchet, Mr Mendick? Have you been lying to us?" His eyes exuded detestation for anybody who stood in the way of his Chartist dreams.

"Stand aside, Mr Armstrong," Mendick advised. "I know little of politics, but this is work I do understand." Walking slowly along the front rank, he looked into each face, watching as the chins stiffened and the mouths hardened under his gaze. He nodded slowly.

"Right, lads," he addressed them quietly, foregoing the bullying rant that so many drill sergeants considered necessary. "We have a lot of work to do, and I'm just the man for the job." These men were volunteers for a cause, not a variety of misfits to be hammered into regimental unity; rather than raving, he would encourage.

"You don't know me yet, but I am James Mendick, late sergeant of the 26th Foot. I am here to turn you into soldiers fit to fight for the cause, men who will turn the tide of history, remove injustice from the country and ensure that everybody has a fair chance."

The volunteers were listening intently, some craning forward to hear better, others stepping closer. When he paused, one volunteer raised a thin cheer.

Mendick stopped that nonsense with an uplifted hand. About to blast the man's impertinence, he thought of the pitiful streets from where these people came.

"It's not time for celebrations yet, my friend. Let's achieve something first."

Shocked at his own mildness, he realised he was sliding from his real purpose and beginning to empathise with the Chartists. He had already gathered enough information to have Monaghan and Armstrong hanged and these poor deluded fools transported to the other side of the world. Forcing himself to look at them through the eyes of a policeman, rather than victims he saw potential rioters and revolutionaries, miscreants and murderers. And then Eccles approached him.

"Thank you, Sergeant Mendick." Eccles thrust forward his hand, ducking in a nervous bow. "Please teach us how to fight." He hesitated for a second. "I lost my sister to the fever last year, and my mother died the year before."

His face was drawn and pinched, yet Mendick recalled Armstrong's words about the short life span of men in Manchester and guessed that he was not above twenty years.

"I'll do what I can," he promised, suddenly hating Eccles for his pathetic gratitude. He must push his primary mission aside to concentrate on the present task, which was to turn this tatterdemalion mob into soldiers. If he convinced Armstrong of his commitment, he might learn who was financing this rabble.

Raising his voice, Mendick addressed the Chartists, "Right then, let's get started. Has anybody here got any military experience?" They looked at him blankly.

"No? All right then, let's see you march around this field. Keep moving until I stop you." He watched them as they marched like Johnny Raw recruits with clumsy limbs and stiff bodies.

Armstrong tapped his shoulder. "Most of these men have never been out of their parish before," he said quietly, "but we've been looking for a reliable drill instructor for some time. The last man was a lush. We had to get rid of him before he got in his cups and spoke too much." Again he tapped the bulge in his jacket.

The tramp of shuffling Chartists was suddenly sinister. They trailed in front of him, their boots thudding in the mud and their faces taut with concentration. The setting matched their appearance, with the trees stark in their nudity, gaunt branches clawing at a sour grey sky.

"How did you get rid of him?" Mendick tried to make the question sound innocent.

Armstrong dropped his hand. "Peter was a prize fighter; he took him for a walk and came back alone."

"I see." Mendick attempted indifference although Armstrong's words hung in the air like a verbal shroud. He remembered Peter's light tread and the width of his shoulders. Despite his obviously limited mental capacity he would be a formidable adversary. He watched as the volunteers reached the edge of the field, tried to turn and collided in a confusion of arms, legs and frustrated curses.

"Let's hope I come up to the mark then."

"Let's hope you do," Armstrong said.

The volunteers straightened themselves out and reformed their lines to straggle back, with those most impatient to impress outpacing the slow and stolid.

And now Mendick had his chance to impress. The ragged ranks halted in front of him, hoping for some magical spell that would transform them from an underfed rabble to a disciplined force capable of defeating the British Army and toppling what was probably the most stable government in Europe.

"Right, then." Mendick mentally pushed Armstrong's pistol and Peter's mighty muscles aside. "Let's get to work."

The men were as enthusiastic as any recruits he had ever seen, driven by desperation to muster together and all the more determined because of the knowledge that discovery would mean certain transportation. They responded willingly to his commands, coming fiercely to attention as soon as he showed them how, presenting their puny arms with near savage force and marching with such concentration that he sighed in empathetic sorrow.

Did these fifty forlorn men genuinely hope to challenge the government? Mendick shook his head, and his volunteers immediately looked downcast, as if they had made some cardinal error. These men were so responsive and eager to please that any line regiment in the British Army would have welcomed them.

"There's a sight to frighten the Whigs," Armstrong commented sarcastically.

"Let's hope that they're not spying on us," Mendick said, sincerely. He was already growing strangely attached to his volunteers. "At least we're secluded here." He nodded to the trees that formed a backdrop to the field. "How far does that woodland extend?"

"About a hundred yards, but Trafford's policies start half way through." Armstrong sounded casual.

"So close?" Mendick looked around. A buzzard keened overhead, the call intensely lonely as it patrolled its territory. "Is it wise to train beside Trafford's land? Any inquisitive gamekeeper can poke his nose in."

"Believe me, there is no need to worry about Sir Robert Trafford." Armstrong smiled. "You concentrate on the training and leave the politics to us."

Mendick shrugged. 'As you wish, Mr Armstrong." If Trafford reported the Chartist gathering to the police, his job would be made much easier.

Within a few hours most of the volunteers had the knack of marching correctly, their right arms and left legs moving in approximate unison, and Mendick called them to what they imagined was attention.

"Right, lads, you have learned the basics of marching. Let's try something more advanced." He grinned at their sudden surge of interest. "Before I'm finished, you'll know all the tricks of the soldier's trade, and today we'll have a small taste of skirmishing, scouting and all the excitement of standing sentinel."

Mendick had already decided it would be best to teach only a simplified version of each military skill, for he did not know how much time he had. The volunteers listened as he sketched the outlines, and followed his lead immediately. There was no doubting their willingness, but they lacked stamina and were pitifully thin.

"How are they?" Armstrong had been standing at the edge of the woodland, watching Mendick's progress.

"Weak. They need decent food."

"They shall have it," Armstrong promised, "when they have earned it." He raised his voice. "You hear that, lads? Sergeant Mendick wants to feed you more, although there are women and children starving in the streets. Do you want to take the food from their mouths? Or do you want to take the food from the tables of the landowners who oppress our people?"

The reply was less of a roar than a whimper, but the message was clear. The Chartist army would continue to drill on short rations and fight with hope rather than strength.

"There you have your answer." Armstrong sounded satisfied.

"We'll see," Mendick said. He had no desire to aid the cause of revolution, but having experienced hunger, he would not see men suffer needlessly.

Armstrong combined a sour shrug with his poisonous glare. "Will we indeed?"

When the dull day faded into dismal night, Armstrong permitted the training to end.

"Enough for today," he said, and nodded to Mendick. "Come with me and I'll show you where you'll sleep."

Mendick was surprised at the size and quality of the cottage Armstrong had allocated to him. The spacious living room was lined with shelves for books, one of the two bedrooms even boasted a real bed, and the privy was separate and moderately clean. Emma would have loved the splendid tiled floor of the kitchen, and she would have clapped her hands in ecstasy over the magnificent Welsh dresser and pine table. The iron grate, oven and boiler for water completed what was undoubtedly the finest cottage Mendick had ever seen.

"Impressive, eh?" Armstrong noticed Mendick's surprise. "Mr O'Connor and Mr Monaghan want only the best for the people."

"Utopia indeed," Mendick agreed. If this was the quality of life that the Chartist leaders planned for the people of Britain, it was no wonder so many gathered to the cause. "This must have cost something to build."

Armstrong's response was so savage Mendick knew he had touched on something important. "That's hardly your concern, Mendick! You attend to the training and nothing else. Do you understand?"

"Of course," he agreed immediately.

"Good. You'll be snug here," Armstrong promised, pausing at the door with his last words, "and safe as the bank. After tonight I'll instruct Peter to stay with you, and Eccles sends out regular patrols to make sure that no nosey gamekeepers come a-calling."

Or to make sure that newly arrived drill instructors did not stray, Mendick realised.

"I'll be back at seven tomorrow morning. Have a good night's sleep, for I want the men hard at work by dawn tomorrow."

As soon as Armstrong limped away, Mendick moved to the lock-up. He could hear Peter whimpering from three yards away, and when he opened the door the ex-prizefighter scuttled out at once, his face wet with tears.

"I'm sorry, Mr Armstrong, I won't drive like that again, I promise, only . . ."

"Mr Armstrong is not here," Mendick told him. "He wants to leave you inside all night." He watched Peter glance over his shoulder at the crowding dark. "But I don't agree."

Peter looked up, his face crumpled as he waited for orders.

"So this is what we'll do," Mendick told him. "I'll let you out, and you will stay in the cottage with me tonight, but tomorrow morning, before Mr Armstrong arrives, we'll put you back in the black hole and pretend that you've been there all night."

Peter nodded eagerly. "And we won't tell Mr Armstrong?"

"No, we won't," Mendick said, "or he'll put us both in the black hole." He held out his hand, knowing that if Armstrong put him in a hole, it would be with a shovelful of dirt on his face and a pistol ball in his brain.

For a moment Peter stared at Mendick's hand, and then he smiled as innocently as a baby and extended his own.

"After all, Peter, we're both fellow Chartists." Mendick felt Peter's paw slide around his like a huge iron glove.

"Fellow Chartists," Peter said, gently shaking hands and repeating the phrase he obviously liked, "Fellow Chartists."

Mendick smiled tautly; he had hoped to slip away during the night and find Sergeant Ogden, but his own weakness had spoiled that idea. He should have attended to his duty and left Peter exactly where he was. Now he would have to manoeuvre his way around the giant.

Once inside the cottage, Peter closed the door.

"In case the night gets in," he said and grinned. "We'll be like brothers, Mr Mendick. Fellow Chartists." Sitting on one of the two chairs beside the deal table, he produced a pack of cards. "We'll play for the bed," he said. "Loser gets the floor."

Glancing at the wooden floorboards with their scattering of straw, Mendick grunted. He had slept on worse, but he had never enjoyed suffering for its own sake. However, when Peter began a clumsy shuffle of the cards, sweating with the effort, and Mendick saw the breadth of his forearms, he looked again at the bed, wondered which unfortunate had last infested it and decided that it would be no hardship to lose. He would prefer a few hours of discomfort to a collection of broken bones, and anyway, he had no intention of spending the night indoors.

"Is there anything to drink in the house?"

In a lightning change of mood, Peter frowned at him.

"A lush, are you? The last soldier-boy was a lush too." He shook his massive head disapprovingly. "Tell you what, let's share the bed and play for the blue ruin. There's nothing better than a flash of lightning at this time of night."

"You have the bed," Mendick decided. "I just want a bottle of Old Tom."

Peter ruffled the cards. "You'll have to win it, first." His laugh was loud and unpleasant. "Come on soldier-boy; let's see how good you are."

Gliding to a corner of the dresser, Peter produced a large bottle of gin and placed it carefully in front of him, where it tempted Mendick with its memories.

"Twenty-one."

It was probably the simplest card game of all, and one that Mendick had played from Calcutta to Canton, but it was best not to let Peter know that. He avoided looking at the gin.

"What are the rules?"

"Don't you know?" Peter emphasised his superiority with a laugh. "It's all right, I'll teach you." Removing the cork from the bottle with his teeth, he took a preliminary swig while Mendick watched, fighting his desire. "The winner of each hand gets a drink." He leaned over the table, grinning hideously, "but the loser gets nothing."

Mendick nodded and played deliberately poorly for the next half hour, while Peter enjoyed a winning streak that saw him empty a quarter of the bottle and grow increasingly raucous.

"You're useless," he crowed as Mendick called for another card when he had a hand of nineteen, and, "Beat again!" when Mendick put down thirteen to his seventeen.

After an hour Peter's speech was slurred and the level of gin had lowered significantly, so Mendick slammed down his cards.

"You can't be this good," he said. "You must know exactly what I'm doing!

"What?" Peter looked up, his eyes hazed by gin. "How can I know that?"

"By cheating." Mendick pressed his advantage. "You must be looking at my cards."

"I'm not." Peter sounded hurt by the accusation. He shook a confused head. "You just can't play good."

"I know what game I can play," Mendick said. "I'll fight you, by God!" He rose from the chair and lifted his fists in the approved prize-fighting manner, hoping that Peter would take the bait and hoping even more that the gin had slowed the his reactions as much as his speech.

"I would kill you." Peter sounded amazed that anyone would willingly choose to fight him. "You're wrong, Mr Mendick. I wouldn't cheat you; we're fellow Chartists, and you let me out of the Black Hole. I'm just better at cards than you; have a drink and forget about it." He pushed the bottle across the table and spread his hands in a gesture of reconciliation.

Mendick hit him. It was a beautiful punch, straight to the point of the jaw, but Peter merely shook his head.

"What did you do that for? Now we will *have* to fight," he said, and Mendick wondered if he had made a major mistake. He was experienced in barrack room turn-ups and in the formal affairs for which Her Majesty had paid him, but Peter was a different proposition entirely. The prize-fighter was a good five inches taller and broader than him and was trained and knowledgeable in his brutal art.

The first punch hissed past Mendick's head with a sound like a passing cannonball, the second numbed his upper arm and the third smashed against his chest and knocked him against the door. He lay there, stunned from the force of the blow as Peter loomed over him, gesturing for him to rise, but instead Mendick yanked open the door and fled.

"Hey, come back, Mr Mendick! Please! If you run away Mr Armstrong will put me in the black hole! Please! I'll let you win!"

Mendick ran into the welcoming night, trying not to listen to Peter bellowing in his wake as he jinked into the trees that sheltered Chartertown. He winced, rubbing his chest and arm where the prize-fighter's fists had caught him; if Peter had that sort of power when half drunk, he would be unbeatable sober.

Within a few minutes he was struggling through brittle briars and stumbling over a half-tumbled wall as he climbed the small knoll where he had stopped only that morning. Looking back, he saw only darkness, but when he reached the summit he nodded his satisfaction. The countryside spread out before him like a black sea interspersed with the twinkling lights of cottages and villages and with one vast array of lights a few miles to the south. That could only be Manchester, and ignoring the confusion of paths Mendick struck directly across country, hoping he could find his way to Ogden's house.

He had memorised the address Smith had shown him and had spent the train journey north perusing a map of the Manchester area, but Armstrong's carriage had driven for a good hour beyond the town, which Mendick estimated would be around six miles. He would have to find the city first and then work out where Ogden lived. Mendick hurried, using the infantryman's quick marching pace and hoping that he was moving in the right direction as he repeated the instructions he had been given.

Sergeant Ogden lives in White Rose Lane in the northern outskirts of Manchester. He is in a cottage within a walled garden with a single brick shed.

The urban build-up began gradually, a cottage here, a cluster there, and Mendick moved rapidly, searching for names and landmarks, thankful that his night vision had always been good. Pushing through a belt of trees, he slipped over a gate in a hawthorn hedge and stopped at a tall stone wall. The name was painted white on a square piece of wood: *White Rose Lane*. Mendick sighed his relief.

It was a village of well-kept cottages with gardens front and back. Fruit trees told of a rural past, and geese honked a warning behind closed doors.

There were two buildings standing side by side, but whilst one looked neglected, the other had a crisply painted front door and an immaculate garden, just what Mendick would expect from the orderly mind of a police sergeant. Taking a deep breath, he tapped on the door and flinched when even that small sound set a dog barking.

A heavy chain stopped the door from opening more than an inch, and a whiskered face peered at him inquisitively.

"Sergeant Ogden?"

The whiskered face nodded suspiciously. "Yes?" The long barrel of a shotgun thrust through the gap between door and wall.

"I am Detective James Mendick from Scotland Yard."

There was a second's silence before the man spoke.

"Scotland Yard! Creation! Come on in, man!" The shotgun withdrew, the chain dropped, and Ogden threw open the door.

He looked about thirty, a few years younger than Mendick had expected, but already a paunch pushed at his long nightshirt. Despite the shotgun he looked more surprised than aggressive.

"What a time of night to come!"

"Who is it? Nathaniel, who is it?" A woman's voice floated from the upstairs room. "Shall I set the dog on him, Nathaniel?"

"No you shall not, Jennifer; it's a gentleman from Scotland Yard." Sergeant Ogden smiled to Mendick. "That's my wife. You'll have to forgive her; she can be a bit emotional sometimes."

Mrs Ogden appeared with a candle in her left hand and a border terrier on a lead in her right.

"Scotland Yard?" She was slender, with her hair in papers and her worn nightdress flapping over bare feet. "Well, shall we bring him in and feed him, Nathaniel?" She smiled uncertainly, hauling back the terrier which seemed more interested in sniffing at Mendick's boots than in any sort of household defence.

"Come in, man, and welcome." Ogden opened the door wider and stepped back to allow Mendick access.

"Scotland Yard in my house?" Mrs Ogden glanced at her husband as if for approval. "That's a rare honour, a rare honour indeed, sir, and you are most welcome to stay the night."

"I thank you for the invitation, Ma'am." Mendick felt himself bowing, happy to be among people with whom he could relax. "But I am afraid I do not have the time. I must spend a few minutes with your good husband and then return to my duties at once."

"Duties!" Mrs Ogden shook her head understandingly. "Of course, men must always perform their duties." She glanced at her husband and smiled, slightly timidly. "Nathaniel is just the same. You will stay for a jug of ale, though, and maybe some bread and cheese?"

Suddenly Mendick realised he was hungry. He nodded.

"The bread would be most welcome, Mrs Ogden, but I must decline the ale; perhaps a cup of tea, if you will be so kind?"

While Mrs Ogden busied herself in the kitchen, Ogden unhooked a lantern from behind the door and ushered Mendick into the back garden, where a brick-built shed stood immaculately to attention. The interior smelled of fresh soil and stored vegetables, with a slightly musty odour that Mendick could not identify.

"We'll get some peace out here," Ogden said, "and I have a number of items that you might find useful." Twirling a large finger through his whiskers, he sat heavily on a wooden stool. "I'm glad you came along, Detective Mendick, although I'm not at all sure what you can do alone."

"Call me James." Mendick had already formed a liking for this couple. "And I am not sure either. There are a lot of angry people up here."

Ogden nodded. "Can you blame them? The times are hard, cruel hard. Of course the people are restless, with unemployment so high and all this talk of Chartism and Radicals overturning the government." He shook his shaggy head so that his whiskers vibrated around plump cheeks. "Creation! There are even Chartists within the police up here. I don't know who it is safe to talk to." He looked up, his eyes suddenly stern. "Don't trust the police, James, whatever you do. Man, but it's good to meet a loyal man in these times of troubles. You have no idea how good."

"I feel the same way," Mendick agreed.

"Creation," Ogden repeated, "things were looking better with the good harvest last year, then came this wet summer and . . ." He shrugged. "I don't know what will happen now. Have you seen the country? There's starvation in the streets and that will lead to a bloody revolution, mark my words."

Mendick nodded. Although the trade and markets of London protected him from the realities of rural life, a country childhood had taught him the importance of the weather. While a good harvest created comparative comfort, a bad summer inevitably brought hunger and deprivation.

"Well, Sergeant Ogden, let's hope we can do something to save the country from that. We both remember the turmoil back in '42." He forced a grin. "If we can let Scotland Yard know exactly what's happening up here, we should be able to nip this sedition in the bud." He thought of the bitter eyes of the men in Manchester, the hostility of Armstrong and the determination of the volunteers, and doubted his own words. "So what do you have for me, then?"

"Quite a lot." Ogden began to rummage inside a heavy chest. "A Mr Smith sent them up by the railway, with a note telling us they were for you." Straightening, he produced a multi-barrelled pistol. "This is one of Harrison's pepperpot revolvers. You see? It has six short steel barrels and a self-cocking hammer, so that all you have to do is pull the trigger and the cylinder rotates, giving you six shots one after the other."

"I see." Mendick placed his hand around the black chequered grip, testing the weight of the revolver. "Six shots without reloading, eh?" He narrowed his eyes, marvelling at the prospect. "It's horrific: six men's lives in my hand; where will it all end?"

"It will fit inside this," Ogden handed him a leather holster, "which you can wear under your shirt. Just be careful you're not caught."

Remembering the force of Peter's punch, Mendick nodded; although percussion caps had reduced the chances of a misfire, he would hate to face the prize-fighter with only a single- shot pistol. This multi-barrelled weapon might just save his life.

"I'll be careful," he promised.

"And there is this too." Ogden handed over a long, needle-bladed knife. "It's called a stiletto, and they use it in Italy, I believe."

Mendick weighed the knife. "It's an assassin's tool, made for murder."

"Aye, but it might be handy in a tight corner," Ogden told him seriously. "I always carry one in case of emergencies; maybe you should do the same."

"I might take your advice." Mendick slipped the stiletto inside his boot, feeling the steel cold and criminal against his ankle.

"There's also a bull's-eye lantern." Ogden handed it over. "And lastly, there is this." Slipping to a dark corner of the shed, he returned with a wickerwork basket about two feet square.

"My lunch?" Mendick hazarded, until Ogden opened the simple catch at the top revealing three pigeons.

"Your couriers," he corrected, grinning. "All you have to do is tie a message to one leg, throw them into the air, and they fly to Whitehall. When there is a return message, the pigeon will fly back here."

"What?" Mendick stared at the nearest bird. The same blue-grey colour as a normal pigeon, it was taller and more slender, with a large cere above its beak. "What's wrong with using the telegraph?"

Since its invention ten years previously, the telegraph had revolutionised communications across Britain, with every main post office possessing the apparatus that could send a message across the country in minutes. He had intended to use the telegraph to send his intelligence to London.

"You can't trust the operators," Ogden said quietly. "The Chartists have infiltrated the network. They have men in just about every telegraph office between Glasgow and the Solent."

Mendick glanced down at the basket of pigeons. "Is it really that bad?"

"It is."

He whistled. "These people are more dangerous than I realised; Scotland Yard knows that there's something brewing up here, but if the Chartists control the telegraphs . . ." He stared at the pigeons, realising that the musty smell and the rustlings both emanated from this basket. "How will these beasts find their way?"

"They are specially trained." Ogden was obviously pleased at being able to educate the Scotland Yard man. "People have been using pigeons to carry messages for thousands of years, and mine are among the best, believe me," he said. "Indeed, pigeon racing is something of a speciality of mine. Unfortunately, the Chartists also communicate by pigeon; that's how they organise their rallies so competently."

He gave precise instructions in the elementary care and feeding of pigeons. "Do you have somewhere safe you can keep them?"

Mendick shook his head. "I share a cottage with a rather large Chartist," he said, "and I'll have to get back soon or he'll become very agitated." The prospect of an angry Peter was not pleasant. The prospect of Armstrong returning to find Peter loose was worse.

"Then you will have to keep them in the basket and feed them daily," Ogden said. "And hope that they're not closed in for long." He looked doubtful at the thought of allowing his precious birds into the care of an amateur, but finally relented. "I suppose it'll be all right," he said. "You *are* from Scotland Yard."

Mrs Ogden's voice sounded through the night.

"There's tea for you both and a nice hunk of bread and cheese for Mr Mendick, if that's all right with you, Nathaniel?" The papers in her hair made her look ridiculously domestic in a setting of pepperpot revolvers and secret messages.

The table was carefully set with a china teapot standing proudly on a fresh linen cloth and a candle stretching tall from its brass holder.

"Thank you, dear." Ogden drew back a chair for his wife before sitting down himself. He said a few words of grace as Mendick waited awkwardly, hoping he could escape quickly without causing offence. While Mrs Ogden watched and ate nothing, her husband asked questions, wanting to know how he had infiltrated himself and what his cover story had been.

"I just told part of the truth," Mendick said, cautiously, "about my time in the army, but I said that I was part of a Chartist group in the Indies."

"Oh, do tell me more," Mrs Ogden asked, and glanced at Ogden, "if you agree, Nathaniel?"

"I do not." Ogden held up his hand. "I don't think we should know too much."

Jennifer nodded. "If you say so, Nathaniel; you know best." She bowed her head in submission.

After they had eaten, Mrs Ogden excused herself. "I will retire now and leave you men to your duties. Come back to bed whenever you are ready, Nathaniel, and Mr Mendick, it was good to make your acquaintance."

"Surely you don't have to return to the Chartists," Ogden said, "if you have already gathered so much information?"

The prospect of catching the next train to London was so tempting that Mendick almost agreed, but he knew that the job was not even half done yet. He had a few names and the address of one meeting place, but when did they intend to act, and where? Would they march on London, or set the north alight? Even more importantly, was there somebody funding them, and if so, who was it?

He shook his head. "I have to go back." He was not foolish enough to believe there were only fifty men being trained, but so far he had no proof there were any others. He would have to return, sit out the danger and see what he could learn.

After the cosiness of the Ogdens' cottage, the night seemed unfriendly. Mendick crouched against the wind, holding the basket close to his chest as he entered the woodland behind Chartertown. Even using the bull's-eye lantern it took him an hour to find a suitably sheltered hollow in which to conceal the basket, and another ten minutes of fumbling to tie his message to the leg of the first pigeon.

He watched the bird flutter into the dark sky, its wings flickering for only a minute before it disappeared into the night.

"God speed, little messenger."

Suddenly he felt very alone; the hour or so of domesticity had reminded him of Emma, and he sighed as he tramped through the dark toward his cottage, with the pepperpot an unaccustomed weight against his body and the stiletto uncomfortable in his boot. What would Emma have thought about him carrying such things?

He was still wondering when the heavy hand closed on his shoulder.

"So there you are!" Peter's voice grated in his ear.

CHAPTER FIVE

Lancashire: December 1847

Mendick froze, wondering if he should draw the revolver or stoop for the stiletto, but Peter's next words dispelled both ideas.

"Thank goodness you're back," he said. "I thought that I had chased you away." He thrust forward his hand in his familiar, abrupt gesture of friendship. "I did not mean to hurt you; it was the drink, and I wasn't cheating, I promise." He looked around at the trees, nearly invisible against the pre-dawn dark.

"I don't think you would cheat, Peter," Mendick reassured him. "It seems that you are just a better card player than I am." He took Peter's hand again. "I had no desire to fight you either." He rubbed his arm, where a bruise was steadily spreading. "You're a far better fighter than I am too, and you looked so angry I thought that I had better stay away for the night."

Peter shook his head, repeating his apology. "Please don't tell Mr Armstrong what happened, James." He was trembling with genuine fear. "He'd put me in the black hole for days, he would."

"I won't tell him anything," Mendick promised. "We'll keep it between ourselves." He looked curiously at Peter's muscles.

"But Peter, why do you let him treat you like that? You could kill him with one finger."

Peter fidgeted uncomfortably.

"But it's Mr Armstrong, I can't touch him; it's not allowed. Besides, if I did, they'd lock me in the dark again forever and ever, Mr Armstrong said, always in the dark, forever." Just the thought had brought a sheen of sweat to Peter's forehead, and Mendick nodded.

"I see. Well, Peter, you have nothing to fear from me. I won't say a thing, and I promise never to put you in the black hole, or any other dark place."

Peter looked at him with total gratitude. "You promise?"

"I promise," Mendick said. "Now, I got myself lost running away from you, Peter, so I'll need some sleep before I start work again."

"You can have the bed." Peter seemed genuinely pleased to make the offer. "But I didn't cheat, Mr Mendick, because we're fellow Chartists."

*

Armstrong appeared almost as soon as Mendick's men were assembled on parade. "How are they?"

"Like nothing I have ever trained before," Mendick told him. "They're as keen as mustard."

"Are they ready to fight?"

"They're willing to fight, rather, but not yet ready. They need arms, and they're weak as kittens. Unless they're better fed, they won't last an hour against regulars."

"Weapons I can supply, but food is hard to come by this season; agricultural depression, don't you know." The sneer was obvious, and Mendick suddenly realised what was happening. Armstrong was deliberately keeping his men on short rations so they would be desperate to fight.

"As you wish, Mr Armstrong, but even Boney said that an army marches on its stomach."

"Aye, and look what happened to him." Limping away, Armstrong withdrew the bolts on the lockup door. "Out you come, Peter. Your time is up."

Mendick was surprised that Peter had the sense to look terrified as he emerged, blinking in the grey light of dawn. He looked at Armstrong like a rabbit at a circling stoat.

"Well, have you learned how to drive?"

"Yes, Mr Armstrong." Peter augmented his words with a vigorous nod.

"I hope so." Armstrong jerked a thumb toward the assembled volunteers. "Now, Mr Mendick is here to train the men in military matters," he said, "nothing else. I do not want him to leave Chartertown for any reason whatever, and if he does, I'll lock you in the black hole for a week. You keep him safe and secure, Peter; do you understand?"

"Yes, Mr Armstrong." The prize-fighter nodded, eager to please. "He'll be safe with me." He glanced at Mendick. "We're both fellow Chartists."

"That's it Peter, fellow Chartists all, and we must stick together, mustn't we?" Armstrong waited for the nod of agreement before continuing, "Well, you stick to him like two peas in a pod."

"I'm sure we can have interesting political conversations together," Mendick said, searching in vain for a spark of intelligence behind Peter's dull eyes.

"Fellow Chartists, all." Peter repeated the words as if they were a mantra.

"You remember that, Peter. I'm relying on you."

"Yes, Mr Armstrong." Peter was nearly glowing with embarrassed pride when Armstrong hunched away.

"He didn't find out, and he's relying on me." He looked curiously at Mendick for a second, with his face screwed up in puzzlement. "You didn't tell him."

"Of course not; we're friends." Mendick held Peter's dull eyes. "You could have killed me last night, Peter, but you did not. I challenged you to fight, remember, and you went very easy on me."

Peter shook his head. "You still didn't tell him."

"Well, it's too late now, and I hope that you don't object."

Shaking his head, Peter backed away, but his forehead was creased, as if his slow brain was struggling with a new problem, and twice Mendick caught the prize-fighter's puzzled eyes on him. However, Peter was a minor worry; far more important was the passage of his message to London. For a moment he pictured the pigeon fluttering over the damp fields and through the filthy smoke of industrial England, and wondered that so much depended on such a vulnerable little creature.

*

"We can't play cards tonight." Peter sounded disappointed. "You'll be all alone."

"Oh? Why is that, Peter?" After a week of Peter's company, Mendick hid his delight at the prospect of an evening to himself.

"Mr Armstrong needs me. I'm to drive him to meet somebody important."

"Oh?" Mendick tried to appear disappointed. "When are you going?"

"We're going now," Peter said. He pointed to the stable lad who had obviously delivered the message. "So you'll be alone all night."

"I'll be fine," Mendick told him, "but you drive carefully, or he'll put you back in the black hole."

For a moment there was dread in Peter's face, but he recovered quickly. "I'll drive carefully," he promised.

Following Peter to the stables, Mendick kept in the shadow of the trees as Armstrong lifted himself on board the blue and yellow coach, and then he trotted in their wake. His first idea had been to follow from a distance, but he decided that it would be easier to hitch a lift. Perhaps Peter's 'somebody important' was the man who financed the Chartists. If so, he could find out tonight and catch the first train back to London tomorrow.

Waiting until the coach jolted over the first ruts, he hauled himself on to the luggage step at the rear, holding on to the rail with both hands and relying on the mudguards to protect him from the worst of the dirt kicked up by the wheels. He knew that if he crouched low he would be safe from observation, for there was no rear window, while Peter was far too fearful to take his eyes off the road.

The coach jolted over the atrocious tracks for half an hour before turning left between a pair of stone pillars and grinding on to a smooth gravel road. With his arm muscles screaming in protest and his face and body spattered by mud, Mendick tried to see where he was. Lamps pooled yellow light onto a manicured lawn surrounded by flowerbeds, so they were within the grounds of a large property. As the coach slowed further, he guessed that they were nearing their destination, dropped off and quickly rolled away into the darkness.

He watched as Peter turned the brougham in a tight circle to halt beside the front door of an impressively elaborate lodge house. Lights glowed behind Venetian windows that flanked a columned door while the roof rose behind a castellated parapet. The door opened the moment the carriage halted.

Expecting to see a manservant, Mendick was surprised at the elegant appearance of the man who stood there. Over six foot tall, he was between forty and fifty years old, with long dark hair swept back from a high forehead, and a frilled white shirt that surely belonged to an earlier era.

As Armstrong stepped hunched from the coach the tall man moved forward to meet him, one hand extended in greeting. Although they were some distance away, the still night air carried their words quite clearly.

"Mr Armstrong! I am delighted you could come!"

"Sir Robert! I am glad that you sent for me!"

Sliding into a shadowed fold of ground, Mendick repeated the name. Sir Robert? In this part of the world, that could only be Sir Robert Trafford, but he was one of the old school, a noted Tory and utterly unlikely to have any dealings with the Chartists. Why was he meeting Josiah Armstrong in a lodge house? Mendick shook his head; it made no sense at all.

As Peter huddled in the driver's seat, Mendick crawled past the carriage, hoping to find an open window or some other means of access to the house. He would dearly love to listen to any conversation between Trafford and Armstrong, to see why two men with vastly opposing views were meeting with such cordiality. He swore as he came closer; for all the Gothic pretensions of this lodge, Sir Robert seemed to have it perfectly secure, with barred windows and a back door that was locked and bolted.

There was a sudden flare of light in a downstairs room, and he ducked down, keeping his head beneath the level of the sill, trying to listen to any conversation inside. He heard the low rumble of a man's voice, punctured by a short, explosive laugh, and then Armstrong crossed to the window and looked out. Only a few inches below, Mendick could clearly hear every word.

"It's good to have a man with your influence on our side, Sir Robert."

His companion came to the window. A full head and a half taller than Armstrong and as straight as a lancer, he spoke with the unmistakable confidence of the upper class,

"Something needs to be done about the suffering of the industrial workers, Armstrong. I only wish that these damned Whigs had not allowed things to get so bad."

Mendick looked up. The two men stood side by side, staring into the dark. Both held a glass in their hand.

"I have always said that the Tories and the workers are natural allies," Trafford said. "I have always been on the best of terms with my tenants; dammit, man, where would the estate be without them, eh?"

"Indeed, Sir Robert," Armstrong agreed. "It is the industrialists who are exploiting the workers, with their lust for profit and more profit."

"Damned upstarts." Trafford seemed to detest the rising middle classes more than he supported the exploited workers. "But together we can put them in their place, eh?"

"With your help, Sir Robert, we can curb their power and make the country a better place." Armstrong spoke carefully.

"And how much help do you expect, exactly?"

Even from outside the window, Mendick could sense the hesitation in Armstrong's pause. However powerful the man was amongst his peers, he still had sense enough to defer to a member of the ruling class.

"We need arms, Sir Robert. We have men enough but we lack weapons, and the Whigs . . ."

"Blackguard scoundrels!" Trafford's voice contained venom equal to anything Mendick had heard from Armstrong. "How many weapons do you wish?"

"We need as many as possible, Sir Robert."

"I'll see what I can do." Trafford sounded suddenly bored. "And now, if you would be so kind, I have personal matters to see to."

Keeping low, Mendick hurried to the front of the house, intending to resume his place on the luggage step, but Peter had parked with the horses facing down the gravel drive, and the back of the coach was in full view of the front door. It was impossible for him to climb on board. He cursed as Armstrong and Trafford came out together, speaking quietly as Armstrong boarded the coach, and then Peter flicked the reins. The coach began to move slowly over the gravel roadway with the lamplight bouncing from the shrubbery and Trafford standing watching with his glass in his hand and a small smile on his long face.

Mendick sighed and shifted into the long loping stride that would carry him to Chartertown. The distance was irrelevant compared to the startling intelligence that he had discovered. Sir Robert Trafford, the arch Tory, was supporting the Chartists against the Whigs. He knew he could not yet return to London; nobody would believe the connection until he gathered some tangible evidence. In the meantime he had to remain with the Chartists.

*

"On your feet, lad!" Mendick glared as a man staggered and fell, but he knew that it was weakness of the flesh, not the spirit, that caused the stumble. He looked over his command again, seeing them with new eyes. Even in his youth, not sixteen years ago, the standard of recruits for the army had been higher; the men had been taller, broader and fitter than these products of an industrial society. Most of the volunteers were under average height, some were actually misshapen from a childhood spent crouched in unnatural positions in mills or factories; others were racked with coughs or so thin it seemed a gust of wind would blow them away.

If these fifty men were a fair representation of the might of the Chartists, then God help Monaghan. The correlation, of course, was also correct; if this was the best that Britain could produce, then God help the nation if there was another war. In their constant quest for profit, the factory owners had brought terrible harm to the people of Britain. Once again Mendick wondered if he were fighting on the right side in supporting the establishment with their zeal for industrialisation, rather than the Chartists with their Land Plan and desire for human dignity.

Hardening his heart and voice, he played the part of the drill sergeant, blasting the volunteers towards a standard of perfection he knew they could never attain.

"Get those feet up, you idle blackguards! You're moving so slowly I can see the dead lice falling from you!"

The volunteers responded with astonishing urgency. Rather than resenting his verbal assaults, they showed a willingness curbed only by their physical weakness. Within a week Mendick had his little band at the level of army recruits of a month's standing. Within two weeks they could march as smartly as most line regiments, within three they could advance in open order and he was teaching them how to skirmish and scout.

He trained them in the driving rain, when every step plashed through muddy puddles. He trained them in the whispering snow, when the background trees were ghostly beautiful but the volunteers' hands were red raw with cold. He trained them on the frosty days when his breath froze against his whiskers and every sound was magnified in the brisk air. And all the time he hoped for news from London.

He had sent a second pigeon south with news about Trafford's Chartist connection, and every evening he disappeared into the woods for a walk, promising Peter that he would be back within an hour. He fed his remaining pigeon, looked in vain for a reply from Scotland Yard and upon his return always found Peter waiting anxiously for him.

Mendick had grown used to sharing the cottage with the prize-fighter. They spoke little but played cards each evening, with more equable results.

"Peter, I'm going to take some of the men on a night exercise."

"Mr Armstrong won't like that." Peter sounded alarmed.

"So we won't tell him," Mendick said and manufactured a grin, "or even better, you can come with us and keep an eye on me in case I find a public house and get bung-eyed, or lose the men in the dark, or run and tell a peeler all about this army that I've been training."

"No, I won't do that." Peter shook his head. "I know you'll come back."

"I always do." He had guessed that Peter would prefer not to enter the night-dark woods. He held out his hand. "You're a good man, Peter, and a fellow Chartist."

Peter took his hand with the edge of his fingers, his face confused.

"Fellow Chartist."

*

The volunteers stood at attention in the damp gloom of the December afternoon. A persistent drizzle soaked them while the trees behind them cowered in shivering misery.

"Right, lads," Mendick said softly, "it is nearly Christmas and we are surviving on starvation rations. That does not seem right for the vanguard of the new utopia, so I think it is time to do something about it." He enjoyed the surge of interest. "We're going to combine our training with a spot of Christmas preparation. Tonight some of us are engaging in a very valuable military procedure. We call it foraging, when we rake the countryside for food," he cheered them with a grin, "and anything else we can get our hands on." He had expected the resulting laugh and waited until it subsided.

"I've been watching you, and I know you now. I know the smart and the quick, the best at drill and those who are ready to employ sly little tricks to get off work."

This time the laugh was a little uneasy as the men looked at one other, wondering what he was about to say next.

"Right. I want Preston, Eccles and Duffy."

He selected the most devious of his men and the ones least likely to have any scruples. Foraging was far more a matter of individual initiative than drill and discipline.

"The rest of you are dismissed; report as normal tomorrow morning."

Even as he hefted the canvas bag into which he had packed a few useful items, he wondered about the legality of his movements. He, who had vowed to obey the laws that kept him on the side of respectability, was now not just bending those laws, but smashing them into splinters. He shook his head, grinned encouragingly to his chosen men and marched them into the darkness.

It was strangely nostalgic to lead a small patrol again, and if Lancashire was certainly not China, the local gamekeepers were probably more efficient than the Chinese army had proved to be.

"Keep close, lads, keep quiet and remember what I've taught you." He led them through the winter woodland and halted just outside Trafford land.

"I know this place," Eccles said quietly, more relaxed that Mendick had ever seen him. "I used to go poaching here as a lad."

"So let's go poaching again," Mendick said, "but I want food for fifty men."

"That's a tall order." Eccles sounded doubtful as his nervousness quickly returned. "Sir Robert is careful of his property. There's mantraps and spring guns all over the place, and as many keepers as we have soldiers." He shook his head. "Bastard."

The policeman in Mendick began to ponder. A man who put so much effort into security must have something to protect, or something to hide, which made this trip into Trafford land doubly interesting.

"Let's see what we can find."

"If you'd given me warning," Eccles said, "I'd have made some traps and caught us some rabbits."

"You can have time off tomorrow to make them," Mendick promised. "In the meantime, you can guide us in."

Eccles grew in confidence as he negotiated the outskirts of Trafford's land. Using brushwood as protection against the jagged glass, he slipped over the boundary wall with ease and slithered across the bough of a tree to descend the trunk.

"Sir Robert is careful always to lop the lower branches from any tree close to the wall," he explained, "just in case of men like me." His grin showed white in the gloom. "But there are always ways in."

Trafford's trees were spaced out, with an occasional exotic rhododendron set between native plants.

"Careful!" Eccles stretched out his hand. "Watch your feet here." He pointed downward, where metal gleamed through the leaf litter. Bending down, he brushed carefully with his hand to reveal a metal plate. "Man trap," he said, pointing to the saw-toothed jaws that were intended to slam shut on the leg of its victim. "Step on that and you're crippled even before the beak sends you to Van Diemen's Land."

As so often before during the last few weeks, Mendick wondered about his loyalties. Obviously the law of the land had to be maintained or there would be anarchy, but to allow landowners to employ such brutal devices simply to defend their game against hungry people seemed positively immoral. Trafford may be a supporter of the Chartists, but where his property was concerned he continued to act like the most selfish member of the upper class.

"Watch for spring guns too," Eccles warned. "The landowners rig trip wires attached to a blunderbuss or something similar. If you're lucky you'll only get peppered with bird shot, but a blast of *that* in your belly is bad enough."

Preston swore foully while Duffy vowed vengeance on any gamekeeper that crossed his path. They eyed the mantrap with loathing and moved ever slower as they neared Trafford Hall.

"There won't be much game near the building," Eccles warned, but Mendick shook his head. "We're not after game," he said. "We won't ever find enough to feed the five thousand . . ."

"But there's only fifty of us," Preston said, but Duffy nudged him and explained the Biblical reference.

"So we're going into the house itself," Mendick said.

Duffy nodded his approval, but Eccles, more knowledgeable about the law, warned of the consequences:

"If we go into the house it's called house-breaking, Sergeant; it might mean the rope."

"What do you think they'll do when they find you drilling and planning a revolution?"

"Sweet God in heaven, I hadn't thought of that." Eccles shook his head; after living the dream of Chartist utopia for so long, he obviously found it hard to bring himself back to reality. "Come on, then." He thrust back his hand. "No, wait!"

A tall man had emerged from a side door of the house, smoking a long cheroot.

"That's Trafford himself," Eccles said, and everyone stopped to watch the man whose property they were invading.

Dressed in a black frock coat, Trafford swept one hand over his unfashionable mane of glossy black hair as he looked out into the night.

"Handsome bugger, isn't he?" Mendick watched as Trafford finished his cheroot, flicked the butt into the grass and sauntered casually around the building to the front door, where he consulted the gold hunter suspended from his waistcoat. "It looks like he's waiting for somebody."

"And here somebody comes now," Preston indicated the landau that ground up the drive, its metal shod wheels scraping over the neat gravel. Leaving his seat, the coachman opened the door and bowed as a woman emerged, so swaddled in a heavy cloak that it was impossible to see her face.

"That's him occupied for the night then," Eccles said. "He likes the ladies, does Sir Robert." He looked around at Mendick. "Especially the Dutch ones, so I've heard."

There was a muted murmur of conversation, and then Sir Robert escorted the woman inside the house, with the front door opening smoothly before them.

"Right," Mendick decided. "Let's observe for a while."

Trafford Hall had occupied its present site for centuries, but a succession of owners had augmented and altered the original mediaeval building. The simple Norman keep was now only a small part of a complex of different architectural styles, its identity lost amidst an array of various wings. Waiting in the fringe of the trees, Mendick watched as flickering candles signalled the progress of servants checking the windows and closing the doors for the night.

"Will there be food in there?" Preston wondered, and Mendick nodded.

"With a staff that large, there will be more than enough food."

Without a watch, it was difficult to judge time, but he estimated that it was eleven at night before the final yellow light died and he could creep closer to the Hall. He toured the building, searching for an open window, but after twenty minutes he realised that Trafford had trained his servants well.

"All the windows are locked," he said, "so we'll have to break in."

"And how do we do that?" There was bitter cynicism in Duffy's voice.

"Watch and learn, my friend," Mendick promised.

Rounding a dark corner to one of the projecting wings, he directed his lantern onto a low window. "We'll go in here," he decided.

"Why choose this one in particular?" Preston asked.

"It's in the darkest corner," Mendick said. "Now, Preston, you keep watch for gamekeepers." He gave what he hoped was a reassuring smile. "You're our ears and eyes." There were iron bars set into the stonework around the window, with the glass of the multi-paned window behind.

"I thought you were a soldier, not a housebreaker." Eccles was watching with professional interest.

"Watch and learn, Mr Eccles." After hunting down some of the cleverest thieves in London, Mendick had picked up some of their tricks. Taking a length of cord from his bag, he drew it around the two central bars, and, using a short metal bar, began to twist, putting pressure on the bars.

"That's clever," Eccles approved.

"If you're taking notes, Eccles, I'll charge a consultation fee." He felt the cord rubbing the skin from his fingers but continued until the bars creaked and began to move. "There we go." he was unsure if he felt satisfaction or relief. With both bars loosened, he took hold and began to pull them back and forth.

"Let me!" Stretching over him, Eccles grasped the left hand bar and hauled it free of the mortar.

"Well done. Stand aside."

Two bars were not enough. Mendick had to loosen the next, which Eccles also removed with a single impressive tug, tossing the metal behind him with an expression of contempt. The sound of iron crunching on to the gravel path seemed to echo around the house. Mendick stiffened, and a score of bats exploded from the eaves far above.

"Quiet!" They crouched in the darkest shadows until Mendick was sure nobody was coming to investigate the noise.

He cut away the putty from the bottom window pane, thrust through his hand and flicked open the catch to ease open the sash.

"Is that what they taught you in the army?" Eccles asked. "Maybe I should sign up and thieve for Queen and country."

"People like me do to property what politicians and generals do to entire countries." Mendick did not have to inject the bitterness into his voice. "But while we would be transported for it, they are given titles and lands."

Duffy looked over to him. "That's the first time I've heard you speak like that, Sergeant."

Mendick grunted but said nothing. He was thinking like a Chartist again.

“There’s somebody coming!” Preston nearly shouted the warning, and Mendick quickly closed the shutter of his lantern and squeezed into the shelter of the wall. Hearing the confident crunch of footsteps on gravel and the patter of a dog’s paws he tried to appear as small as possible. If a lone gamekeeper caught them, they could fight their way clear, but with a score of servants within shouting distance, escape through policies thick with mantraps might not be so easy. The footsteps passed and Preston grunted,

“All clear, Sergeant Mendick.”

Mendick said nothing. He waited apprehensively for a few more moments and then crawled through the open window and inside the house. With his men silent behind him Mendick padded onto a stone-flagged floor in a dark room that smelled of mould and neglect.

“Lantern!” Mendick hissed, and Eccles obliged, directing the narrow beam around the room. Heavy wooden tables lined three walls, while unmarked boxes sat solidly on a shoulder-high shelf.

“It’s some sort of store room,” Duffy said.

“So I see,” Mendick said, as Eccles flicked the light around boxes of soap and candles, polish and paint. “No food, though.”

“That would be too easy,” Eccles said. “Let’s keep going.”

Closing the window, Mendick pulled a piece of dark paper from his pocket and placed it over the missing pane.

“If anybody should look in now, they won’t see anything or feel a draught. Now keep quiet.”

“Jesus, Sergeant, that was impressive.” Eccles looked at him with new respect.

“Aye, we learn lots of interesting skills in Victoria’s army.”

Their boots echoing on stone slabs, they moved through the ground floor, with Mendick not sure exactly for what he was searching but hoping for some sign. Duffy cleared his throat.

"Is the food not usually stored in the cellars?" Mendick berated himself for missing the obvious.

"Find a stairway, then," he ordered, and within minutes Duffy was leading them down a twisting stone stair, feeling their way along a rough wall that took them to a short corridor lined with doors.

"Cellars. Maybe wine cellars." Preston licked his lips.

"They'll be locked." Duffy looked to Mendick.

"Not for long." The army had taught him a plethora of tricks for foraging, but it was the people he had met as a police officer who showed him how to pick locks. The cumbersome, old-fashioned doors of this part of Trafford Hall were not even a challenge. The first cellar contained racks of bottles, filmed with dust.

"That'll do me." Preston reached for the nearest until Mendick pulled him away.

"Food," he reminded him. "We've got an army to feed."

The second cellar was filled with sacks of meal, interspersed with rounds of cheese and boxes of apples.

"That's better," Mendick approved. "Everybody select a sack of meal, some cheese and whatever else you fancy. I'll see if I can find anything else."

"Right, Sergeant." Eccles had already taken a huge bite of an apple and was chewing lustily, while Duffy was sampling one of the rounds of cheese.

To the delight of Preston, the next cellar was filled with jars of honey and jam, but the fourth was double locked, with a massive padlock holding a heavy chain in place. Mendick frowned as his police-trained mind switched on; what could Sir Robert Trafford possibly have that was so valuable it merited such precautions? He selected the most intelligent of his volunteers.

"Eccles, you lead everybody home and for the love of God, don't get caught."

"Are you not coming, Sergeant?" Eccles sounded nervous at the sudden responsibility.

"You just go ahead," Mendick ordered. "I'll not be long behind you."

Waiting until the volunteers had slipped into the dark, he knelt down to work, but after five minutes of frantic jiggling with the stiletto he realised that it would take an expert to pick this padlock. He swore and then froze as voices echoed along the corridor. There was the flicker of candlelight, a yellow glow that bounced along the wall in his direction and a deep-throated laugh.

"Dear God." He glanced behind him to where the corridor ended abruptly in a brick wall that blocked any prospect of escape. There remained only the food cellars, so he slid into the nearest just as two figures loomed at the far end of the corridor. Closing the door with his foot, he crouched in the dark and cursed again when the lock failed to connect and the door creaked open. With no time to close it a second time, he could only hide and hope that nobody noticed.

He looked around, momentarily panicking as he realised how vulnerable he was. The cellar was a place of stone. Stone walls sloped upward to a groined stone ceiling, while deep stone shelves held various sacks and boxes. Where was best to hide? Ducking down, he crawled into the lowest and furthest away shelf, dragging a sack of meal in front of him for additional concealment.

There were two voices; one belonged to Sir Robert Trafford, and the other to a woman who shared his confident, educated upper class accent. No doubt she was the same woman who had arrived in the landau. Why were they down here at this time of night?

The voices became louder until it sounded as if they were just outside the storeroom, then they abruptly stopped. Mendick tensed, wondering if he had been seen, but just then he heard the rattle of a chain and realised Trafford was entering the neighbouring cellar. Silence stretched for long moments, but as Mendick crawled out of his hiding place Trafford began to speak again.

The acoustics of the cellar created a frustrating echo; Mendick only caught the occasional word, but Trafford appeared to be an entertaining speaker for the woman was laughing. The sound was distinctive, with a curious whoop of breath that he had heard before, although he could not recollect where. Weighing the fear of discovery against his duty to ferret out information, he peered through the gap between the door and the wall.

Trafford was locking the padlock and speaking with the woman, who had one hand on his arm in a most companionable fashion. He seemed to listen with only half his attention, but then he smiled to her, bent closer and kissed her briefly on the lips.

Mendick choked back his surprise as the lantern glow fell fully on the woman. Last time he had seen her she was dressed in worn clothing and had the rough voice of a mill worker; now she wore a fashionable dress and her accent was entirely upper class. The woman who returned Trafford's kiss was Rachel Scott.

CHAPTER SIX

Lancashire: December 1847

"Oh, Robert, how forward you are." Scott pressed against him, hands moving down his flanks and on to the hips of his skin-tight trousers, and then she smiled, said something in a harsh, foreign language and pushed him away.

"Speak English, at least," Trafford commanded; Rachel Scott shook her head.

"If the Germans are good enough to pull you out of a hole, Robert, you could have the courtesy to learn their language."

"Courtesy be damned, woman! Ernie's not pulling me out of any hole. He's using my misfortune to set his damned white horse galloping all over his cousin."

"Temper, temper, Robert. That's no way to speak of kind Uncle Ernie." Scott's tone was mocking, but Mendick sensed the steel behind the words. "Don't forget what will happen if he decides to withdraw his offer."

"I won't forget, but damn you, Rachel, you know that I'm right." There was almost a whine in Trafford's voice as Scott again gave that curiously indrawn laugh and slapped his arm teasingly.

"Oh, Robert, don't be so serious. Just do what Uncle Ernest wants, and everything will be fine again. Think of the money, and remember I'm here to help you."

Trafford's laugh was loud but unconvincing.

"Of course you're here to help me, Rachel, but . . ." His tone changed from cajoling to sudden anger, "Damn these idle servants! Look at that, the blasted door is open, despite my explicit instructions!"

Mendick shifted back, trying to merge with the shadows and not make any noise as Trafford put his hand on the door handle.

"I'll have somebody's job for this."

Scott laughed again, "Luckily, it was *that* cellar."

"Only I have the key for the other," Trafford said, as their footsteps receded. "It's an inconvenience, though, all this sort of thing." His tone changed again and he seemed to be confused. "We're damned odd bedfellows, don't you think? Us and the Chartists?"

"It's the times in which we live, Robert. Everything's changing, so we have to make sacrifices and compromises." She then said something Mendick did not catch.

"The Traffords have been here for centuries, dammit. We're part of the blood and bone of England, and now I'm pandering to Radicals and . . ."

"Oh, Robert, there you go again. Just think of the end result; think of the power you will have. Uncle Ernest will be as much in your debt as you are in his. You might even be able to fly a white horse yourself."

Mendick was unsure if Trafford was laughing or grunting as he walked up the stairs, but he remained still for some minutes, pondering over their words. It made no sense that Rachel Scott should be in Trafford Hall at all, yet alone that she should be speaking to Trafford. Even more strange, why should she come to the house by coach, with her own coachman, and dressed in such fashionable attire? And what were the allusions to Germans and Ernie and a white horse?

Mendick shook his head; there was a lot here that did not add up. He already knew there was a strong link between the Chartists and Trafford, but where the mysterious Ernie came into it, he could not imagine. It was obvious that Sir Robert Trafford was a central figure, but how and why, was unclear.

Even more startling was Scott's chameleon-like ability to alter her accent depending on her company, and he wondered if Monaghan knew about this nocturnal visit to Sir Robert. Obviously, she was not just the factory hand she had claimed to be in the Beehive, but who or what she was Mendick did not know. However, he suspected that some of the answer lay within that carefully locked cellar. If he could get inside, he might have some valuable information for Mr Smith, but that would mean borrowing Trafford's key.

Very aware of the night time sounds in this ancient house, Mendick hugged the darkest shadows as he followed the voices. Candlelight bobbed ahead of him as Trafford and Scott meandered along the corridors, and Mendick followed as closely as he thought was safe. Twice he had to duck into deep doorways as floorboards creaked alarmingly, but in a building as old as this such things were to be expected and aroused no suspicion from the couple ahead.

Scott seemed jumpy, though, turning to look behind her on three separate occasions and Mendick kept further back than he liked. Eventually Trafford unlocked the door of a room, disappeared inside for a bare two minutes and reappeared.

"Now to more amenable pursuits," he said, and Scott laughed again, lifting her face to his.

“Oh, Sir Robert,” Her tone was mocking. “You do like to live up to your reputation, don’t you?”

Gliding an arm around her waist, Trafford whispered something which made her smile before he led her gently away. As soon as the candlelight had faded along the corridor, Mendick tried the door. The lock was simple, responding immediately to his stiletto, and he slid inside.

Trafford’s library was large and surprisingly modish with glass-fronted bookcases lining three walls and tall windows taking up most of the fourth. There were only three pictures. One showed Sir Robert as a young man in full hunting fig, the second was of a young, stern-looking woman with blonde hair and direct blue eyes and the third was a surprisingly cheap print of a distinguished-looking man on a white horse.

“The white horse,” Mendick said, looking at the picture for inspiration. The man glowered belligerently down on him, his whiskers neatly combed and his nose aristocratically curved. “So who the hell are you?” He shrugged and turned away. “I doubt it matters very much.”

Faint light from the windows revealed a roll-top desk standing proud with a brass candlestick on top and a leather-bottomed chair squared underneath. Trafford had been in and out of the room in two minutes flat meaning he must have thrown the key either on top of the desk or in one of the drawers. It took just a second to scratch a Lucifer from the box on the desk and apply it to the wick of the candle. Faint light illuminated the room.

He carefully rolled the desk open and was surprised to find it immaculately neat, with a brimming ink well, a blotting pad and a selection of quill pens. A penknife sat at their side, with the blade gleaming in the light of the candle.

There were three brass-handled drawers; the first contained a box of cigars and a notepad, with a short barrelled pistol placed carelessly on top; the second a small box of loose change, a collection of pornographic prints showing plump blonde women in various positions, a wash leather bag containing shaved dice and a pack of well-used playing cards. The third was empty save for a map of Chartertown and a folded document tied with a linen ribbon.

Holding the candle close, Mendick unfolded the document and attempted to interpret what was obviously legal jargon. He cursed and shook his head as candle wax dripped on the paper while the single flame cast fitful shadows across the page. Neither his police nor his army training had prepared him to decipher such terminology. Retrieving the notepad from the top drawer, he dipped a pen in the inkwell and began to copy the words, hoping to analyse the contents when he had more time.

It was tedious work, laced with the anxiety that somebody might walk in. After fifteen minutes he thought he heard voices outside the door. Shielding the light, he ducked behind the desk with his heart hammering and one hand hovering on the revolver inside his jacket.

The voices rose and fell, ending in a laugh as they passed. He returned to his pen, dripping ink on the paper as he scribbled.

"Sweet Lord," he said, as the import of the words gradually became clear. "Sweet Lord."

The document was from Dobson and Bryce, a firm of London solicitors, demanding that Sir Robert paid a large sum of money that he owed to their client. If the monies were not paid, the solicitors would take legal action, including seizing Sir

Robert's property and lands, and if their sale did not realise a large enough sum in such depressed times they would have Sir Robert thrown into a debtor's prison until his creditors were paid.

It seemed that the rich Tory aristocrat of Trafford Hall had exceeded his income and was in the hands of moneylenders. So how could a man in such a precarious fiscal position promise help to the Chartists? He could hardly supply what he did not have and surely would be too preoccupied with his own misfortune to be concerned about members of the working classes. Suddenly the contents of the locked cellar increased in importance.

Carefully replacing the document, he closed the drawer. Only then did he notice the candlelight reflecting off a small brass object beneath the desk.

"There you are," he whispered, and lifted the key. Dousing the flame, he cut a small piece from the candle and trimmed the wax until he had a useable wick. Putting the miniature light in his pocket together with two of Trafford's Lucifers, he left the room and negotiated the dark corridors, grasping at the wall for guidance as he fumbled down the stairs.

The key opened the padlock to the cellar in seconds, and he unravelled the chain before using his stiletto to push back the lock of the door. The chamber was dark but the perfume of gun oil was very familiar. He scratched a Lucifer on the wall and lit the wick of his candle stump.

"Good God!" When the flame rose he saw the walls were lined with long crates. Although most were securely sealed, the one nearest to the door gaped open, and Mendick peered inside.

Having recognised the shape of the crates, he was not surprised to see a dozen Brown Bess muskets, smoothly greased and neatly packed in straw.

"Third model India Pattern," he told himself, lifting the topmost like it was an old friend. He cocked the gun with the ease of long practice, sighted along the barrel and experimentally squeezed the trigger.

The sound of the falling hammer reawakened old memories. For a moment he was back in uniform amidst the humidity and horror of China, but he shook away the image; that past was gone. He remembered that Trafford had promised to find weapons for Armstrong but wondered again how a man as deeply in debt could afford such expenditure for a cause so far from his own interests. He smoothed his hand over the thirty-nine-inch barrel; there seemed to be a great deal of mystery surrounding Sir Robert Trafford and his friend Rachel Scott.

Replacing the musket, Mendick moved around the cellar. There were many more crates of muskets augmented with boxes of the lethal seventeen-inch bayonet used by the British Army. There were also barrels of black gunpowder, boxes of lead shot and a single box of long-barrelled pistols.

He swore. Training the unarmed volunteers had seemed like play-acting; he had never expected them to possess muskets. Now Trafford had enough firepower to equip half the population of Lancashire, let alone a few score Chartists. He shook his head as he thought of his eager, disciplined men marching through England, well armed and as full of bitter hatred as a lifetime of repression could make them.

Scotland Yard had to know about this development. He had to inform Mr Smith so the uprising could be halted before it became deadly serious. He ran his eyes over the crates, calculating the quantity of weapons, and wondered where they had come from. Unless there was a very corrupt quartermaster at Horse Guards, they had not come from the War Office, so they must have another source.

That thought was interesting for there were not many manufacturers who would be able to mass-produce quality muskets. As the candle began to gutter he scanned the crates for a factory name, but they were plain wooden boxes with no distinguishing mark. In an age of blatant commercialisation, the manufacturers had neglected to proclaim their affiliation to the wares, which was nearly as mysterious as a debt-ridden landowner aiding the Chartist cause.

The candle finally died, leaving him in the dark. He sighed. He would send this intelligence tonight and let his superiors worry about the meaning. With luck they might recall him back to London where he did not have to share a cottage with a brainless giant and did not have to be careful of everything that he said and did. He quietly blessed the forethought of Sergeant Ogden in providing him with a clutch of pigeons to carry messages. But first he would have to return the key.

By now he was familiar with the layout of the house and hurried through the unlit passages, almost running up the stairs and through the corridors. He was nearing the door of Trafford's library when he turned the last corner and walked straight into somebody soft and pliable.

"Oh, my God!"

Mendick swore with the sudden shock of collision, automatically putting out his hands. He felt the rounded warmth of a woman's body and started as her alarmed howl echoed around the house.

"Who's that? Mary, are you all right?" A man's voice sounded from further down the corridor, and Mendick turned and ran.

"You! Stop!"

The accent was rough, a servant rather than a master. Mendick cursed that he had not bluffed it out, but it was too late now. He must have disturbed some clandestine romantic liaison and it was just bad luck they were in the corridor at the same time as him.

"Stop! Thief!"

Mendick swore again, for those words would rouse the house. He heard confused calls, the sound of opening doors and saw the glimmer of a candle while dogs barked and the unknown woman still screamed in alarm.

"Why is there all this shouting?" There was authority in the voice, even through the blurring of sleep.

"I thought I heard a noise, Mr Sims, and I came to investigate. There's a strange man in the house."

"Some blasted thief no doubt! Bring lights and we'll soon have him by the heels!" Mendick thought the voice belonged to the butler.

"You! Make sure nobody enters the Master's rooms! Oh God, why did this have to happen tonight when the Master has company? Move quickly now!"

Mendick could see more candles and hear the baying from what sounded like a mastiff.

"Keep that damned dog quiet or Sir Robert will have our hides!"

Mendick dashed into a side corridor feeling more like a hunted thief than a Scotland Yard officer. If he were caught, he could hardly explain his presence by saying he was stealing food for the neighbouring Chartists. He cursed and felt for the key. Trafford was sure to miss it and would know that his secret was discovered; no casual sneak thief would break into his library only to steal a key.

He would have to return to the library.

"For the love of God, don't disturb the Master."

Mendick heard the phrase repeated as candles flickered along the corridors and soft-footed servants peeped nervously into darkened rooms. Silently blessing his good fortune that he had chosen a night when Trafford was busy with a woman, Mendick edged cautiously forward, dodging into door recesses when servants came close, padding along the echoing corridor whenever it seemed safe.

He heard voices as he approached the library and saw a stout man standing outside holding a lantern in a shaking hand. Mendick watched for a second, saw the man test the door handle nervously before sighing audibly and walking away with the lantern casting erratic shadows all around.

Easing forward, he slipped his stiletto behind the lock and slid into the library, sliding shut the catch behind him. Replacing the cellar key exactly where he had found it, he stepped toward the door.

"What's all the blasted commotion in this house?"

Mendick recognised the rich tones of Trafford and froze as a strong hand rattled the door handle.

"Sims! Have you checked in here?"

"The door's locked, Sir Robert."

"I know it's locked, Sims! Have you checked inside?"

"No, sir." The voice ended in a yelp of pain.

Mendick ran quickly to the window, but a brief glance revealed a group of servants standing immediately outside. He would have to sit tight and hope that nobody came in.

"Damn you, Sims, can you not perform the simplest of tasks? Find the key and check the damned room!"

Mendick heard scurrying feet and then the strange, indrawn laugh of Rachel Scott.

"My, Robert, you *are* masterful when you are angry, but should you not dress yourself?" There was the sound of a soft slap. "You might shock the servants."

"I'll dress any way I like in my own house, Rachel - if the servants don't like it, they can damned well leave."

Rachel laughed again. Very slowly, Mendick unlocked the door and peered out, to see Trafford, stark naked, grasping a riding whip and facing away from him with Scott at his side. She wore what appeared to be a white sheet inadequately draped over her body, so her right leg and left shoulder were left shockingly bare.

"Light every damned candle in the house and search every room!" Trafford flicked the whip through the air as he took charge, his rich voice penetrating into every recess as he organised the hunt.

"Rouse everybody out of their beds, even the blasted tweenies; I want the house turned upside down, dammit! I want this blasted thief found and I want to see him swinging at the gallows!"

Mendick pressed hard into the darkest shadows on the wall as a host of servants appeared; he was quite aware that Trafford had the power to carry out his threat. Although burglary may not be a capital crime, a major landowner like Sir Robert could say anything he liked in court. He could claim the burglar had threatened violence, which could be enough to have him sentenced to death, and suddenly Mendick remembered Mr Smith's words: "If you are discovered . . . we may not even be able to admit you are one of ours."

The prospect was alarming. Previously, when he had faced danger, he had had the security of a uniform and an official position. The regiment would support him, the police force had been there to back him up, but now he was truly alone, trapped in an English country house with a vengeful proprietor after his blood and scores of staff only too eager to help.

But what exactly had he learned? Mendick thought of the muskets in the cellar and the legal document in the desk. The law did not forbid anybody owning muskets and many landowners were in financial difficulties, but taken together with his knowledge that Sir Robert was befriending the Chartists these isolated facts could be significant. The quantity of muskets was particularly worrying. Mendick was not sure exactly what his intelligence meant, but he knew that he must escape and inform Mr Smith of all that he had discovered.

Candles were being lit all over the house as servants ran this way and that, dressed in their night clothes and shouting contradictory orders as they got in each other's way. For a second Mendick contemplated waylaying a footman and swapping clothes, but he discarded the idea at once; there was bound to be noise, and where could he put his victim? His only sensible option was to find somewhere to hide until the initial panic had subsided.

He waited until the corridor was clear before he slipped away, but then shadowy figures ahead and the glow of a candle made ducking through the nearest door prudent.

He was in the withdrawing room, with a huge piano against one wall and a selection of chairs and small tables crouching on an Axminster carpet. As voices sounded outside he ducked behind one of the largest chairs. He was suddenly aware of the hammer of his heart and the dryness of his mouth.

"Check in here!"

There was the butler's authoritarian voice, and a young man then entered the room. He was ludicrously dressed with his trousers pulled over a baggy nightshirt and a nightcap on his head, but there was nothing amusing about the stout stick in his hand. When he held up a candle in a brass holder, shadows jumped around the room.

"Hello?" The man did not penetrate far, peering nervously into the room. "Is there anybody here?"

Mendick kept still. He knew that it was almost impossible to distinguish shapes in a half-lit room, but any movement would mean instant discovery.

The servant brandished his stick. "I can see you," he said and moved cautiously across the carpet to the mantelpiece with the candle guttering in his hand and his nervous breathing audible in the otherwise silent room. Without lingering he lit one of the candles on the mantelpiece and withdrew quickly, obviously relieved that the room appeared empty.

"There's nobody in here, Mr Sims."

Mendick sat tight, listening to the scurry of passing feet, the querulous voices of servants and the banging of doors, until the sounds faded into the distance and he emerged from behind the chair. Now he had to escape from an alerted building and send his message to London.

He was fortunate that the withdrawing room had large windows which opened directly to the terrace; it was simple to slip the catch and roll to the ground outside. Although the terrace was empty, there were men in the policies with their lanterns high and their voices raised to give each other courage. Mendick tried to gauge their numbers and swore softly as he saw the whitely naked form of Trafford leading a small patrol of the outdoor staff.

"I want this thief caught, and I want him hanged!"

Standing in the shadow of the wall, Mendick knew that he would be reasonably secure once he reached the woodland. The danger was in crossing the immaculate sweep of the lawn. With half the lights in the house blazing, the immediate surroundings were as illuminated as one of those new-fangled Christmas trees that Prince Albert was blamed for bringing over from Germany. For a moment he was back before the walls of Amoy, with the lights flaring and the Chinese Army waiting for the assault, but he shook away the memories.

The sounds died down as the servants moved to a different section of the house. Mendick counted to ten, took a deep breath and ran across the short grass, not bothering to dodge as he relied on speed to carry him to safety.

"There he is!"

It was almost inevitable that somebody should see him but rather than hesitate, Mendick ducked his head and ran all the faster. He heard the sharp crack of a firearm but the shot was so poor that he did not even hear the wind of its passage. Somebody was running behind him, other people were shouting uselessly, that damned dog continued to bay and then he was amongst the trees with darkness a cloak and the servants crashing behind him clumsily, beating the bushes with their sticks.

"Come out, you bastard!"

"I saw him; he went that way"

"Should we be doing this? Would it not be better to just let him go?"

After dodging Tartars and Mongolians during the Opium War, Mendick was not concerned about a score of British house servants although he was slightly wary of the gamekeepers. He was also nervous that he might trip one of the man traps, so he moved slowly through the trees until he found the boundary wall. The final barrier, but Mendick was in no mood to be delayed and scrambled up the bole of the nearest tree, gathered his courage and leapt into the darkness.

He felt the sharp pain of a twisted ankle, but the relief of leaving the policies of Trafford Hall was more than adequate compensation, and he limped back to his remaining pigeon. It seemed pleased to see him as he fed it a handful of seed from the jar beneath the basket. He composed a short note: *Trafford friendly with Chartists. Has large quantity of arms.* He pondered for a while, wondering if he should mention the lawyer's letter and the white horse but decided that they were not so important. Instead he added, *Will remain in position.* He tied the message to the pigeon's leg and launched the bird into the air.

"That's all I can do for now," he told himself, but the image of those muskets remained with him together with the memory of Trafford and Rachel Scott. It was not until he returned to his cottage and the anxious face of Peter that he realised he may have been wrong. Perhaps Trafford was not friendly with the Chartists? Perhaps Rachel Scott was a Chartist plant in Trafford's house and he had just sent misinformation to Mr Smith?

This possibility left him very troubled. He also began to wonder why Scotland Yard had not sent back any of his pigeons.

CHAPTER SEVEN

Chartertown: December 1847

Mendick permitted himself some slight satisfaction as he walked around Chartertown. With the meal and delicacies the volunteers had liberated from Trafford Hall, the people of Chartertown enjoyed their first decent Christmas in years. He started as Preston's wife smiled to him. Normally she greeted him with a suspicious glower, as if he was personally responsible for leading her man into danger.

"You'll be coming to our Christmas, then?" Mrs Preston asked, her thin face taut but with new warmth in her eyes.

"I would dearly love to come, Mrs Preston, if I am not inconveniencing you."

"You made it possible," Mrs Preston told him. "It's the first time in their lives my children have had full bellies." She turned quickly to rebuke her son. "John Frost! Stop pulling at your sister's hair!" Her slap lacked any force. "We've called all our children after the great Chartist leaders," she explained. "They're all we have, really."

Mendick smiled and nodded. John Frost had led the Chartists to disaster at Newport in 1839. He was hardly the most auspicious of heroes.

With so many working class people gathered together, Mendick was surprised that most of the celebrations involved little of the heavy drinking he had come to associate with an

English Christmas. The absence of alcohol did not seem to spoil the general feeling of goodwill, however, and he was even more pleased that Armstrong had called Peter away on some private mission.

Following a series of muted protests from the wives, he had cancelled his programmed Christmas Day training, and everybody gathered at the simple church where a Chartist pastor delivered a traditional Christmas message of peace and goodwill.

"We are gathered in hope for a better future." Dressed in respectable clothes but with no pretence of formality, the pastor addressed his congregation as if they were friends, rather than speaking down to them in the clergy's usual patriarchal manner. "And although we prepare for the violence of war, let us all pray for a peaceful resolution to our difficulties, an extension of the franchise and a better life for everybody, with co-existence rather than conflict."

Following the sermon, there were carols with a Chartist message, and a communal meal to which everybody had contributed. The pastor raised his hand in blessing.

"May God grant peace to everybody here and to everybody in this country. Let us pray that the government can find it in their hearts to accept the Charter and bring a more equable society to us all."

The messages of peace heartened the congregation as they filed outside to enjoy the warmth of the bright fire outside the church wall. Mendick was struck once again by the philosophy that these Chartists embraced. Used to seeing his volunteers as prototype soldiers, when he saw them mingling with their families he realised they were husbands and fathers first, and for a moment he saw them, however distantly, as the inheritors of exactly the utopian community that they desired. He saw them working their few acres as independent yeomen, much as their ancestors had done before industrialisation; he saw them with a say in this country that had cheated them of so much, and he wondered if he had the right to destroy their dream.

At that moment it would have been easier to join them, to throw in his lot wholeheartedly with these hard-used, stubborn, undernourished people and fight against the inequalities of the established system.

Until he remembered the stacked boxes of Brown Bess muskets, and the prospect of the horrors that Civil War would create. There was no utopia in war, only blood and agony, broken minds and mutilated bodies. Looking around the gathered families, he shook his head; if these people were not volunteers for a glorious, just cause, neither were they raging revolutionaries. They were all victims of two contrasting ideologies, one of selfish privilege and the other of bitter resentment.

In the eyes of the chief protagonists these people, these intense, suspicious, impetuous, emotional people, counted less than an indrawn breath. Did it matter if it was Monaghan or Earl Russell, Josiah Armstrong or the Duke of Wellington who consigned them to the muzzle of a musket? Either way they were doomed to be blown this way or that, dependent on the whims of their political masters, and that was the real tragedy of their lives.

Whatever they did, and however well they did it, did not matter. They would leave no mark on the world, they could only live their brief lives and disappear, unknown, unrewarded and unrecognised by anybody in any way.

"God save you all," he whispered, "for I am an agent of your destruction."

He saw Mrs Preston lifting young John Frost Preston in the air, laughing at the simple pleasure of having a full belly. He saw Eccles's sardonic face split into a huge grin as a young woman slipped her arm into his and presented her lips for a kiss. He saw Duffy pull a bottle from inside his jacket, take a sly sip and hand it over to the eager hands of a friend.

These were not bad people, so why in God's name did they have to live in such misery?

The church bells rang joyously, celebrating the anniversary of the birth of Christ as the Chartist families exchanged greetings and good wishes. Mendick smiled as for one brief day they embraced something of the utopia for which they hoped. He could almost sense the peace that descended on them as he looked around the scattered community.

Here was the church, a symbol of hope in a land of oppression, and the Christmas tree, green amid the stark branches of winter. Here were the people, dressed in their threadbare best, and all around were good wishes and a tangible feeling of friendship. Some families were already disappearing into their homes, keeping the doors open to allow their neighbours free access, and the sound of carols sweetened the air.

"Merry Christmas, Chartists," Mendick said quietly, "and please God you are all here to see the next."

"Here comes Josiah!" Eccles pointed a slender hand to the track which led from Chartertown to the uncertainties of the outside world. "And he's coming in style."

"Oh, no," Mrs Preston said quietly. She pushed her son, noisily munching an apple, into her house. "Stay indoors, John Frost, and keep your sister with you."

Armstrong's coach swayed alarmingly as it creaked along the rutted track. Peter was driving, his forehead furrowed in concentration, and he halted the horse with an expression of utter relief. Mud from the wheels spattered onto the ground and the horse stood, head bowed in the traces, with froth along its flanks and its breath clouding around its head.

"Here we are, Mr Armstrong." Peter's voice matched the relief on his face.

Armstrong disembarked, one hand holding his red cap to his head and the other placed for balance on the door of the coach. He wore a smart chesterfield with a velvet collar, but none of the wives smiled at him.

"Here we are indeed." He looked around the settlement as if he had never seen it before, his mouth twisted by that sinister scar. "Where are the men? Where are the soldiers of the Charter?"

"Celebrating Christmas with their families, Mr Armstrong," Mendick said. He could almost feel the spiteful chill emanating from the man.

"There'll be time for celebrating when the fight is won." Armstrong sounded more smug than angry. "Get them formed up, man; I've brought them something that will transform their lives forever!"

"But it's Christmas." Mendick tried to gain an extra few minutes more for his men, but he knew that the day had already changed.

"Tell that to Finality Jack." Mendick grunted. Trust a Chartist to use the nickname attached to Lord Russell ever since he had called the 1832 Reform Act the final solution. Armstrong frowned.

"Now get them out here, or I will send Peter to do it for you."

It took ten minutes to prise the volunteers away from their wives and children, and Mendick had to close his mind to the expressions of dismay on so many faces as he paraded them beside the coach. They stood to attention, each man more erect than his neighbour and for a moment Mendick was proud of the progress he had made. He could feel the families gathering behind him, asking questions and wondering why their Christmas was being disrupted. The sound of sobbing children nearly obscured the song of a solitary robin.

"They're coming on." Armstrong ignored the disappointed families as he glowered at the volunteers. "They look fit and healthy." He raised his eyebrows. "And better fed than before."

"We did some foraging," Mendick admitted. He was unsure how Armstrong would view his independent actions.

"Aye? Be careful. We don't want to draw attention to ourselves in any way. Not yet." Armstrong nudged him with a sharp elbow. "But we've not long to go now. Wait until you see what we have inside the carriage." His sudden grin reminded Mendick of a week old corpse, and then he signalled to Peter, who plunged inside the coach and dragged out a very familiar crate.

"Do you recognise this?" Armstrong asked, and for a second Mendick wondered if he had been seen in the cellar after all, but Armstrong continued with hardly a pause. "I'll wager that you do! These crates are exactly the same as those used in the

British Army, and we both know what they contain." His voice cracked with excitement as he opened the crate.

"Look at this, boys! Just look at what I have for you!" Holding up a musket, Armstrong grinned to the men, who remained in rigid lines as they had been instructed. "This is an India Pattern Brown Bess, the same as the redcoats use. Come over then, and look!"

While a few of the men surged forward, most looked for Mendick's approval before they moved, some to grab a musket and hold it as if were made of gold, others to glance apologetically at their wives. Only Mendick saw the shock on the faces of their families; while training with sticks and staves had made violence seem only theoretical, these muskets brought home the reality of what might happen. Armstrong might have brought gifts, but they were not the embodiment of the Christmas spirit.

"*Now* we can overturn the government," Preston said, running a calloused hand up the length of the brown barrel. "*Now* we can bring work and houses and feed the people. *Now* we'll show these bastards." He was shaking his head, his eyes moist with emotion.

As most were, Mendick realised. He had expected an outpouring of rage, expressions of hatred and the desire to slaughter, but instead he saw mostly relief, a hope for a better life and a yearning to get the job finished as soon as possible. Yet again these Chartists had surprised him, increasing his affection for the men he was training to be slaughtered. Only two volunteers hung back, one youngster who could not have been more than seventeen and a balding, middle-aged man who held his musket as if it were the handle of a plough and clung to the arm of his wife.

"They're good men, Mr Armstrong," Mendick said. "I don't want them wasted."

"Wasted?" Armstrong guided him away from the volunteers as Peter unloaded a box of bayonets and handed them out. "I can't tell you too much yet, but I can reveal a little now that you've proved yourself. Peter says that you have been very dedicated, training the men hard, and not only in simple drills but in skirmishing and foraging too."

"Of course." Mendick resolved to let Peter win their next few card games, at the very least. "These muskets are impressive, Mr Armstrong; they appear to be quality weapons, not some Brummagem rubbish for the African market. If they're the India Pattern or the 1842 Short Land Pattern, then they're equal to the best used by the British Army!" He tried to sound casual. "Can I ask from where they come?"

Armstrong shook his head. "That I am not at liberty to say. But I can reveal that we have help in high places. Unexpected places too." The warped grin seemed only to augment the acid in his eyes. "We will make an impact this time; that I promise you."

Mendick decided to push a little harder. "We'll need more than fifty men, then, if we want to make an impact," he said. "Fifty men won't last long against the whole Queen's army."

"We have more than fifty." Armstrong's grin writhed around his mouth as he watched the Chartists examine their muskets. "We have a few more in other places."

"A few more?" Mendick was uncertain how far to probe, but any fragment of information could help nip this insurrection in the bud. He saw Mrs Preston exchange a child for her husband's musket and hold it at arm's length, as if it were something vile. Should he condemn that woman to widowhood? Or should he break her dream and send her man back to the hellish long hours and shockingly low pay that industry demanded of its victims?

"How many is a few?"

Armstrong lifted a musket, his fleshless claws closing on the stock. Keeping both eyes open, he sighted on the church tower and pulled back the hammer.

"I can say that this unit is only one of several that we have stationed all around the country." He pressed the trigger and the hammer clicked down ominously.

Mendick nodded. "I thought that we were too small a group to overturn the government." He would have to relay this intelligence to Mr Smith as soon as one of his pigeons returned. "So how many of us are there, Mr Armstrong?"

"Again, I am not at liberty to impart that information." Armstrong's face closed. "But suffice to say that the *establishment,*" he made the word sound like a sneer, "will be dismayed at the power we can command."

Mendick forced an eager smile. "So when do we act? When can I lead these men against the Whigs?" He hesitated a little. "I would like another few weeks, if possible. They are good, but not yet up to the standard of regular line infantry. For one thing, now they have muskets, they have to be taught to shoot."

"Which I am sure you will do very well." Armstrong seemed pleased at Mendick's enthusiasm. "We have more than sufficient powder and ball, and I can assure you that you will be given advance warning."

"And the noise?" Mendick probed deeper, pushing Armstrong as far as he dared. "Fifty men volley-firing creates a tremendous shine; the neighbours will be bound to hear. . ."

Again Armstrong looked gratified, his red cap bobbing as he nodded.

"You mean Sir Robert Trafford? Don't you worry about him. Mr Monaghan has Trafford well numbered and filed. You shoot away all you like, and remember that every ball is a tiny lead nail in the coffin of the government! He's a fine man, is Mr Monaghan, and a first class leader. Indeed, he wants to see you." Delving into the tail pocket of his coat, Armstrong produced a sealed letter. "This is your invitation. I think he's going to tell you . . ." Armstrong shook his head. "Perhaps I should not say, yet. Although I can guarantee that you will find the meeting very interesting."

Mendick kept his face immobile although he felt the tension build inside him at the prospect of discovering more about the mysteries that surrounded this surreal insurrection. Armstrong seemed to be watching him very closely, as if gauging his reaction.

"Thank you, Mr Armstrong." He held the letter, feeling the rich quality of the paper. "It will be an honour to meet Mr Monaghan again."

His name was written in neat, bold characters, but there were no other words on the front. He was aware only of a premonition of evil tidings as Armstrong gave his twisted smile.

*

Sitting by the evening fire, he watched Peter stare blankly into the flames as he opened his letter.

Mr Mendick, the letter read. *Pray attend a meeting at the Beehive on the 7th January at 9 PM*. There was no signature, nothing incriminating to send to Scotland Yard.

“Very clandestine,” he said and shook his head when Peter asked what he was reading. “Just an invitation to meet somebody,” he said, showing the single sheet of paper.

“I’m no scholar,” Peter told him, staring at the letter in incomprehension. “I never went to school.”

“I see.” Mendick once again wondered if the Chartists might have a point about the shocking division of society.

“I’ll learn sometime though.” Peter leaned closer, as if proximity would clarify the mystery of the printed word. “I’m not stupid.”

“No, you’re not,” Mendick reassured him. “Stupid people can’t drive coaches.”

“That’s right,” Peter said seriously. “They can’t, can they? Stupid people could never drive a coach as good as me.” Fetching the cards, he cut and dealt. “And stupid people can’t count the numbers in a pack of cards, either.” He pulled his chair over to the table. “Fellow Chartists?”

“Fellow Chartists,” Mendick confirmed, hating himself for the trusting pleasure in Peter’s eyes.

*

The barman waved him straight into the back room of the Beehive, and Mendick entered the familiar combination of stale tobacco smoke and gaunt faces. On his last visit, every man present had been suspicious, but now they nodded a quiet welcome; they had accepted him. Even Armstrong looked less hostile than normal as he lowered himself into the seat nearest to the door, although the bulge in his jacket was a reminder. Mendick pushed away the thought of the pepperpot revolver which lay concealed under a slab in the cottage; if the Chartists caught him carrying it he would be as good as dead.

“You are all familiar with the work that Mr Mendick has been doing.” Monaghan rose from his position at the head of the table. “He has spent the last month training a detachment of our men, and by all accounts, they are now among the best we have.”

The atmosphere lightened further; some of the anonymous faces even relaxed into cautious smiles.

“So you are continuing the good work you started in the East.” Rachel Scott emerged from behind the fug of tobacco smoke. Mendick watched her step to the head of the table, her clothes patched and her accent once more rough-edged. “You are part of the movement now, Mr Mendick, and that no man can deny.”

“Nor would want to,” a balding delegate said quietly. He looked over to his companions. “I heard that you have also trained your volunteers in foraging and picketing?”

“I have, sir,” Mendick confirmed, but let’s hope that there is never a need to test their skills.”

The delegates nodded their approval and the balding man spoke soberly, “Aye, we would all agree with that. Nobody wants to shed blood, but the best defence is to possess the means of attack.”

“Please God it does not come to that,” an elderly man whispered, “I was at Peterloo when the dragoons charged. I saw what sabres can do to unarmed people, and God forbid we ever witness such a thing again.”

Monaghan’s Liverpool Irish accent was very prominent as he replied, “If they do unleash another Peterloo on us, we will be ready for them, thanks to Mr Mendick and those like him.”

"Aye," the elderly man agreed, still whispering. "I was ten at the time, but I still remember the panic."

Mendick did a quick calculation; if the elderly man had only been ten at the time of Peterloo in 1819, then he was under forty years old now. Such was the effect of industrial living conditions that he looked at least twenty years older, with grey skin pulled taut over a deeply lined face.

"This time," Rachel Scott said, "the dragoons will be met with men trained and carrying muskets equal to anything that the British Army has."

The balding delegate began to clap, and one by one the others joined in, until they were standing around the table in a show of Chartist solidarity, respectable working men driven past the point of toleration until they were willing to challenge the might of the established state.

"Our muskets are superior to those carried by some army units." Mendick thought it might do no harm to reveal a little of his expertise. "We have the 1842 Pattern, with percussion caps. This means they are more reliable than the old flintlocks, particularly in wet weather." He remembered the hectic affair outside Canton, when rain had rendered the British muskets useless and the Chinese attacked with spears.

Scott gave her unique laugh. "Perhaps we should only fight in the rain?"

"We? *You* won't be fighting at all," the balding man said sardonically, and for a second Scott looked surprised, as if she had not expected such a reaction.

"We all fight in our own way," Monaghan soothed away the tension, "but I have a question or two to ask." Again Mendick experienced a feeling of dread.

"Of course," he said, automatically measuring the distance to the door. There were half a dozen delegates in his way, and Armstrong sat in the chair nearest the door with one leg stretched in front of him and that sinister bulge inside his jacket. Mendick wondered if Peter was waiting outside.

"You are an experienced soldier," Monaghan said, "and you have spent some weeks training our volunteers. If it comes to actual fighting, do you think that our men will stand against regulars?"

It was an obvious question, but one that could not be easily answered. Should he praise the men and possibly encourage the Chartists to rise, or say that they were not ready and endanger his position and possibly his life. If in doubt, tell the truth.

"That depends on many factors," he said. "On who leads them, on why they are fighting, and on the behaviour of us and the enemy on the day."

It seemed strange to be referring to the British Army as the enemy, and with a jolt he realised that the men he had trained might be facing the 26th Foot, his old regiment.

"That we understand," Monaghan said, "but if conditions are favourable, will they stand?"

Mendick thought of swarthy, clever Eccles, the straightforward Preston and quiet Duffy. They would be good men in any army.

"Aye," he said. "Aye, they will stand." And they will die, he thought, once the regulars fire their aimed volleys and the artillery find the range. Mrs Preston would be a widow, grieving hopelessly as her man lay, a smashed ruin on his own native soil.

"Good, that's their job." Monaghan nodded his satisfaction. "And one more question: will the Army fight against their countrymen?"

Would he have fought the Chartists? Mendick pondered for a few moments before replying.

"Some will not," he said. "Some would rather desert, and a handful might even switch sides, but most will fight for the regiment as they did at Newport in '39. The habit of discipline is hard to break."

The silence in the room told him that the delegates were considering his words.

"Then so be it," Monaghan said quietly. "We will welcome the deserters as brothers and face the rest musket to musket." The delegates agreed solemnly.

"Thank you, Mr Mendick, you are doing a sterling job." Monaghan was first to shake his hand, with a surprisingly silent Armstrong close behind, and one by one every delegate came to him with a smile of fraternal acceptance. Rachel Scott was last, her hand softer than that of everybody else but her congratulations sounding no less genuine. She held his eye for a fraction longer than necessary and brushed her hip against him as she turned away.

"It is good to belong to such an organisation," Mendick said, and, shockingly, he realised that he was speaking the truth. He looked around at the company of men, with their haggard faces and eyes bitter with repression, and he realised the fundamental decency within them. Even Armstrong may have been sincere behind that bitter exterior.

They were fighting in the only way left open to them.

Suddenly he understood the true meaning of fraternity; not the camaraderie of the army, where enforced suffering thrust men together, but the day-by-day struggle of life, the knowledge that everybody shared the same hunger and everybody was part of a greater whole. He swallowed, choking back the salt tears he had suppressed since the death of Emma. He was accepted here; these men trusted him, and he was duty bound to betray them to the very authorities whose repression they were attempting to remove.

"Now, a drink, I think." Monaghan made the decision, adding further cheer to the room, and within minutes he was pouring measures of gin into eagerly held tumblers and the grim-faced men were exchanging greetings with Mendick and asking him about his experiences in the army.

Monaghan allowed them a few minutes before he rapped on the table and called for order. For the next hour they discussed the finances of the Chartist movement, the growing unrest in Ireland and the political turmoil in the Italian states before Monaghan closed the meeting with a few words.

"Thank you for your time, gentlemen, but some of us must continue to pursue the cause." As expected, he received a ripple of laughter. "Mr Mendick, I would appreciate your company for the remainder of the evening. Mr Armstrong and Miss Scott will also be required."

Mendick glanced at Armstrong, who held his eyes but retained his cynical sneer, while Scott did not look up from the scrap of paper that she was studying.

"We'll use your coach, Josiah," Monaghan decided, "and your driver."

It was a short ride through the frosty streets of Manchester, with Mendick jammed hip to hip with a constantly restless Armstrong while Monaghan and Scott sat opposite. They travelled in silence broken only by the drumming of the horse's hooves and the low grinding of the wheels on the road.

"Here we are," Monaghan said as the coach came to a surprisingly gentle halt, and Peter appeared, opening the doors and helping Scott to the ground. They had driven through an arched gateway into a courtyard surrounded on three sides by high, near-windowless brick walls. A rising wind drove flurries of snow against dark corners and somewhere a loose shutter banged irregularly.

"The gates, Peter," Monaghan ordered.

They closed with an iron clang that echoed for half a minute and Peter ensured they remained that way by rasping two long bolts into their slots.

"This used to be a working mill," Armstrong mused. "There were nearly two hundred people employed here, but look at it now, lying idle in this slump, and all those people scraping for survival on the streets. And what about the mill owner? Is he suffering too?"

Mendick said nothing, waiting for the point.

"Hardly," Armstrong spat on the ground. "He's living off the cream of the land in London, dancing away the winter while his workers starve."

"Pray come this way." Monaghan stepped into a side entrance, where panelled walls still smelled of beeswax polish and a brass handrail decorated a varnished stairway. "This was the mill manager's entrance," he said, "Not quite what the workers were used to."

Monaghan led them along a long passageway. Dirty windows overlooked a factory floor where canvas covers protected idle looms.

"This is where the managers ordered the overseers to strap the children," Monaghan said and strode deep into the bowels of the mill, passing portraits of severe-looking men as they turned into a deeply carpeted corridor.

"Here we are." Monaghan stepped into an office with a single oak desk and an array of leather chairs. "This room was used by the owner, when he deigned to attend. He held his meetings with the managers here." He extended his hand. "Sit down."

Mendick did so, noticing that Peter remained standing, with his back to the door. The room was surprisingly large, but bars protected windows overlooking the courtyard.

"We use this room to conduct some of our . . ." Monaghan glanced at Armstrong, "less savoury business. I like the irony of using the owner's room to work against his interests."

"By 'less savoury', Mr Monaghan means things that we have to do, rather than things we really want to do," Armstrong explained. "You'll understand what we mean in a minute."

Monaghan placed himself in the armed chair behind the desk. He leaned forward with his hands pressed together as if in prayer.

"I've been studying you, Mr Mendick, and I've asked Mr Armstrong to keep an eye on you too."

"Oh yes?" Mendick felt himself tensing. He wondered if Scott had recognised him when he made that mad, scurrying run away from Trafford Hall, or if he had betrayed himself at some other time. He glanced over to Peter, who was watching him intensely, his massive prize-fighter's arms folded across his chest.

"Oh yes, I think it is time we were straight with each other." Monaghan glanced down at the desk for a second and sighed. When he looked up, there was a new light behind his eyes, as if he had come to a very difficult decision. "Mr Armstrong made a few enquiries about you and discovered some interesting things."

Mendick tensed. He could feel the force of Peter's glower and prepared for a leap that might catch the prize-fighter by surprise. He would have to get in the first blow, or Peter would kill him. He planned a feint to the eyes with forked fingers, followed by a high knee to the floating rib.

"You were recommended for bravery in the army," Monaghan said softly, "during the operations outside Canton, and promoted to corporal."

"I was."

Mendick remembered that terrible day, when thousands of Chinese had attacked the 26th in a rainstorm. With their flintlock muskets useless, the 26th had resorted to the bayonet and there had been some desperate work before a force of marines had arrived to help. He remembered the bravery of the Tartar soldiers and the long scream as Private Higgins slumped forward, ripped open from breastbone to crotch, his intestines spilling obscenely out.

"You told us you were a sergeant," Monaghan said, "but we'll let that pass. And afterward you lost your rank."

"I did," Mendick admitted. He wondered when Monaghan would come to the point.

"A private soldier under your command was sentenced to be flogged, and you argued for him," Monaghan said softly. "You stood up to the colonel for the sake of your man." Monaghan was on his feet. "That was enough for me. You put your own career and skin at risk for one of your men; that is the sign of a true Chartist!"

"Thank you," Mendick acknowledged the stupidity that had lost him his rank and the favour of his colonel. He remembered the drunken buffoon who had started a fight with a Chinese barman in Hog Lane. The ensuing riot had lasted for two hours and incapacitated a dozen men, but he had still felt some responsibility for the man and argued his case.

Scott raised her eyebrows and allowed her eyes to drift from Mendick's face to his feet and back before she gave an approving nod.

"Men like you are a rare commodity," Monaghan told him, "and we think you could be a valuable, no, a *very* valuable, asset to the cause."

Mendick had not expected this conversation. He began to relax a little. "Thank you, Mr Monaghan."

"But first, we must show you the true face of the enemy." Monaghan nodded to Armstrong. "Bring him in."

As Armstrong and Peter left, Scott gave a long smile.

"When I first saw you at the rally, I thought you had something; it was a sort of tension beneath that surface calm that you portray. I was slightly disappointed when you did not immediately display the fire we require, but you have more than justified yourself since. You are doing well, Mr Mendick; if you keep it up, who knows where it might lead."

"Who knows indeed," Mendick agreed, aware of Scott sliding toward him, her hips swinging in slow provocation. He heard shouting outside the room, and then Armstrong crashed in, followed by Peter carrying a man who struggled and swore.

"Here he is." Peter let his bundle drop and placed a booted foot on top. "The spy."

"The police spy," Armstrong said and landed a vicious kick that rolled the man over onto his back.

"Good God in heaven!" Mendick stared down. Despite the bruises covering one half of the man's face, despite the swollen jaw and the clotted blood, he recognised the friendly face of Sergeant Ogden.

CHAPTER EIGHT

Manchester: December 1847

"There's nothing godly about this one." Pulling back his foot, Armstrong kicked hard into Ogden's ribs. The policeman groaned and tried to curl into a protective ball, but Peter reached down and pulled him to his feet. "This is Sergeant Ogden of the Manchester police."

Ogden tried to straighten, but the pain of broken ribs forced him into a crouch. He gasped as Armstrong slapped him hard across the head.

"Sergeant Ogden is a spy for the government, aren't you, Sergeant Ogden?" Punctuating each question with a savage slap, Armstrong continued, "You have been spying on us, haven't you, Sergeant? And you've been watching what we're doing, haven't you, Sergeant? And you've been sending messages down to your masters in London, haven't you, Sergeant?"

"That's enough." Mendick grabbed Armstrong's wrist, feeling the frailty of bone and the lack of muscle. "We're Chartists, not savages."

"Mr Mendick is right." Scott stepped forward. "Anyway, it's not what Sergeant Ogden has been doing that matters, it's how much information he has sent down to London."

"I've sent nothing to London." Bright blood dribbled from Ogden's mouth and onto the carpet. "And that's God's own truth. I swear."

"Ask him again," Armstrong said quietly, and Peter landed a slashing chop to Ogden's kidneys that sent the sergeant reeling back to the floor. He writhed, clutching his back and gasping at the fresh agony.

"For God's sake!" Mendick stepped forward. "You can't treat the man like that!"

"We don't want to." Monaghan placed a restraining hand on his shoulder. "But we have to. I told you we would show you the true face of the enemy, and here it is."

"He doesn't look very dangerous to me. For mercy's sake, let the man go!"

Monaghan shook his head. "You are a compassionate man, Mr Mendick. I admire that trait, but sometimes we have to push our natural sympathy, aye, even our Christianity, aside for the sake of the greater good."

Peter lifted Ogden and punched him again, twisting his fist to direct the blow inward, and the sergeant screamed his agony.

"Please! I tell you, I didn't send any messages."

"Maybe he's telling the truth." Mendick tried to pull Peter back, looking to Scott for support, but again Monaghan intervened, shaking his head.

"There is no secret that the various branches of the Chartist movement use pigeons as carriers," Monaghan explained. "We have done so for years. But the authorities have grown wise to that, so they have borrowed our ideas. You see," he nodded to Ogden, who was trying to straighten up, "that man is one of the leading experts in pigeon racing in this area. Obviously we have been aware of him and only a few days ago we intercepted one of his messages."

"Intercepted? How?" Mendick stared at Monaghan. "How can you intercept a pigeon?"

"With a hawk," Monaghan said bluntly, and Scott looked shrewdly at Mendick.

Dipping into her pocket, Scott produced the slip of paper she had been reading earlier. She handed it to Mendick, who read it quickly: *Trafford friendly with Chartists. Has large quantity of arms. Will remain in position.*

"Jesus!" The blasphemy was unintentional, but he felt suddenly sick at seeing his message in the hands of the Chartists. The shock was twofold. Firstly, if his message had not got through, then Smith was unaware of the full situation up here, and secondly, an innocent man was now carrying the blame. He looked up at Ogden, who gave a tiny shake of his head.

What should he do? If he admitted his guilt, then he would be failing in his duty, he would probably be killed and the insurrection would go ahead anyway. On the other hand, his conscience would be clear and Ogden might be saved. Mendick read the message again, looking for some salvation.

"Trafford? That's utter nonsense." He tried to sound like an angry Chartist. "Trafford is no friend of ours."

"Maybe Ogden got it wrong then. Ask him again," Monaghan ordered, and Peter took hold of Ogden's arm, bending it behind his back until the policeman moaned in agony. Mendick stepped forward; conscience had to take priority over his duty.

"No, you can't do that; he's an innocent man!"

Ogden looked up at that, his face screwed with pain. Blinking away the blood that streamed over his eyes, he spat at Mendick.

"We know you, you treasonous bastard! You're Mendick! You tried to incite mutiny in the army, you bloody Chartist!"

The message could not have been clearer; Ogden did not want Mendick to reveal himself. Stepping back, hating what he had to do, Mendick drew himself erect.

"Maybe he's not so innocent." Unable to look away, he stared into the face of the man he was abandoning.

Ogden screamed as Armstrong pulled back his boot and kicked him full force in the groin.

"What other messages have you sent? What other damage have you done to the people?" Stamping his foot on Ogden's instep, Armstrong twisted his heel to increase the agony as the policeman writhed, his mouth wide in soundless anguish.

"Enough, surely!" Mendick looked desperately at Monaghan. "We can't create a new country based on torture!"

"So says the soldier, a man who was paid to kill and to whom violence was a way of life." Scott put a light hand on his arm, squeezing slightly. "But you are right, Mr Mendick. We are getting nowhere here." She nodded to Monaghan. "The spy is either very stubborn or very ignorant."

"Dispose of him," Monaghan agreed.

Armstrong nodded to Peter, who dragged Ogden out of the room.

This time Mendick could not meet the policeman's eyes.

"What are you going to do?"

Monaghan gave a small smile. "We'll kill the bastard and stuff the body under a collapsed building so it looks like he died in an accident."

For a second Mendick thought of that happy household in the Manchester suburbs with the bustling Mrs Ogden's bare ankles and bread-and-cheese, but he shook away the memory. He could do nothing to help Ogden; he could only hope to avenge him by performing his duty.

Only a couple of hours ago he had felt welcome amongst the men in the Beehive, he had believed that the Chartists were dedicated to equality, but now he had witnessed the brutal reality. Perhaps these people were sincere in some ways, but no respectable person would have acted in such a manner, and nobody who called himself a Christian.

"You do not approve." Scott had her head on one side as she studied him. "You are a good man, Mr Mendick, but you are offended by the practicalities of revolution."

Her sneer stiffened him. "I've seen a lot worse," he said truthfully. "But I am surprised that the spy could have been so far from the mark. How could he believe Trafford was a friend of ours?"

"He was not too far off the mark," Monaghan said.

Mendick raised his eyebrows. "But how can that be possible?"

"Because we have mutual enemies," Monaghan was smiling as he explained. "Sir Robert Trafford is an old-fashioned Tory, a man still living in the past. This new breed of industrialists and factory owners challenge his idea of the correct order of things and he needs our help to put them in their place."

Mendick nodded. "So he's just using us then."

"That is what he believes," Monaghan agreed. "Sir Robert believes that if we remove the Whigs from power, his Tories will return." His smile included the whole room. "He has yet to realise that when we achieve suffrage we will never return to the old ways."

Mendick tried to appear calm, but his mind began to race. Monaghan had given him the information that he required, and he could leave these muddled, contradictory people and return to Scotland Yard.

"I see, so that is why we can train our volunteers so close to Trafford Hall."

"Exactly so," Monaghan nodded solemnly. "We needed land to train our men; Trafford has plenty, so we asked him nicely to borrow some."

So much for the story of raising money by subscription. "And he agreed?"

"Very readily."

Monaghan glanced at Scott and gave a small, conspiratorial smile. "So you see the spy was not so wide off the mark and far more dangerous than you realised."

Mendick nodded. "You are a clever man, Mr Monaghan, but I still do not agree with casual brutality.

Monaghan shook his head. "I do not agree with casual brutality either, Mr Mendick; ours is targeted and necessary." He leaned closer. "But at the end of the day, does it matter? Compared to the suffering of countless numbers of people, does it really matter?"

Mendick realised his commitment to the Chartist cause could be questioned if he gave the incorrect answer.

"Perhaps not," he said. He looked up as somebody screamed: a long drawn-out sound which rose horribly before it abruptly ended.

Although Rachel Scott sounded calm, there was perspiration on her forehead. "That's the end of Sergeant Ogden's worries, and one less enemy for the cause."

When Armstrong and Peter returned, both were splashed with blood. Peter immediately returned to his previous position at the door, but Armstrong was watching Mendick. "You are wondering at our apparent cruelty."

"I wonder at the necessity," Mendick modified.

"I do not," Armstrong said, "for one piece of cruelty may prevent something a great deal worse. I have no reason to love the peelers, or their spies; if I may?" He glanced at Monaghan, who gave a brief nod of approval. "Look."

Armstrong slipped off his jacket, unfastened his braces and slowly unbuttoned his shirt, which he removed with obvious effort. Apparently oblivious to the presence of a woman, he unbuttoned his trousers, let them fall and stepped free, naked and unashamed.

Although his face and arms were deeply tanned, his body was as white as that of any city clerk and so thin it was nearly emaciated. Mendick could count every rib down to the sunken stomach, but it was the scores of ugly scars wrapped around Armstrong's sides that held his attention. He heard Scott's sudden indrawn breath and looked round at her.

Scott's mouth was pursed and she dropped her eyes briefly before jerking them back up.

"And now look." Armstrong turned slowly around, and Mendick winced. Scars and weals criss-crossed him from the neck to the back of his knees; some were crusted and weeping, others ridged white, but there was hardly a square inch that was not disfigured, and not an ounce of fat anywhere. With all the spare flesh ripped away, the muscles and sinews writhed obscenely beneath his skin whenever he moved.

"You can see why I use a coach rather than ride a horse." He indicated his buttocks and thighs, from which the flesh had been virtually stripped.

"God in heaven!" Mendick looked away. He had seen enough floggings in the army to recognise the distinctive clawing of the cat-o'-nine-tails, but he had never seen anybody scarred so badly before.

"There is no God in Van Diemen's Land," Armstrong said, "and many of the inmates would welcome the chance to ascend to heaven, or even to hell, for either would be preferable to that place." He turned round, fingering his twisted mouth as he glared at Mendick.

"Did you never wonder about my scarred face? That was just one flick of the cat's tail. The rest you have seen; now you know why I have no cause to favour the authorities. If Ogden had his way, we would all be sent back to Port Arthur." Supremely uncaring of his nudity, he stared at Scott. "Women are treated no better."

"I think you have made an excellent point," Scott said. Stepping forward, she lifted Armstrong's clothes from the ground and handed them to him, holding his eyes. "Perhaps you had better get dressed; it is cold in here."

She watched over him as he gently eased his shirt and jacket over his warped body.

"And now, Mr Mendick, perhaps you had better take a seat?" Although Scott's voice still held the grittiness of the mill, her eyes seemed more troubled. "You have seen both sides of us today. You have seen the fraternity of the Charter and the steps we sometimes have to take to achieve our aims. You have also seen . . ." she indicated Armstrong, "why we must take these steps."

The words hung in the air for a few seconds, and Mendick wondered if Scott was attempting to justify the murder of Ogden. She was watching him, her head cocked on one side and her eyes mobile, until he turned away.

"Drink?" Monaghan posed the word as a question but did not wait for a refusal as he produced a decanter from the cupboard that sat against the far wall. "These factory owners lived in fine style, Mr Mendick, and it seems a waste to neglect their luxuries."

"Indeed." Mendick wondered how Ogden had died. Had Peter beaten him to death, or simply broken his neck? The memory of that final scream lingered.

The brandy splashed into crystal balloons, swirling in an amber invitation he knew was dangerous to accept. He put out his hand, suddenly desperate for the comfort of alcohol after the sordid murder of his comrade, but determined to only sip the contents.

"You'll be wondering what sort of people we are," Monaghan said calmly, "but we're not monsters, I assure you. Mr Armstrong has very effectively shown you the price of failure; many of our comrades were transported to Van Diemen's Land back in '42; most remain there. Others were shot or imprisoned in this country. That's what we're up against, but you already know that." He drank deeply of his brandy, waiting for Mendick to join him.

"That spy knew of you," Scott leaned closer. "He knew you had tried to incite a Chartist mutiny."

Mendick blessed Ogden's presence of mind; even when facing a horrible death, the Lancashire policeman had remembered the detail from their brief discussion across the kitchen table.

"It was nothing," he said, truthfully, "an exaggeration."

"I'm sure it was no exaggeration." Leaving her seat, Scott allowed her hand to drift over his shoulder. "I think that there's more to you than meets the eye. You are a soldier and a Chartist, a man who is not afraid to act alone, yet a man who faithfully follows orders, a man with enough Christian humanity to plead for the life of a sworn enemy . . . you are an interesting man."

Mendick shrugged. "Not really."

A swallow of brandy fortified him, the smooth spirit warming him against the malignant chill that emanated from these people. They had calmly and brutally murdered an officer of the law and were now speaking as if nothing untoward had happened. He took another drink, closing his eyes in remembered pleasure.

"Oh, I think you are," Scott said softly.

Monaghan finished his brandy with a quick jerk of his head. "Like the rest of us, Miss Scott, Mr Mendick is only one individual fighting to restrain the excesses of the Whigs and to bring work for all through reforms to the electoral systems." Monaghan shook his head as if bewildered that the authorities did not immediately accede to the demands of the Chartists. "Is that too much to ask? To improve the lot of the people?"

"Revolutions are never easy." Scott barely sipped at her brandy. Her voice had softened in conjunction with her eyes which never strayed from Mendick's face.

By now the alcohol had entered his bloodstream, relaxing him so he leaned back on his chair, stretching out his legs as Monaghan smiled at him over the rim of his glass.

"As Miss Scott says, Mr Mendick; you are an interesting man. I believe that we can trust you." As he leaned closer, the amiability hardened into something vicious. "Indeed I think we have to trust each other now, for you are deeply involved. You have knowingly trained men for a revolution, which is treason, and have participated in the death of a police officer, which is murder."

"I understand that, but you have no need to distrust me. I am as dedicated to the Charter as you are." Even a single glass of brandy had made Mendick loquacious.

"Aye?" Armstrong raised his skeletal face. "You were the Queen's man once, and still you fomented mutiny."

"And in doing so, proved his loyalty to our cause," Scott's eyes still washed over Mendick.

"Even so," Monaghan mused, "even so." He looked up. "You've done a good job so far; I feel sure that you will continue. I would not be pleased if you were to revert to any earlier loyalties."

"I assure you, Mr Monaghan, I only have one loyalty,'" Mendick told him.

Reaching for the decanter, Monaghan refilled Mendick's glass. "Let's hope that it's the right one, shall we?"

The second brandy was even more warming than the first, and Mendick felt himself mellowing, although the image of Ogden being dragged to his death was horribly imprinted on his mind.

"It will be." Scott was smiling at him, and then she shook her head. "Oh, how I hate all this formality. We have already dispensed with titles and ranks, so we should not need such things as misters and misses. Mr Mendick, if you permit me, I will call you by your given name, which is?"

"James." With two glasses of brandy inside him, he found it easy to return her smile. "And may I call you Rachel?"

"I would be offended if you did not!" She gave that strange, whooping laugh that he remembered from Trafford Hall.

Mendick allowed Monaghan to refill his glass once more. By now the brandy was an old friend, warming him as it removed his reserve.

"Then Rachel it is, and Josiah?" He raised his glass to Armstrong, who nodded coldly.

"Mr Armstrong will do nicely; as will Mr Monaghan."

"I see." Mendick shrugged; he knew that brandy affected his judgement, but it seemed that only Rachel was friendly here, and he smiled to her again.

Monaghan was examining him as if he was some strange creature dropped from the heavens.

"Are you certain that you were a soldier, Mr Mendick?"

"Of course!" He lurched to his feet, holding the brandy glass as if it were a weapon. He glared at Monaghan. "What sort of damn-fool question is that?"

Monaghan smiled slowly, lifting a placatory hand. "Now, now, there's no need for that attitude. My point is that you're the first soldier I've met who can't handle a mere three glasses of spirits."

"Handle three glasses?" Reaching for the decanter, Mendick filled his glass to the brim, spilling brandy on to the desk. "I can handle a hell of a lot more than three."

"No, no." Scott laid a soft hand on his arm. "I do not think you are a drinking man, James."

When Scott leaned closer her face seemed to metamorphose into somebody entirely different until Mendick imagined that his wife sat next to him, with that serene smile hiding her mischievous nature and her husky laugh ready to tease him to distraction.

"I am all of that," he said, but he did not object when she gently removed the glass from his hand and replaced it on the desk.

"Come on." She was shaking her head, a sister chiding her wayward brother, a mother her son. "You're in no state to travel, James. We'll bed you down here for the night." Her touch was so gentle that he could not resist as she guided him into a small anteroom, where a splendid red coverlet lay atop a single bed.

"Sleep tight."

As Scott helped him remove his outer clothing, Mendick allowed the brandy to drift him away to a place where Ogden's screams resounded through his mind and Emma was standing in the shadows, shaking her head disapprovingly.

CHAPTER NINE

Lancashire: March 1848

"Have you heard the news?" Armstrong eased himself out of the coach even before it halted. "It's revolution, red, raging revolution."

"What? Is the Queen still on her throne? When did it start?" Mendick stared at him, suddenly feeling very sick. He had been training his men in volley shooting, extolling the stopping power of the Brown Bess musket while his mind raced over the mysteries that he had yet to unravel. The arrival of Armstrong's coach upset his entire parade; the volunteers were crowding around listening to the news and raising undisciplined cheers. He looked around, contemplating the chilling prospect of his men facing the rolling volleys of regular British infantry.

"Not over here but on the Continent – Naples, Palermo, Paris; the monarchs are tumbling like skittles." Armstrong grabbed his arm, jerking it like the handle of a water pump. "Our revolution is going to happen, Mendick, and you and I are going to be right in the middle of it. Just imagine, we can boast to our grandchildren of the day we toppled the Whigs and established the Charter."

"So it's not happened yet." Mendick tried to calm Armstrong down, holding both thin shoulders. "We've not had a revolution here."

"Not yet," Armstrong admitted, "but soon. Monaghan has called a general meeting of all the delegates, including you and me."

"Where and when?" If he could inform Scotland Yard about such a meeting, the police could pick up all the Chartist leaders simultaneously and end any insurrection with a minimum of violence. As he could no longer use the pigeons, he would have to slide away to the railway station and get the next London-bound train.

"This afternoon, at Trafford Hall." Armstrong's words ended any hopes of a swift resolution. "So come on, Mendick, nearly everybody is already there; just you and I are missing."

"Trafford Hall? Sir Robert's place?"

Armstrong's wink revealed how light-hearted he was feeling. "Why not?"

*

It felt strange to roll up to the front door of Trafford Hall in Armstrong's coach and to have a stony-faced flunky open the door for him as if he were somebody important rather than a masquerading police constable.

Feeling as apprehensive as he had when approaching the walls of Amoy, Mendick stepped up the broad steps and into a hall that had obviously been designed to impress. Fluted pillars soared upwards from the marble floor to explode in Corinthian splendour on an ornate ceiling. Between them, two crystal chandeliers swung low, their multitude of sparkling lights amplified by mirrors that covered half the walls. Classical sculpture added to the splendour, with an array of white marble deities presiding from raised plinths.

The Chartist delegates appeared ill at ease amidst such opulence; a few were affecting loud bravado, but others were shrinking into the corners or standing with arms folded and faces furrowed. Only Rachel Scott appeared relaxed as she contemplated the muscles and manhood of Michelangelo's David.

"A good copy," she said.

Monaghan swept into the room, puffing on a cheroot and wearing a very plush morning coat.

"This way, gentlemen." He indicated a side door and the entire gathering trailed through, some slouching, others putting on a betraying swagger.

Monaghan took them through a lancet arch door into a much simpler hall, a primitive chamber with a flagstone floor and an oak-beamed ceiling. Great logs crackled in the huge fireplace as servants set out rows of wooden benches for the convenience of the delegates. Mendick found a space close enough to the wooden platform to hear what was being said but far enough back to appear inconspicuous. He avoided Armstrong, who sat right at the front, but was strangely disappointed that Scott walked past him with hardly a glance.

"I won't keep you long." Monaghan spoke so quietly that everybody had to strain to hear him. "We all have a great deal to do. You will have heard about the revolutions taking place all across Europe, and now it is our turn."

They cheered at that, simple, desperate men alongside the cynical and the cunning, the honest worker and the devious politician, all ostensibly committed to the Chartist cause.

"You are all aware that Feargus O'Connor has organised yet another petition and a massive march that will end in a rally in Kennington Common in London. If Parliament accepts our five points – only five, note, not six, for we are allowing them some leeway – then we will have won." Monaghan waited for the excited buzz to fade away before he continued.

"But if they do not," he said, and his voice had a new edge to it, "if Parliament does *not* accept the Charter, then it will be our time, brothers, and all our work here will be needed. If Parliament ignores our demands, then we will be embarking on more direct, and much more physical, action."

This time the cheers were shorter, ending in a general chant of "Tell us how" and "Name the hour" from a small but vociferous group at the front of the meeting. Recognising Armstrong as a prominent member of these men, Mendick reasoned that Monaghan had instructed them on what to say and when to say it.

"We will take part in O'Connor's march and rally, so if the Charter is turned down, we will be in London and ready to rise. We will gather in the Midlands and travel south in our units, with our weapons carried in carts."

The hiss and crackle of the fire seemed a suitable backdrop as the delegates listened to Monaghan's words.

"We will not make a Moscow of Manchester, instead we will strike at the political and economic heart of this nation; we will take over London and dictate our terms to our oppressors!" Monaghan paused, allowing the audience to wait for the final words they knew he would announce: "We will achieve the Charter!"

Strangely, the climax sounded weak. Mendick had expected something more inspiring, but the Chartists still erupted in spontaneous applause. Monaghan had to raise both arms to achieve quiet.

"O'Connor's rally at Kennington Common is planned for the twelfth of April, so we will start to travel south a fortnight before. That is only a few days away. Our brothers in London will welcome us, and we will recruit them to our cause."

April the twelfth. Mendick closed his eyes. Now he knew the plan, and he knew the date. Monaghan intended to infiltrate his Physical Force Chartists into what would otherwise be a peaceful gathering, and if the government did not accept the Charter, he would lead an uprising in London itself. It was very simple but could also be very effective, with hundreds, perhaps thousands, of armed and trained men already in position amidst a disgruntled and angry populace. The recent uprisings across Europe had showed how easy it was to topple an unpopular government; perhaps it was Great Britain's turn next.

He tried to ignore the secondary mystery of Scott's Uncle Ernest and that teasing mention of a white horse. The relationship between Scott and Trafford was unimportant compared to ensuring that this attempted revolution did not go ahead. He would have to act like a Chartist this afternoon. Later, he would slip away and return to London with his information.

Standing up, Mendick cheered and thrust his fist in the air to announce his approval of the plan to turn London into a city of devastation and horror, with dead bodies in the gutters and half-trained Chartists exchanging fire with the Brigade of Guards.

"We will achieve the Charter!"

Armstrong was beside him, hand extended in comradeship.

"The day is announced, brother: the day of our liberation!" He was grinning, his eyes brighter than Mendick had ever seen. "The process will be painful, but picture the results: a full franchise, full employment and equality."

Taking his hand, Mendick shook it vigorously, realising that all around him, men were doing the same. They were cheering their own revolution before it had taken place, congratulating themselves for initiating their own destruction. If he closed his eyes, he could recall the sordid reality of that faraway war in China, the valour and slaughter of the assault on the Bogue Forts, the rotting corpses, the shrieking wounded, the row after row of the sick on their hammocks; did these people really want that here? Did they have any idea what a civil war would do to the country? And then he remembered the misery of the brick streets of Manchester, the dripping cellars with their hopeless occupants, the dying children and weeping mothers; did the moneyed classes understand what they were doing to the country? Did they care, so long as it did not impinge on their own comfortable lives?

"Go now!" Monaghan was back on his feet. "Return to your volunteers and prepare for war! Prepare for government!"

There was a last cheer, a final triumphant roar, and Armstrong began to sing. Although he knew the tune of *Rule Britannia* well, it was the first time that Mendick had heard those particular words:

"Spread, spread the Charter
Spread the Charter through the Land
Let Britons bold and brave join heart and hand."

Others joined in, and then the tune and words altered to Armstrong's favourite Chartist song. Others joined in until the entire room was roaring out the words, and Mendick saw the tall figure of Trafford standing behind Monaghan, a glass in hand as he joined in,

"Truth is growing – hearts are glowing
With the flame of Liberty:
Light is breaking – Thrones are quaking-
Hark! The trumpet of the Free
Long in lowly whispers breathing
Freedom wandered drearily
Still, in faith, her laurel wreathing,
For the day when there should be Freemen shouting
Victory!"

The Chartists were still singing as they began to dissipate, in small knots or individually. Mendick edged toward the door, now knowing exactly what intelligence he had to carry with him to London. All he had to do was get to the railway station in Manchester and within hours he could put a stop to all the impending trouble.

"James," the voice was low and feminine, "James, it's me."

He looked up. Scott stood in the shadow of a recessed doorway, smiling to him.

"This way, James."

"Rachel?"

"You fell asleep on me last time, James." She shook her head, eyes mocking, "You really must avoid the drink in future." Her smile broadened. "But there's no drink here, James, only you and me and a host of excited delegates who cannot think of anything but power for themselves." She moved slightly, stirring her hips suggestively.

"I must go . . ." Mendick tried to slip away, but she held him with a small hand. He stared at her, confused but not tempted, until she laughed.

"You look like a small boy in a sweetshop, James. You have seen all the treasures, but you're undecided which one to pick first. Which is it, James, the Charter or the woman?"

"I must attend my duty."

"Of course you must," Rachel agreed, "but you must also admit that I attract you." She nodded to the rapidly emptying hall. "Look at them all, James, eager to run back and start a war that may kill most of them. The Chartist symbol is the beehive, and they are just the drones, destined to work and die for others, whoever is in government." Her contempt startled him, but he could not fault her logic. He shivered as she echoed his own thoughts from earlier.

"What does it matter to them who is in power, which voice makes the decisions, Finality Jack Russell or Vociferous William Monaghan? Whoever it is, they are destined to remain at the bottom of the heap, with or without the vote or the six points of the Charter, they just don't matter."

"They?" He lifted an eyebrow. "Don't you mean *we?*"

Scott shook her head. "We are different, you and I, James. We don't belong with the drones.' She looked at him with a cynical twist to the side of her mouth. 'The problem is, I am not sure where you belong at all."

"I must do my duty," Mendick repeated, and she mocked him with a laugh.

"Your duty? Duty is the old standby of the lazy and the confused. People who *do their duty* don't have to think, do they? They allow other people to do their thinking for them, and thereby allow others to rule their lives." Very deliberately, she shifted her position, thrusting that provocative hip further towards him. "Well, James? Are you going to do your *duty,* or are you going to do *me*?"

He looked at her. She had supported him when he tried to help Ogden, and had spoken up for him in front of Monaghan, and despite, or possibly because of, her mysteries, she was an alluring woman. Nevertheless, her attempt at seduction was as attractive as the hiss of a serpent. Even as a siren, she was so inferior to Emma that he would not have considered even talking to her except as part of his job.

"I'm sorry, Rachel, but I must do my duty."

The sound of a slow handclap made him turn around, and he saw Armstrong a few steps behind him and Peter towering in the background.

"Well said, Mr Mendick, a man has to do his duty." Armstrong stepped closer. "The only question is your duty to whom, and what exactly does that duty entail?"

"What?" Mendick looked at him, shaking his head. "I do not understand, Mr Armstrong. My duty to the Charter, of course."

"Of course." Monaghan slipped from a side door. "Of course." He nodded to Scott. "Well done, Miss Scott. You played your part to perfection."

Scott gave a graceful little curtsey as Monaghan glowered at Mendick.

"You were about to scurry to your masters in London, were you not?"

"Which masters in London?" Mendick tried to bluff, but he felt sudden sick dread. His memory of Ogden writhing on the floor was vivid. He glanced back, preparing to run, but Armstrong gripped his arm.

"Come with us, Mr Mendick; we have things to discuss."

He shook away the hand.

"I don't think there is anything left to say." He stepped toward the door, but Peter was there first, balancing on the soles of his feet with his hands clenched and his head lowered like a young bull.

"Best do what Mr Armstrong says." Peter raised his head, his eyes dazed. "Please, James, I don't want to hit you."

Mendick nodded; he remembered Peter's strength and speed; he knew that he could never defeat him in a fair fight.

"You just had to ask," he said. He glanced at Scott, who favoured him with a simpering smile. "There was no need for the subterfuge." He nodded to Peter, who remained immobile in the doorway. "Or the threats."

Armstrong grunted and produced the pistol from within his jacket, caressing the barrel lovingly.

"No threats, Mendick, just a reminder."

Monaghan took them to a large, draughty room immediately beneath the hall, his feet rapping on the floor of stone slabs. He scraped a Lucifer, waited until the phosphorous flare calmed down and lit a brace of candles. Yellow light immediately illuminated an oval table and a single chair, on which Monaghan sat and extended his legs.

"This was the kitchen, when the original hall was first built, and then it was used for storage before the new store rooms were built." He glanced at Mendick. "But you know all about them, don't you?"

Still faintly smiling, Scott took up position on one side of the huge fireplace, with Armstrong directly opposite. Armstrong tapped his pistol against the long spit that was slowly rusting against the wall.

"How should I know about the new store rooms?"

"You were there," Monaghan said quietly. "The day that you robbed Sir Robert's larder to feed your men, you snooped around and discovered the weapons store."

"What?" As Mendick tried to simultaneously look confused and angry he measured the distance to the door, where Peter stood immobile with his arms folded. The muscles stood out like wire hawsers.

"Of course we knew it was you," Monaghan said, his voice very quiet. "We always knew who you were." There was triumph in his smile. "Why else would Miss Scott single you out at the meeting, and why else would we bring you into the fold? We played you like a fish and you bit on our bait every time."

Mendick tried to keep the horror from his face as he edged closer to the door, but on a nod from Armstrong, Peter turned the key in the lock and enclosed it within his great fist.

Armstrong pointed his pistol directly at Mendick's face. The barrel seemed as wide as a nine-pounder cannon.

"Show him, Miss Scott."

"With pleasure."

Reaching into his inside pocket, Scott withdrew a folded document, which she handed to Mendick.

The letter from Scotland Yard proclaimed his guilt with seven simple words: *Chartist Rally,* it read. *Infiltrate and join the cause.* Mendick stared, unable to say anything. The Chartists must have broken into his London home and found that. But how? The question screamed in his mind; how did they know who he was, and where he lived? Somebody must have told them, and only then did he remember that notebook of faces that Mr Smith had shown him. Somebody in Scotland Yard must have informed the Chartists who he was, there could be no other explanation.

Scott smiled to him with her head tilted on one side.

"Cat got your tongue?"

"And you thought that you were so clever, too." Monaghan shook his head in mock sorrow. "You came here from London, inveigled yourself into our midst, and you even made a good job of training my soldiers."

"God!" Mendick felt his mouth drop. "But . . ."

"But?" Rachel mocked him again. "But why? But why not just kill you as soon as you arrived?" Her laughter bounced around the bare stone room.

"Because if we did," Monaghan told him, "Scotland Yard might just send somebody that we don't know about, or even worse, somebody who was actually *good* at their job. This way, we could keep an eye on you and ensure that you didn't tell your bosses anything important."

"What's wrong, James? You look pale." Stepping forward, Scott stroked his face with a soft hand. "Not as clever as you thought?"

"Pale? It must be the chill. It's cold in here." Mendick tried to keep his voice light as he thought furiously. His life was unimportant, but he had to escape and warn about the horrors that Monaghan was about to unleash on London. He glanced around the room. With Peter holding the key to the only door, and Armstrong cradling his pistol like a beloved baby, he only had one, very unlikely, chance.

"We'll soon make it warmer for you," Armstrong promised grimly, with a significant glance at Peter.

"Look on the bright side, James." Rachel was still smiling. "At least we won't have to question you. You don't know anything we haven't already told you, and you haven't sent any information to Scotland Yard." She leaned closer so her moist breath washed his face. "We caught all your pigeons."

"Mr Armstrong," Monaghan spoke in a conversational tone, "could you and Peter take Mr Mendick for a walk, please? And don't bother to bring him back."

CHAPTER TEN

Lancashire: March 1848

The knowledge that he had only one slender chance to escape before Peter's iron fists closed on him awoke a long dormant madness; Mendick feinted joyously for Armstrong's eyes, watched him jerk backward and swung a savage uppercut to his groin. For a second he relished Armstrong's high squeal of agony, and then he swept his hand sideways at the candles. The first went out immediately, but the second rolled along the table top casting dancing shadows until he snatched it up and rammed it against Monaghan's face. Monaghan screamed and all light was extinguished.

Mendick hoped Peter would be so petrified by the sudden darkness that he would remain static, blocking the door. There was only one other exit from the windowless room, and he gambled that nobody had even considered it. Pushing past the still yelling Monaghan, he ducked under the chimney breast and thrust his head up the flue. The once familiar smell of soot and the cool downdraught from outside spurred him onward and upward, blessing his luck. In choosing the old kitchen for his interrogation, Monaghan had given him the widest chimney in Trafford Hall.

Generations of soot had coated the stonework, but there were still sufficient hand and footholds to pull himself upwards. He was suddenly grateful for his childhood years as a climbing boy, spent clambering up and around choking flues with his master lighting straw in the grate to encourage greater speed. He remembered that most of these old buildings had their chimneys placed in stacks where the flue was common to two or more fireplaces.

As a child he could have scrambled straight up and out the topmost chimney; although he was now far too large for that route, the lower part of the flue was still spacious enough to accommodate him. He pushed upward, feeling the stonework rough under his hands, coughing as soot dribbled down upon him.

"Where is he?" A sliver of light glinted from below, and he heard the distorted echo of Armstrong's voice. "Where in hell's name did he go? He must have sneaked past you, Peter, you useless bastard!" There was the sound of a slap and of Peter whimpering.

"He didn't get past me, Mr Armstrong, I swear. I was here all the time. He must be a ghost."

"Some ghost." That was Scott's voice, taut with fury. "He's gone up the chimney!"

Mendick stopped moving, clinging on with his fingertips and the toes of his boots. He had hoped to escape through the fireplace of the great hall, one floor up, but the flue was more restricting than he had expected.

"I can't hear him!" That was Monaghan's voice. "It's so bloody dark I can't see anything up there either. Are you sure that's where he is?"

"He can't be anywhere else," Scott told him.

"I'll get the bastard!"

Mendick cringed from the deafening crack of the pistol; the ball smashed against the wall of the flue a few inches away from his leg, dislodging a torrent of soot.

"For God's sake, Josiah!" Scott's words halted in a bout of coughing, and Mendick hoped that she choked to death. "You're as stupid as Peter!"

"Fetch a glim!" Armstrong's voice echoed up the chimney.

Mendick could feel his fingers slipping on the soot-smoothed ledge and knew that if he did not move soon, he would fall. There was cold air and faint light coming from above, but it was impossibly far away, and he knew he could not squeeze through the narrowing passage. He had trapped himself. He saw a yellowish flicker from below as somebody thrust a candle up the chimney.

"Is that him?" Armstrong must have stepped into the fireplace. "Mendick, you bastard, come down!"

With his fingertips trembling from the strain, Mendick kept still. He knew how hard it was to make out bodies against a dark background and hoped that Armstrong would give up and try the door.

"I can't see a bloody thing up there." The light withdrew, and Mendick heard scrapings from the room. He eased himself further up, but the movement dislodged more soot, which showered down onto the fireplace below.

"There! I hear him! He *is* up there! Light a fire on the grate and we'll smother the bastard!"

For a second Mendick was a child again, balancing on a tiny ledge while his master lit a pile of straw. He remembered the feeling of utter panic amidst the suffocating smoke, and the pain of scorched feet as he had danced to keep away from the rising sparks. He would not allow himself to be roasted alive half-way up one of Trafford's chimneys.

Throwing himself upwards, he searched for handholds, trusting as much to luck as anything else as he clambered up the flue. Coughing, he swallowed soot, feeling the stonework tearing his clothes and ripping the skin from his body as he frantically tried to escape. He had gambled on this chimney being connected to another in the room above, but he could not see any opening in the unrelenting black stone, and the flue was becoming progressively narrower. Soon he would not be able to climb further; he would either have to stay and be suffocated, or return and face whatever ugly death Armstrong had in mind for him. The finality of death did not matter with Emma waiting, but the knowledge of defeat did.

Voices echoed hollowly. "Break up the chair and throw it on; if we get the old soot on fire, we'll roast the peeler's flesh from his bones!"

"Jesus!" He remembered Restiaux's prayer as he had waited outside the Holy Land, *"Lord, I shall be very busy this day; I may forget thee, but do not forget me."* The words did not give him any comfort as he heard the crackle of flames, and felt the heat beat on to the soles of his feet. He coughed desperately; the smoke was burning his lungs and stinging his eyes, but he also noticed that the smoke was not rising straight up; it was veering to the left a few feet below him. If the smoke was moving in that direction, there must be an alternative passageway, hidden in the black of the flue. He edged down, towards the leaping flames and heard Armstrong's triumphant laugh.

"Come down and burn or stay there and smother, you peeler bastard!"

Something large was thrown onto the fire, sending an array of sparks upward; he flinched but continued to inch downwards, seeking the outlet that was redirecting the smoke. Beneath him the sparks lengthened and slid to one side, and he felt them scorching his legs and smelled his trousers burning as he eased himself lower, towards that elusive gap in the stonework, towards the fire.

He gasped as a tiny flame licked up the calf of his trouser leg, but even that small flaring light revealed the break in the flue, an opening barely wide enough for him to squeeze into. It was still beneath him, closer to the dancing flames, but with no choice he edged down, choking in the smoke, wincing as the torrent of sparks smouldered through his moleskin trousers, burning his calf and spreading onto his thigh. He chewed his lip, unwilling for Armstrong to hear him groan as the biting pain halted his downward progress.

He glanced toward the tiny opening, blocked as it was by a spiral of sparks and the lick of yellow flame. If he descended further, he would be within the fire, but to remain was to roast slowly; he had to go down. Retching, with his lungs a smoke-filled agony and the flesh of both legs now smouldering, Mendick forced himself further down. Knowing that Armstrong and Monaghan would be standing close to the fireplace as they listened for his agonies, he kicked violently, sending red-glowing soot showered down towards them, and then suddenly he was level with the opening.

Close to, the gap looked even smaller, and he was unsure where it would lead, but he knew he had to try. The alternative was a terrible death.

Thrusting his head into the reeking darkness, he wriggled his shoulders, felt his jacket tearing on the stonework, felt something ripping at his skin but pushed desperately onwards. The heat of the walls was intensifying by the second, while the smoke was so dense that every breath was a searing agony.

He heard a new terrifying roaring and knew immediately what it was. Unswept for years, the soot coating the flue had caught fire and was flaring upwards. It would only take seconds for the flames to reach him, and then he would die in slow agony. The flames would scorch away his flesh and race on upwards, leaving him flayed and trapped to die screaming in the dark. The heat increased, roasting his legs, driving the air from his lungs. He gasped, coughing furiously as every whooping breath increased his torment.

"Burn, you bastard!"

The voice came from beneath him as he writhed. He thrust himself into the narrow gap heedless of the pain as skin and flesh was flayed from his shoulders and burned from his legs.

There was cool air on his face as he scraped forwards, and then his hips jammed. In front of him was a small square where the blackness lightened to gray, but the narrowness of the opening stopped him, and he screamed, giving way to the pain of the flames that tormented his feet and legs.

"Jesus, help me!" Mendick felt panic overcome his sanity, remembering the terror of his childhood years, and sobbing with desperation he hauled himself on, shrieking at the combined agony of fear and fire and ripped skin.

"There he goes, squealing like a baby!" Laughter followed Armstrong's words, and the prospect of their pleasure spurred Mendick to a final effort. Grabbing hold of the stone with already shredded fingers, he screamed away his pain as he plunged forward, feeling his trousers rip and his skin peel away as he forced himself through the last obstacle.

After the horror of being trapped, the cool dark was heaven, but he knew that he could not pause to savour it. He crawled on only to fall headfirst into gaping space. There was hardly time to yell before he landed with a clatter in an empty fireplace.

He lay still for a second, cradling his agony. He coughed, the smoke was rasping at his lungs, and forced himself to look at his legs. He felt massive relief when he saw that although his trousers were scorched and smouldering, his burns were only superficial, although no less painful for that. Swearing, he crushed away the last glowing sparks with the flat of his hands, and only then did he inspect his surroundings.

He was in a bare room with walls and floors of undressed stone, no furniture, no floor covering, but two doors and a shuttered window. He flinched when somebody spoke outside and looked hopelessly for somewhere to hide. He knew he was too exhausted to put up a fight if he was caught here and breathed a sincere prayer of gratitude as the voices died away.

"Thank you, Lord," Mendick intoned, "for saving me from the fires of hell." For a moment he was tempted to curl into a ball on the cold stone floor, nurse his pain and relive the terror of those flames curling around his legs.

"No," he dismissed the thought, "keep moving or the wounds will stiffen. Get out now." He had seen a lot worse out East, but he was shaking with reaction at the remembered horror.

Forcing himself upright, he staggered to the shutter and eased it open, but the ancient windows were barred against intruders, and he had no tools. For a second he cursed his bad luck, stared outside at the dark grounds leading to freedom, and then he closed the shutters and limped across the room.

The first door opened onto a cupboard, the second gave access to one of the panelled corridors that threaded through Trafford Hall, and he moved out cautiously, very aware of the echo of his footsteps.

"Well, now we know exactly what we must do." The voice was Scott's; she had reassumed her educated accent, and Mendick felt the sudden batter of his heart. Backing into a recessed doorway, he tried the handle and eased himself inside as Scott and her companion walked along the corridor.

"We will use O'Connor's march and Monaghan's insurrection to our advantage." Scott was speaking quite casually, as if witnessing attempted murder was a daily occurrence.

The room he found himself in was dark, with chairs arrayed around a central table and with a sideboard loaded with decanters. The footsteps stopped right outside, and Mendick looked for somewhere to hide. There were no other exits, and he refused to contemplate the fireplace.

The door opened and as Scott stepped in, Mendick rolled under the table, smothering his pain as his shin scraped along the carved wooden leg. There was the rasp and flare of a Lucifer and the soft glow of a candle.

"Let's have a drink."

"Feel free to use my brandy." The second voice had the well-remembered arrogant drawl and slight lisp of Sir Robert Trafford. "You treat it like your own anyway."

"It's as much mine as yours, Robert," Scott responded coolly.

Mendick kept very still, hoping nobody would look beneath the table. There was the gurgle of liquid, the click of a glass stopper and a brief exchange of a toast.

"To the white horse."

"The white horse, damn his evil hide." The arrogant drawl paused. "Can you smell smoke? There's a most damnable smell of smoke in this room."

"I can't smell a thing," Scott sniffed loudly. "It's probably a backdraught from another fire. One of your flues was on fire earlier; shocking stench there." She gave her distinctive laugh. "It was like something had crawled up the chimney and died."

"Oh. That must be it then." There was a sharp clink as Trafford replaced his glass on the table. "So with this revolution in France and all the troubles in Italy, the Whigs are really shaking. They will be on the alert."

"Indeed they will," Scott agreed. "And the Chartists will give them exactly what they expect. When O'Connor's rabble rally on Kennington Common and Monaghan's volunteers create mayhem up and down the country, the government will be hard pressed to keep control."

"Everybody will be watching the Chartists," Trafford agreed. "Finality Jack cannot afford troubles in London, so he'll send in the army and then order them up here to finish the job. I expect there will be hundreds executed or transported to the Colonies. The Chartists will be destroyed."

"Exactly," Scott said, "and all that commotion will mean that our target is more vulnerable."

"Excellent." Trafford gave a sudden high laugh. "Bang, bang and little Drina is dead, the government collapses, people fear revolution on a European scale, and I am out of the woods."

"And Ernie's white horse is back in his own stable," Scott murmured, "ruling Britannia." There was the swish of brandy again and a second clink of crystal on crystal.

"And far more importantly, your father will be paid, and my creditors will be yapping at the heels of somebody else," Trafford added, sniffing again. "I was right though, Rachel, there is a most abominable stink of smoke in here."

"Perhaps we should go elsewhere, then," Scott decided. "We can dodge these blackguard Chartists and find somewhere private."

"By God, Rachel, I will ensure that once I am back above par, no radical will ever enter my policies again or set a single foot on my lands." The glasses clattered onto the table, and they left leaving the door open wide.

"Merciful heaven."

Mendick crawled from under the table and slumped onto a chair, rubbing his legs as tenderly as he could while he tried to make sense of what he had heard. It seemed that Scott and Trafford were only using the Chartists as cover for another plot, but he could not fathom why. He did not know who Drina might be or what the white horse signified, but neither really mattered to his duty. He had been sent here to find out what the Chartists were planning, and he had done just that.

Whatever double game Rachel Scott was playing, Monaghan and Armstrong were undoubtedly dedicated to the Chartist cause, and they intended to use O'Connor's planned gathering in London to cause revolution.

Mendick looked down at himself; even with his clothes frayed and scorched and his legs screaming their agony, he carried an important message. He knew exactly how dangerous these men were, but he had one advantage: they believed that he was dead. Now all he had to do was remain undiscovered until night, slide away from Trafford Hall, catch a train to London and warn Scotland Yard. He looked up instinctively as somebody walked into the room. Monaghan stood there with a lighted candle in his hand.

"You!"

For a second they stared at each other, and then Mendick moved. Although he was exhausted and injured, he was also a trained soldier and an experienced police officer, while Monaghan was only a politician. Feinting to the left, Mendick dodged Monaghan's clumsy lunge and landed a perfect punch straight to the politician's throat.

Unable to yell, Monaghan folded to his knees, making strange gargling noises. For one mad moment Mendick wondered if he should kill Monaghan now and end the threat of revolution, but he pushed temptation aside. He was a police officer, not an executioner. Ignoring the pain in his legs, he pounded into the corridor. As he did so, he heard voices, recognised Armstrong's Northumbrian accent and knew that he had delayed a fraction too long.

The corridor stretched ahead punctured by a score of doors, decorated by portraits of long-gone Traffords and as friendly as the teeth of a fighting dog. Mendick knew he could no longer hide; Monaghan would scour the building. He had to leave the house and run.

But how? The doors would be guarded, and every ground floor window seemed to be barred. He swore in frustration then remembered the kitchen where he had broken in so many weeks ago. Fighting the searing agony of his burns, he hurried along the corridor, shoving aside a startled servant as he slammed open the kitchen door.

"What?" A maid stared at him, backing away as he entered. "There's no Chartists allowed in here, sir."

Mendick ignored her and strode to the window. As he had guessed, the broken pane had been replaced but the bars had not. He wrestled with the catch, swearing. The window held; escape was a fraction of an inch away, but he was still trapped. The frightened squeals of the maid had attracted attention, and he heard male voices and the thunder of booted feet.

Careless of the noise, he lifted a box of soap and threw it at the window, kicked away the worst of the fragmented glass and squeezed through the gap in the bars. Cold iron raked painfully across his torn hips.

"There he is!"

"Shoot the bastard!"

He dropped, rolling on gravel which scraped his legs abominably, but rose as soon as he heard the penetrating crack of a pistol. He was running even as he smelled the whiff of powder smoke, jinking from side to side with legs trembling and the pain from his burns mounting with every jarring step. There was another shot, the sensation of disturbed air as the ball passed close by his head, and then he was among the trees, cursing the morning light threatening to betray him. Had time passed so quickly?

"Get your servants out, Sir Robert." That was Armstrong's voice. "And loose the dogs. He's a police spy!"

Dawn eased incandescent and pink-grey over policies sugared with the call of early birds and perfumed with new growth. Mendick moved as quickly as caution allowed, aware that the budding branches offered no protection against pistol shots, but knowing that lingering would be fatal. The peace of the country depended on the intelligence he had gleaned.

Gasping as the pain in his legs increased, he dodged among the shrubbery. Something snagged at his ankle, and he tripped.

His head slammed against the bole of a tree, momentarily stunning him. He lay still until the pain in his head was under control and his mind was again clear, and then looked ahead.

"Sweet God in heaven!"

Before him the mantrap gaped open, its saw-edged teeth waiting for a victim. His ankle had scraped against the outside. London life may have its dangers, but living in the country was not idyllic.

Rising swiftly, he headed for Trafford's boundary, watching all the time for mantraps and the equally unpleasant spring-guns. There were men swinging ugly blackthorn cudgels when he approached the wall, their voices pitched high to conceal their nervousness, and he ducked behind the rough trunk of an elm. Somebody laughed, the sound harsh in the still morning, and a dog began a series of staccato barks until its keeper kicked it quiet.

Burrowing close to the tree, he watched the servants pass before he moved forward. After surviving the flue, scaling a twelve-foot wall was nothing, but the broken glass at the top removed more of his clothing and more of his skin. Dripping blood, he staggered through the woodland, jumping at every sound. If Armstrong had alerted the Chartists, they would hunt him like a fox.

He heard voices close by and fought the temptation to hide; he struggled on, dragging his torn legs through the undergrowth, sobbing with pain and exhaustion, still coughing away the smoke in his lungs. At that moment he had no idea what to do except to continue running and head for London. He shook his head; that horse would not run. He needed a more practical plan. With no money in his pocket and his legs shaking beneath him, he would not be able to manage a quarter of the distance. He needed somewhere to rest, recuperate and regain his strength.

"The police," he told himself. "I can go to a police station," immediately realising he could not. The police would telegraph Scotland Yard, and the Chartists who infested the telegraph system would probably withhold the message and would certainly know his whereabouts. Indeed, Sergeant Ogden had mentioned that the Chartists had even infiltrated the police ranks. He would have to get his message to London in person, but in his present condition he could not. The thought of Jennifer Ogden's cheerful, capable face came to him. She would help; he could find sanctuary in White Rose Lane.

CHAPTER ELEVEN

Manchester: March 1848

He was nearly staggering with exhaustion when he reached the familiar lane with its uneven cobbles and squat cottages, but nothing was quite the same. The Ogdens' garden door sagged open, and the shed, once so redolent with industry, gaped to the world. There was no rustle of pigeons nor of anything else in the house that was as silent as Ogden's grave.

"Mrs Ogden." He hammered on the door. "Please let me in." He leaned against the wall with his heart thundering and agony gnawing at his legs, but there was no reply. He tried again, desperately pounding the door until it was opened. It remained at a cautious gap, secured by a stout chain.

Jennifer Ogden gripped a poker in her right hand; the nightcap perched on her head dispelling any appearance of aggression. Her eyes were clouded, but her voice was clear and very precise.

"Oh, it's you, Mr Mendick; if it's Nathaniel you seek, I am afraid that he is dead."

"Mrs Ogden." He thrust his foot forward to prevent her from closing the door. "I know about Mr Ogden—it's you I want to see."

Mrs Ogden stared at him, making no move to lower the poker or to unhook the chain.

"You must be mistaken, Mr Mendick. I cannot comprehend any reason that we should see each other."

"Help me," Mendick begged simply. He felt himself sag and straightened up.

For a second Mrs Ogden did nothing, and then she ran her gaze over him.

"Oh, I see," she said before motioning him to move his foot and pushing shut the door. He heard the rattle of the chain and the door reopened. Mrs Ogden ushered him inside and lit a candle. She surveyed him quietly, shaking her head, and only when she seemed satisfied that he was no threat did she place the poker on top of the table.

"Look at the state of you," she said. "What on earth have you done to yourself?" She shook her head. "You've heard about Nathaniel, then?"

"I have," Mendick admitted.

"They said he was killed by a collapsing building, but I don't believe it."

"I know," Mendick said. "I don't believe it either."

"They killed him." Mrs Ogden sounded surprisingly calm. "Those Chartist people he was after. And then they killed my dog." She shook her head again and looked closely at him. "But that can wait," she said, stepping back. "You're hurt. You're all bloody, and your legs are burned."

"Yes," Mendick agreed.

"What happened, Mr Mendick?"

"The same people who killed your husband tried to kill me," he told her. "I have to stop them, or they'll start a revolution."

Mrs Ogden did not appear perturbed at the news. She brushed a loose strand of hair from her face, her eyes examining him.

“We’ll have to get you cleaned and patched up first,” she decided. “You can’t stop anything in that state. Come along now.”

She ushered him into the kitchen where a fire was laid but not lit. The table was as neat as ever, with a linen cloth covering the bare deal boards and a vase of newly cut daffodils in the centre.

“If your hurts are not treated, they’ll get poisoned,” Mrs Ogden told him, somewhat severely, “and then you might lose a leg. Do you want that?”

“No,” Mendick said.

“Then keep quiet and let me do what I have to do.”

“I am sorry about your husband,” Mendick began and then realised he did not know what more to say.

“Are you?” Mrs Ogden sounded suddenly accusing. “You hardly knew him, so why should you be sorry?”

“I lost my wife. I know what you must be going through.”

She held his gaze for what seemed a long time. “Do you? I wonder if any man ever knows what a woman has to go through.”

Mendick looked away. She must have been hurting very badly to be so abrasive. “Maybe you’re right,” he said, “no, not maybe. You *are* right.”

“And how would you know if I am right or not?” Her continued bitterness surprised him. “Nathaniel was good at his job. They found him under a pile of rubble you know, thrown away like he was nothing.”

Mendick nodded, unable to bear the challenge in her eyes.

“I would like to meet the man that did it to him,” Mrs Ogden said.

"It was more than one man," he told her, "and it is my intention to see them hanged." She did not react to his words. "He was one of the best men I have ever met," he assured her, "and he was known as a good man even in Scotland Yard."

"One of the best men . . ." Mrs Ogden began, and then nodded, possibly partially mollified, although Mendick suspected tears were not far from her eyes. "Let's get you cleaned up." She fetched a brown bowl from the dresser in the corner. "We can talk about Nathaniel later if you wish."

"Of course."

He moved to help but she waved him away impatiently. He stood impotent as she worked a pair of bellows to bring the fire back to life, piled on some coal and filled a pot with water from the outside well. He watched her bustling around, thankful that he was safe for the time being. He did not realise that he was sleeping until she woke him.

"Come on now, Mr Mendick. Let's have your unmentionables off." She indicated his trousers.

Although Mrs Ogden had washed and changed into a comfortable dress of patterned green flowers and tidied her hair, her eyes were shockingly blank as though she refused to acknowledge the truth of her loss.

"What?" Mendick looked up. "I can't do that!"

"Don't be silly; I have to clean you up, so your trousers must come off. Do you really think that the sight of your legs will shock me?" There was no humour in Mrs Ogden's smile. "I've just lost my husband, and you're just another man."

"It's indecent." He stared at her for a moment as she looked scornfully back at him.

"It's necessary. Shirt too, please; we'd better do this properly."

Her logic was inescapable, and he peeled off his shirt and trousers, gasping at the scrape of cloth against his scorched and blistered skin. He stood naked before her, covering his decency with both hands. She surveyed him, pursing her lips.

"Turn around. You're a mess, aren't you?" She touched the wounds on his left hip, and he winced and pulled away. "Don't be such a baby. What did you do? Fall in a fire?"

"Something like that." Mendick thought it best not to say too much.

"I take it the Chartists lit it." Jennifer Ogden was no fool.

"They did," he agreed. "The same Chartists who murdered your husband."

"We'll talk about them later, too."

She had heated up the water and began to work on him, starting with the minor scrapes on his back and working her way down to his legs, washing away the blood before applying goose grease to the burns, tutting in sympathy whenever he winced but still thoroughly cleaning each wound before moving on to the next.

Embarrassed at first, Mendick soon found it strangely soothing to have a competent woman attending to him. He watched her frown in concentration as she dabbed at his wounds, ignoring his discomfort in her determination to do a good job.

"Thank you, Mrs Ogden," he said, humbled and strangely ashamed. "I am deeply indebted to you."

She looked up, brushed a stray strand of hair from her face and nodded, unsmiling.

"It was necessary; anyway, doing this takes my mind off things." She stood up, cleaning the grease from her hands on a cloth. "I'll find you something to cover yourself with. You won't mind wearing Nathaniel's clothes, will you? And when I make us something to eat, you can tell me what's happened and how it affected my husband." She narrowed her eyes. "And don't tell me that he was not involved, because I know he was."

While Mrs Ogden bustled with pots and plates, Mendick gingerly pulled on Ogden's clothing and related his story to her, glossing over the details of her husband's death but emphasising that he died bravely.

"Of course he did." She seemed to accept Ogden's murder calmly. She had placed a tray of soup, bread and cheese on the table. "He was always a brave man if nothing else. The question you should be asking is why I am not upset about it."

"What?" When he looked up Mrs Ogden was facing him squarely.

"You heard me, Mr Mendick. My husband is dead, yet I am not weeping a bucketful of tears. In truth I have not shed a single one nor do I intend to. Indeed, you may have noticed I am not even wearing mourning togs."

"People mourn in different ways . . ."

"I am not in mourning." Again Mrs Ogden was challenging, waiting to parry the inevitable questions.

"He was my husband, Mr Mendick. During his lifetime it was my duty to love and obey him; now he has gone I owe him nothing, not loyalty, not even a memory. In fact, I fully intend to forget him as soon as I can."

"I am sure you don't mean that; he was a good man . . ."

"Was he? Was he indeed?" Mrs Ogden's voice was syrup-sweet, but there was no mistaking the steel behind those eyes.

His meagre education had taught Mendick that women were not intended for the harsh existence of a policeman or a soldier. Women were to be kept secure, worshipped from afar and, while eminently capable of running a household and caring for any number of children, did not possess a man's capability to deal with life's more severe tasks. Experience, however, had shown him that this perception was untrue. Emma had been his equal in life, and more recently he had seen Rachel Scott intrigue with the best of them, become involved with the nastier side of politics and even participate in the murder of Ogden and his own attempted demise. Mendick realised that Jennifer Ogden had continued to stare directly at him.

"What are you going to do about these Chartists, Mr Mendick?"

The change of tack took him by surprise, but he answered with the truth.

"Tell Scotland Yard all that I know," he said.

"I will help," Mrs Ogden told him. "These people killed my husband, such as he was, and now you say they are planning to kill more husbands, sons, daughters, wives." She stopped and swallowed hard before continuing. "Is that correct?"

"That is correct," Mendick agreed.

"But if you get your intelligence to Scotland Yard, they might stop that from happening?"

"That's right," he nodded.

"So you get yourself down to that telegraph office right away, Mr Mendick, and send off your information." Mrs Ogden folded her arms, seemingly pleased that she had solved his problem so easily.

"I can't use the telegraph," Mendick told her quietly. "The Chartists have infiltrated the system, and it was Mr Ogden himself who told me they were also in the local police force."

"I see," Mrs Ogden nodded. "So what *do* you intend to do?"

"I must travel to London and deliver the information in person."

"I'm coming with you," Mrs Ogden told him. "When do we leave?"

Mendick stared at her. He had not anticipated this turn of events and certainly did not want her slowing him down.

"I'll leave as soon as I can . . ."

"Good. We can catch the train." She spoke as if the decision had already been made.

"All my money is in Chartertown."

"I've got some money," Mrs Ogden said at once. "I'll pay for both tickets. Ogden would approve."

"Mrs Ogden." Mendick wondered how he could dissuade her painlessly. "I would be faster on my own. This information must get through."

"Nonsense." Mrs Ogden dismissed his argument with a single word. "The train travels at the same speed however many passengers are on board, and I have the money. Either we go together, or you find some other method of transport."

Looking at those brittle eyes above a face so determined, Mendick knew he had only one card left to play.

"It might be dangerous," he said weakly.

"So was living with Ogden," Mrs Ogden told him, unsmiling. "Let's leave as soon as we can. I hate this place and all that it stands for. I want a new life with no ties to the past. Now. I want to go now." She stood up, and for the first time Mendick saw there were tears in her eyes.

"All right, Mrs Ogden. Let's go together."

He remembered how he had felt when Emma died and how he had thrown himself into his job, working every hour he could and not caring about time or anything at all. Mrs Ogden was unfortunate—she did not have such an avenue of escape.

"We'll do that." Mrs Ogden put her hand on his arm, shaking her head. "But call me Jennifer and I will call you James. I don't ever want to be known as Mrs Ogden again."

"As you wish," he said and looked away when Jennifer made no effort to stop the tears sliding down her cheeks.

"There's Ogden's second best frock coat," Mrs Ogden said, "and his top hat. You'll look most respectable in that."

As they stood at the front door of the cottage, with Jennifer in a green coat long enough to hide her ankles and with a pretty feathered bonnet on her head, she looked back inside.

"And there we have it," she said. "A house full of memories, the grave of my dog and the physical remains of ten years of marriage and shared existence." When she looked at him, her eyes were bitter. "Do you understand what that means, James? Ten years of your life? Ten years . . . and now it is gone."

Mendick said nothing. He put his hand on her shoulder, but she shook it away.

"I don't want sympathy, James." Her voice was as edged as he had ever heard. "Look inside my home, James. Can you see anything missing?"

"Missing?" He shook his head. "I'm sorry Jennifer, but I don't understand the question."

"No? Then you certainly don't understand, James, do you?" For a second he thought she was about to break into tears again, but she recovered. "Step back, please."

He did so, wondering, as she lit a candle and allowed the flame to play on the curtains by the window.

"Careful!"

"No!" She pushed him back. "Let it burn. Let it all burn down." Her voice was acid but the tears on her cheeks soft and round. "I am burning my bridges. This is ended now, and I won't be back. Take me away, James; take me far, far away."

As they walked down the lane, smoke was coiling from the cottage and orange flames lit up the sky, but Jennifer squared her shoulders and did not look back.

*

"There is no direct train to London," Mendick said. "We'll have to travel to Birmingham first and change at the station there. Wrap up well; there's no glass in the third class windows."

"I'm not travelling third class with all the riff-raff." There was finality in Jennifer's tone. "It is far too long a journey to bounce around on a hard seat in a filthy coach like a cow or a sheep going to market, and I'm not wasting money on foolish profligacy by travelling first, so second it will be." Her smile took him by surprise. "It's all right, James, I have a capital head for figures."

"I'm sure that you have," he agreed, moving closer, but Jennifer stepped back.

"And James," she fixed him with a stern look, "I'm quite sure we'll be travelling through tunnels, and I warn you I am wearing my longest hat pin, so I want no shenanigans in the dark, if you please."

"There will be no shenanigans," Mendick promised. He wondered if she was joking until he saw the pin thrust through her hat. "You are quite safe with me."

"Oh yes," she told him, thrusting forwards her chin. "I am quite safe."

Manchester London Road Station had opened only six years before and was the main departure point for London and all other points south. The station was busy, with crowds of businessmen in frock coats and tall hats pulling at their whiskers as they discussed the latest downturn in trade, a few prosperous-looking gentlemen looking for the first class compartments and a mass of obviously third class passengers talking in hopeless optimism of the jobs they would find in the next town or maybe the one after that.

It still seemed a marvel to Mendick that within the last decade these railways had spread across the country, slicing the time it took to travel from one end to the other. In his youth it had been quicker to travel by steamboat rather than use even the fastest of the stagecoaches, and far cheaper. Now iron rails linked the whole country together and new branch lines and stations were being opened every year. The thought of all this progress jeopardised by revolution and Britain dragged down to the level of some petty European state did not bear thinking about.

"Well, now we are on our way." He had purchased their tickets from a clerk who studied his face suspiciously before accepting his money. He edged close to Jennifer, who moved aside so that not even their clothes touched. Sighing at his inability to understand this woman, he watched the crowd instead.

"Let's hope this train is on time." Jennifer seemed intent on keeping her distance. "I want to see this Inspector Field of yours."

Mendick frowned. "I'm not sure if Inspector Field will actually see you."

"He'd better . . ." Jennifer stopped, grabbing hold of his arm. "James! Look at that! On the wall."

The poster was neatly made: an accurate sketch of his face and a short but bold caption beneath:

This man is James Mendick, and he is an enemy of the Charter. He is dedicated to destroying the hopes of the working classes of this country. If you see him, ensure that you shout out his name.

"God in heaven!"

Mendick stared for a second, wondering at the ingenuity of the Chartists, and then he remembered the notebook with the picture of each Scotland Yard detective. There was obviously a talented artist within the Chartist ranks, and once the picture had been drawn, it would be a simple matter to print off a poster, possibly on the same press that produced their *Morning Star* newspaper. He cursed; no wonder the ticket clerk had stared at him.

"And there's more." Jennifer dropped her hand from his arm. "See?"

There were other posters scattered around the station. On walls, on pillars, even on the outside of the ticket booth – each poster showing Mendick's face, and each portraying him as an enemy of the Charter.

"Keep your head down," Jennifer advised, "and pull down that hat. Thank God that it's too big for you."

He did so, immediately feeling that every eye in London Road Station was fixed exclusively on him.

"Maybe there are no Chartists here," Jennifer said hopefully, "and we can just slip on to the train and keep quiet until we leave Manchester."

"Please God that you are right," Mendick said, glancing around him. He shook his head and rammed the top hat even further down as he felt his stomach heave. "There's Josiah Armstrong himself, in the red cap, and the monster at his side is his guard dog."

Armstrong leaned against a pillar at the entrance to their platform, with his revolutionary red cap on his head, a stubby pipe in his mouth and his arms folded across his scrawny chest. He was surveying the crowds much in the fashion of a police officer at a fairground, checking and identifying each person before passing on to the next. Beside him Peter looked like some circus exhibit—the strong man of Manchester—more than a head taller than Armstrong, twice as broad in the shoulder and with the lowering expression of a stag in the rutting season.

"They must have guessed I'd go straight for the train," Mendick said, hating himself for underestimating the Chartists' intelligence. "And they'll probably have people at every station in the area too."

He imagined Monaghan alerting the entire Chartist network; there could be men, some of whom he may even have trained himself, standing beneath posters all across the North. The thought was frightening, a private army within the nation, scores, maybe hundreds of potential revolutionaries looking for him.

"We'll have to think of something else."

"So that's Armstrong." Jennifer stepped clear for a better view until Mendick pulled her back. "Let me go. I want to see the man who murdered Nathaniel."

"It's not safe," Mendick protested as she shook him off irritably, and he could only watch as she walked forward, her eyes never leaving Armstrong's face.

"God, Jennifer, don't do anything foolish," he muttered, torn between the need to leave the station as quickly as he could and the desire to follow her to ensure she was not hurt.

Jennifer stopped a yard short of Armstrong and spoke a few words. Trying to merge into the anonymity of the crowd, Mendick watched as they spoke for a few moments, and then Jennifer nodded and walked slowly back to him. She was shaking, and he saw that all the colour had fled from her face.

"I wanted to speak to him, just once," she said, with a tremble in her voice.

Mendick nodded; he could empathise with her feelings. After the death of Emma he had wanted to hurt people, anybody, just to express his bitterness.

"That was hard for you," he said.

She nodded. "Take me away from here." Her voice was taut, and she could not hold his eyes. "Ogden could be brutal, James, but I don't think I've ever been so close to pure evil as I was just now."

Mendick agreed although he could not have put his feelings into words. Before Armstrong had been transported he had been known as a vociferous supporter of the Charter, a noted orator and a firebrand, but his experiences in Van Diemen's Land had embittered him. Genuine concern for his fellow workers had warped into a crusade against every factory owner, and he was prepared to use any method to achieve his objective. In a sense, the authorities had created Armstrong from their brutality, and Armstrong intended to unleash the whirlwind of his revenge on London.

"We'll have to stop him," Jennifer said quietly.

"We will," Mendick agreed. "But not by catching a train at this station."

Several men were reading the posters when Mendick hurried from the station and back into the bustle of Manchester's streets. He saw the same pinched faces as before, but now they seemed sinister, as if every eye was watching him and every man's hand was turned against him. Manchester had appeared a place of languishing industry, hectic anticipation and desperate poverty, but now it seemed to host a nest of watchful Radicals, a fermenting broth of revolution and physical Chartism; he had to leave as quickly as he could.

"Where can we go?" Jennifer clung to his arm. Speaking with Armstrong had drained her more than Mendick had realised. "Could we catch the stage coach?" She raised her eyebrows. "We'd be in London in a day or so."

"I doubt they'll have forgotten about that," he said. "I suspect there will be Chartists all over the damned place."

There was a bill-sticker outside the station, busy with paste pot and brush as he plastered portraits of Mendick over every vacant wall. Passers-by stopped to watch, and one famine-thin woman deliberately spat on the poster.

"Whatever we do," Mendick decided, "we can't stay here." He glanced around, fearful of recognition. "Let's just walk."

"Where?"

"Anywhere, nowhere; I just need to think."

Keeping his head down, he chose a street and strode on, hoping to come to a solution. The most obvious would be to walk straight into a police station, say who he was and ask for help, but Ogden's warning of Chartist sympathisers in the police ranks had been very stark. If he could not trust the police, then who was left? Was he the only loyal man in Manchester? Was he the only loyal man in Great Britain?

The thought was appalling and carried its own negativity, for if there were only a few loyal men then he was in a minority, and did that not make *him* the rebel and the majority the true inheritors of the nation? He shook his head; to think that was to discard everything he had ever believed; he must try to be rational. He swore, limping as the burns on his legs began to ache.

"Where are we going?" Jennifer sounded plaintive, and Mendick realised she was lifting her feet in distaste and picking her way through horse manure. He had led her into a narrow lane of arched doorways and stables.

The nearest door was open, and he peered in. There was a single carriage, its dark paint highlighted by a distinctive yellow stripe he remembered, and the shock of recognition was so sudden he nearly ran away. He had taken Jennifer straight to the courtyard of the Beehive, the heart of Monaghan's Physical Force Chartists. He, who had acted been so concerned for her safety, had led her to the most dangerous place imaginable.

CHAPTER TWELVE

Manchester: March 1848

"Sweet God in heaven!" The idea was so sudden and so extreme that it shocked him. He felt his excitement rising and squeezed Jennifer's arm.

"We're going to London, Jennifer, and we're going in style." He stopped squeezing when she violently pulled free.

"Let me be, James."

He apologised at once but continued, "Listen. Your name is Rachel Scott and you're an important Chartist. Can you repeat that?"

"Of course."

She looked at him, forehead furrowed. "My name is Rachel Scott, and I am an important Chartist, but why . . .?"

"Don't think. Just do it. Now, follow my lead and look arrogant."

"What?"

Rather than arrogant, Jennifer only looked perplexed as Mendick straightened his shoulders and marched into the stable. For a second he hesitated in case Peter was inside, but remembering that the prize-fighter was on guard at the railway station, he raised his voice in his best imitation of an officer of the 26th Foot.

"Is anybody here? I said, is anybody here?"

A short man emerged from one of the stalls, wiping his hands on a wisp of straw.

"Who are you?" Recognising the voice of authority, he gave a small, obviously reluctant, bow.

"McGill." Mendick gave the name of the sergeant who had terrorised him as a recruit. "Is Mr Armstrong's coach ready yet? He wants it now."

The man scowled suspiciously.

"Where's Peter? Mr Armstrong always sends Peter for his coach." He leaned back for a better view of Mendick. "I don't know you at all."

"And I don't know you either; nor do I want to." Mendick adopted his most supercilious expression. "You might not know me, but you will know Miss Scott, here. Everybody knows Rachel Scott."

Jennifer stepped forward, acting as one born to expect obsequiousness from underlings.

"And you are?"

The man stepped back, bowing with genuine respect.

"I'm sorry, Miss Scott, I did not know . . . I have never seen you before, although naturally I know all about you . . . I am Robert Peach, the ostler for the Beehive, and of course I'll help you in any way I can."

"I know that," Jennifer said, but Mendick interrupted:

"Put a good horse in the traces," he ordered. The fear of recognition made him more authoritarian than he intended. "And make sure that it's a *fresh* horse, well rested and fed."

"Of course, sir," the ostler agreed.

"And you'll have food prepared for us?" Jennifer asked sweetly, opening her mouth in apparent horror when the ostler shook his head.

"I was not given orders . . ."

"Then I am giving you orders now! Get some food, and fast!" She looked over to Mendick. "I thought Mr Armstrong had matters better arranged that this, Mr McGill. I shall have words with him, severe words."

"I'll send the boy right away," the ostler promised, "but . . ."

"Do that," Jennifer ordered.

"We haven't got time," Mendick began and Jennifer shot him a look that could have frozen lava.

"We have to eat," she hissed.

Mendick gestured outside, where a man was busy with paste pail and posters. He guessed that his portrait was about to decorate even this insignificant alleyway. Jennifer nodded.

"Ostler," she snapped, "tell the boy to make sure he is back before the carriage is ready or I'll take a whip to him."

"You'll both be sorry, by God." Mendick lowered his voice. "So get to it!"

He watched the billsticker slap the poster onto a stable door and walk closer, the pail swinging from his left hand. Jennifer pulled him inside the stables and pushed the door shut.

"You are distracting the ostler," she told him, severely, "and the good man is doing his best for us."

Within ten minutes Mendick was sitting on the driver's seat of the brougham, holding unfamiliar reins in his hand as he manoeuvred out of the lane and into the streets of Manchester. He had no plan except to head for London and no clear idea of the direction, but it was good to be doing something positive again, good to have cocked a snook at Armstrong and his band, and better to be leaving behind the Chartist heartland.

"Let's hope that we don't break a wheel," he said, and Jennifer threw him a look that would have curdled milk.

It was many years since he had driven, and he was out of practice, pulling the horse first this way and then the other, and the brougham rattled uncertainly over the greasy cobblestones.

"Careful, James," Jennifer shouted from inside the coach, "or I'll take over the reins."

"Sit still and keep quiet," he replied, too tense to act the gentleman. Determined to prove himself, he whipped up the horse, which jerked forward and nearly clipped a brewery dray lumbering in the opposite direction. It was only the fact he was driving a private coach and possessed an extremely baleful glare which prevented anything more serious than a brief exchange of insults.

With the centre of Manchester congested, he had to quickly relearn old skills. Wagons and carts, carriages and stagecoaches all crammed onto the roads, and he was too busy controlling the horse to pay much attention to the direction of travel.

"Which way is it?" he asked hopelessly, and Jennifer pointed to a black-and-red coach.

"That's *Peveril of the Peak,*" she said, "the London stage. Follow it!"

As the coachman's horn blared a warning to keep clear, Mendick tucked in behind the *Peveril,* hoping there were not too many stops. Dark rain squeezed through the seemingly permanent pall of smoke oozing from those cotton mill chimneys that were still working, but he tried to ignore the depression. Easing over the River Irwell, he passed the

Cathedral and looked ahead for a sight of the hurrying stagecoach.

"What delicious weather." Jennifer had opened the window and thrust her head outside.

"Oh aye, the day is incapable of improvement." Mendick huddled beneath the rain. "You stay inside the carriage and keep dry."

"How long will it take us to reach London?"

"I have no idea," he admitted. "Two or three days, perhaps, but we don't have to drive all the way. We'll have to avoid the turnpikes too, in case the keepers are Chartists; we can stop further south and take the train when it is safer."

"No." Jennifer shook her head emphatically. "We'll drive all the way. If the Chartists are in one railway station, they could be in them all. We'll find a decent, out-of-the-way inn for the night and rest the horses."

The industrial revolution had given Manchester some fine architecture, but its growth had spawned a city which contrasted a prosperous centre with shocking housing and ugly factories. However, as they drove south, the brick terraces gradually eased into some of the most delightful country Mendick had ever seen. His spirits rose as the city disappeared behind him and the rain eased to a pleasant drizzle.

Spring had enlivened the countryside, pushing the dreary winter away in a blush of green grass and flowers. Daffodils nodded from the gardens of cottages, ploughed fields were already flushed with growth, and birdsong sweetened the crisp air as the brougham pulled further away from Manchester's bitter memories.

“This is better.” Jennifer poked her head out of the window, holding on to her bonnet as the breeze washed her face. “How far will we go today?”

Mendick glanced backward to reply, “As far as we can, or rather, as far as the horse is willing to pull. I’d like to get a fair distance before dark. Armstrong will soon discover that his carriage is missing, and it won’t take him long to guess who has it. If he controls the telegraph system, he’ll certainly warn his minions to watch out for us.”

“I never thought of that,” Jennifer admitted. “So what’s best?”

“Follow your plan of finding an out-of-the-way place to spend the night. A country inn with no recourse to the telegraph would be best.”

Jennifer’s forethought had ensured they had enough food for that day, and in the evening Mendick eased them off the main road and into a village where a handsome inn slumbered under a glorious sunset. With its beams and thunderous log fire, he had never seen anything so inviting. The landlady booked them in as a married couple, and Jennifer, practical as ever, did not object.

“Only married people or a brother and sister can respectably travel together,” she reminded him, “so we will just have to make the best of it.” Her smile softened the confusion in her eyes. “Just remember I have my hat pin.”

“I would not take advantage of you,” he told her.

“You will not have the chance,” Jennifer promised sweetly.

Their room overlooked the village green, where ducks huddled in a pool of muddy water and a gaggle of barefoot children resisted the efforts of their parents to drag them home.

"It's beautiful," Jennifer said. "It's so pleasant after the industry and bustle of Manchester."

Mendick agreed. At one time not too long ago, most people in England would have lived somewhere similar; being forced to the cities to find work must have broken their hearts. No! He shook his head. If he continued with that train of thought he would find himself supporting the Chartists again. He sighed, cursing Armstrong and Monaghan for latching on to what had been a relatively peaceful movement and turning it into something sordid.

"It's a perfectly well-conducted inn, too," Jennifer said quietly, "but we might have a slight problem tonight."

One bed dominated the room, and the chambermaid bustled about cheerfully, talking about the weather and the terrible state of affairs in France while checking that there was water in the triton pitcher, laying out fresh linen and commenting on the fine carriage that they were driving.

"Well, Mr and Mrs Brown," she said, "I'll bid you a good night, then." She curtseyed and left them with a single candle burning and the fire glowing red against the evening chill.

"So here we are." Mendick watched as Jennifer sat gingerly on the bed, testing it for comfort and cleanliness, just as Emma would have done.

"Here we are indeed," she agreed. She was obviously waiting for him to speak.

"So how do we proceed?"

"Simple," Jennifer told him, pulling the hatpin from her hair. It was about ten inches long and looked wickedly dangerous. "You sleep on the floor, and I have this by my side."

"You have no reason to be afraid of me," he tried to assure her. "I would not insult you in any way."

"No." She ran two fingers along the length of the pin. "I have no reason to fear you at all." She raised her chin defiantly, and then suddenly she was crying; her shoulders shaking as the repressed emotion of the past few weeks escaped. She tried to control herself, gulping for air as her face screwed up. "That's just what Ogden said on our wedding night; those were his exact words!"

"Oh God!" He extended a hand in sympathy, trying to pat her shoulder but she rounded on him, jabbing with the pin so he withdrew hurriedly. "I'm sorry, I had no idea. . ."

Her face was twisted as she snarled at him across the breadth of the bed, "No! You have no idea, no idea at all!" She was sobbing violently now, taking great whooping breaths, and then she turned away from him and lay on the bed with her face buried in the covers. He did not know what to do. He would have known exactly how to soothe away Emma's grief, but Jennifer was an unknown entity, somebody with such unexpected mood swings that he was left feeling confused and powerless.

Standing by the bed, unable to help but unwilling to leave Jennifer to suffer alone, Mendick could only watch as she lay there, her shoulders heaving. He cursed Armstrong and the Chartists anew. Whatever their high ideals, all they seemed to do was leave a trail of misery and suffering in their wake.

Blackbirds eased them into the night, and fresh rain softly caressed the windows as the fire gradually faded. Mendick sat on the only chair, occasionally putting out his hand but always withdrawing it before he made contact with Jennifer's tormented body. When the candle burned low he lit another, unwilling to leave her in the dark.

When Jennifer finally looked up, her eyes were red-rimmed and swollen. She swallowed hard, but when she spoke her voice was very controlled. "Can you remember when I asked you what was missing in my . . . the house in Manchester?"

"I remember," Mendick said quietly. In the confusion of trying to escape from the Chartists he had not given the question any more thought.

"So, James, what was missing?" Jennifer seemed to be biting back the words.

"Your husband? Mr Ogden?" he hazarded, and saw the anger flare again, uncontrollable and frantic.

"Not Ogden! Not ever Ogden! What else? What should there be after ten years of marriage?" She nearly screamed the words, heedless of being overheard.

"Children, of course! Children! I have none, can't you see that?"

Mendick backed off from her fury. This was not the demure domestic woman that he had first met, but a spitfire full of bile and bitterness.

"I had not thought . . ."

"Of course you had not thought." Jennifer took a deep, shuddering breath. "But try to think now, James. I cannot have children, James. What do you think of that?"

He remembered Emma carrying their child, he remembered her pride and beauty, the way she swelled and the way she suffered.

"My wife died in childbirth," he said quietly, controlling his own emotion. "If she had been unable to have children, she would still be with me."

Deep in her own grief, Jennifer brushed aside his experience. "You say that *now,* but what would you have said then? I saw the look in your face just now; you despised me."

"Despised you?"

Mendick had been married long enough to realise that he could not console a woman in such a frame of mind. Jennifer was looking for a quarrel and would twist whatever he said. She had been hurt and wanted to hurt somebody else, and he was the most available person. Yet he knew that she was also at her most vulnerable, scared, newly alone in the world, so he must ensure he did not distress her further.

"No, Jennifer, I do not despise you." He braced himself for the inevitable onslaught, but instead she sighed.

"No? You would if you were my husband. You would if you wanted sons to follow you."

Suddenly he thought he understood. Jennifer had nothing of Ogden, no child to carry his memory, and she believed that Ogden would have been disappointed.

"Nathaniel married you, Jennifer, for yourself. As soon as I saw you together, I knew that you were happy. He would not mind; he would understand."

"Would he?" Jennifer raised her eyebrows in a display of such scepticism that Mendick knew he was wrong again. "Would he indeed?" She stood up, still brandishing the hatpin. "No, he would not. He wanted children, Mr Mendick, and I failed him. I was infertile and produced no heirs." She slapped at her crotch, deliberately obscene. "This is useless; I am useless, and he hated me for it."

"No," he tried to console her, "I'm sure he did not."

"You're sure of an awful lot, Mr Mendick, and all your sureties are incorrect. He hated me for it, and . . ." she paused, shaking her head as her face collapsed, her mouth open in howls.

Once again he took a single step forward but stopped. He could only watch and wait for Jennifer to regain her composure. By the time she recovered, the bed was a rumpled mess and her face was blotchy and swollen.

"He beat me, Mr Mendick, that's how much he understood. He beat me, and that's how *happy* we were together."

"Oh sweet Lord." Mendick sat on the bed. "I had no idea."

"No," Jennifer said quietly, 'you had no idea. You saw him as a good man because even *Scotland Yard* knew that. You saw Ogden's public face, the smiling, dedicated police officer who always did his duty, the man with the docile wife and the respectable occupation. I saw the *real* Nathaniel Ogden, the ranting failure who married a woman who couldn't even produce a child. I saw . . ." she shook her head. "I saw a different man, Mr Mendick, and I do not care that he is dead." She looked up through eyes liquid with tears. "Now do you despise me? A woman who can't produce children and a wife who doesn't care that her husband is dead?"

"He beat you?"

Mendick tried to equate his vision of the cheerful Sergeant Ogden with a man who beat his wife. He had encountered other such men, one or two of whom he had arrested, but they were usually drunken brutes who took out their frustrations on the most vulnerable person they could find; he had not thought of Ogden as a failure, a drunkard or a brute. He glanced at Jennifer, searching for some residual evidence, a fading bruise, perhaps, or a swollen lip. She read his look with ease.

"He hit me where it would never show," Jennifer confirmed. "Where only he would ever see it, if you understand?" She passed a quivering finger over her body.

"I think I do." Mendick felt his lip curling. "My God, but I'm sorry, Mrs Ogden . . ."

"Jennifer. Call me Jennifer." Her voice had risen to a hysterical scream. "Never use that name again. I do not want that name!"

"I am sorry, Jennifer. But could you not leave? Go somewhere else?"

"Where would you have me go?" She spread her arms to indicate her helplessness. "A woman apart from her husband has few rights, James. You know that. As you know that the law allows a man to discipline his wife; he was breaking no law."

"Indeed he was," Mendick said quickly. "He was breaking the law, and could have been jailed for what he did."

"But he told me . . ."

"Lies. He told you lies."

"But he was a policeman, and he said it was legal . . ." Jennifer looked up, her face twisted and tear-stained, horrified at this new example of her husband's cruelty.

"It is not legal to hit your wife," Mendick assured her gently. He wanted to hold her but knew that she would not accept his sympathy, nor his embrace, however kindly meant.

"Oh God." She ducked her head, her voice quavering, "It's too late now. He's gone, and you're taking me to London to start a new life where nobody knows me."

Mendick nodded. "That's the sensible thing to do." He tried to sound calm and reasonable, but he felt like shouting at the terrible injustice of life. "We'll drive down to London together, tell Scotland Yard all we know, and then you can build a better life for yourself."

"I won't be telling Scotland Yard anything," Jennifer told him. Her smile was bitter. "Do you really think I *care* if the Chartists take over the country?"

"Probably not," Mendick said, "but whether they succeed or not, their attempt will bring misery to thousands of people just like you."

Jennifer looked at him, her eyes narrow. "Then let them suffer!" She spat out the words. "Where were they when I needed help?" She glared at him, conveying her hurt through wild eyes, until she began to cry again, this time with great, heaving sobs that left her drained and exhausted.

Mendick said nothing, sharing her hurt. He had seen many emotional women in the police cells, the only difference was that he had not cared a button for any of them, and he was beginning to care for Jennifer. He waited for her to calm down.

"I have no intention of talking with Inspector Field or any other inspector. I only want to get as far from Manchester as possible, and you provided me with the means." Jennifer looked up again. "So *now* do you despise me? Now are you going to hit me?"

Mendick shook his head. "No," he said quietly, "and when you have stopped trying to make me dislike you, we can speak again. Until then, I think you had better get some rest, we have another long day tomorrow." He hesitated for a moment. "I will sleep with most of my clothes on, but if you feel more comfortable, you can remove some or all of yours. I promise to respect your privacy."

He looked directly into her eyes, seeing the pain behind the defiance, the fear underlying the aggression. "I told you before that you have nothing to fear from me, Jennifer, and I repeat that statement." He lowered his voice and spoke very slowly, "You have nothing to fear from me, Jennifer, now or in the future. What your husband did was terrible, and I sympathise with you, but I have no reason to despise you."

When he awoke, Jennifer was lying under the top cover, with her hatpin clutched firmly in her hand. She was still sobbing, but he could do nothing to ease her pain. He listened to her for some time, and only when she stopped did he gently remove the pin from her fist in case she rolled onto it and injured herself. She did not stir, so he rearranged the covers to make her more comfortable and looked down on her lying there.

"Sleep tight," he said quietly, and for a moment he saw Emma watching from the corner of his mind.

*

"It's over two hundred miles between Manchester and London," Mendick said as he cracked his whip. "And it might be best to avoid the main roads, so settle down for a long ride."

The horse jolted forward, its hooves kicking up gravel from the drive as he left the inn and steered onto the road. The coach lights glinted in the darkness of pre-dawn, flickering over the roadside trees and occasionally reflecting the yellow eyes of watchful sheep. Looking further afield, he saw pinpricks of light where the inhabitants of lonely cottages were wakening.

"We have travelled about forty miles, so by my reckoning we have two or even three more days of travel ahead of us."

Jennifer nodded. Puffy-eyed from lack of sleep, she had insisted on joining him on the driving step that morning. Saying nothing, she sat at his side, wrapped up in her coat and with a thick coach blanket on top. Only when the brougham jolted over a series of deep ruts, spraying mud on either side of the road did she break her silence, and then to speak very softly.

"He hated me, James," she said quietly. "He hated me for failing to give him a son, and he proved it by making me feel worthless in every way." She looked away again, fighting her tears. "Everything I did, he mocked; everything I said was wrong. 'You're useless, Jennifer,' he said. 'You can't make a child and you can't do anything. You're useless.'"

"Aye?" Mendick guided the horse around a bend, with the lanterns only a meagre guide in the darkness and the horse's hooves slipping on mud. "Well, we both know he was wrong, then."

"I have to *prove* him wrong, James; I have to prove that I am not useless."

Although she used his name, Mendick knew that she was speaking to herself, justifying her actions, assuaging her guilt for leaving her home.

"He failed to stop the Chartists, James, so I must succeed." She looked at him, her face strained. "So maybe I will speak to your Inspector Field after all."

"That could be helpful," Mendick said quietly. "And as you have come to that decision, I think it is time to put things right between us."

"There's nothing to put right," Jennifer said, suddenly guarded again, as if suspecting he would demand some piece of what remained of her fragile self-respect. "And there is no *us*. We are travelling together; I have the money, and you drive the carriage. When we reach London, we do what we have to do and part, never to see each other again."

"Agreed," Mendick said. "But until then? Are we going to sit at rigid attention, with you mistrusting everything I say and do and with me expecting you to plunge that great dagger of a hatpin into me at any second?" Mendick tried to smile, but Jennifer looked away.

"Do you blame me?" Her voice was sharp again. "If my own husband hated me, why should you be any different?"

"I have no reason to hate you. Indeed, I have every reason *not* to; you helped me when I needed help, and when you did not have to."

Jennifer said nothing but stared into the surrounding blackness. Somewhere far away there was an orange glow from a factory fire, its light a focal point for her attention. An owl screeched hauntingly, quickly echoed by its mate, and Jennifer shivered on the seat.

Mendick pressed home what he thought might be his advantage. "And no, I do not blame you, but I think you blame yourself."

Jennifer stiffened at once. "My life is nothing to do with you, and I would thank you not to pry."

Sighing, Mendick laid the whip across the flank of the horse so it bucked forward, jerking the brougham behind it.

"And there's no need to take out your black temper on the horse, Mr Mendick!"

He cracked the whip again, hunched into Ogden's coat and glared gloomily ahead. Here he was, driving down the length of England in a stolen coach, with the future of the nation in his hands, and rather than plan for the best way to deliver his message, he was arguing with an embittered widow.

"We'll have to hurry," he explained needlessly. "The Chartists' meeting is planned for the twelfth of next month."

"That's two weeks away yet." Jennifer's reminder was sharp.

"It's not much time to organise defence against the Chartist hordes."

"Hordes!" Her tone was scathing. "Hordes of unemployed men who only want a decent wage for their families and some sort of representation in the running of the country." The coach slammed into a hole in the road, jostling Jennifer against him, but she quickly pushed herself away. "Not the most dangerous enemy for the government, I would think."

"Thousands of angry and stubborn men, some of them trained and armed, highly organised and led by unscrupulous and ambitious murderers." Mendick put another interpretation on the Chartists. "As you know very well."

"And who is to blame for that? You helped train them," Jennifer quickly altered her angle of attack.

"Perhaps so, but we still have to warn the government." He steered around a series of half-hidden potholes. "And that means reaching London as quickly as possible."

"If you want to be quick, then you had better be careful," Jennifer said acidly, "for there's a fire ahead."

With all Mendick's concentration on the driving, he had not seen the droplets of light. Now he saw them, a score, a hundred, a thousand tiny flames merging together to form a single mass about a mile ahead and to the right.

"What in God's name is that?"

"How should I know?" Jennifer sounded irritated. "But we'll soon find out. Drive on."

Instinctively slowing down, he saw more of the lights, some in untidy groups, and others in regular columns, all gathering at a central point, spreading over the countryside in an impressive incandescent display.

"James." Jennifer pointed to their left where more flickering flames bounced toward them.

"They're torches," he said, "dozens and dozens of people carrying torches."

"Oh, my eye." Jennifer craned over him to look. "Oh, my eye, whatever next?"

A group hurried beside the carriage, panting men marching side by side with their hands aloft and torches sputtering in the air. Mendick looked downward, about to ask what was happening, until he saw the face of the nearest man.

Eccles was leading his volunteers, his swarthy face set, body moving lithely and relaxed as he had been taught, and with his musket carried at the trail. At his back were Preston and Duffy, each with a torch and musket, and the others followed in the regular infantry march in which he had trained them so well.

"Sweet God in heaven, Jennifer, they're Chartists. It's a gathering of the Physical Force Chartists."

Jennifer pressed to his side, momentarily forgetting her reluctance to be close to a man as she watched the assembled hordes. "But why here?"

"Why not?" Mendick shrugged. "It's away from any centre of population. They must have taken the train to the nearest station and assembled on this moorland." He swore, lifting the reins. "Jesus, Jennifer, if they recognise us, they'll kill us dead."

"Keep your head down then, James, and drive like the wind." Jennifer spoke quietly, as if the Chartists could hear her above the drumming of the horses' hooves, the growling of the wheels and the steady tramp of their own marching feet. “There must be hundreds of them.”

About to whip up, Mendick realised he had delayed a fraction too long. The road ahead had filled with marching men, some carrying muskets, others pikes or stout staves or agricultural tools, bill hooks, scythes, even a pitchfork – anything they imagined might make a useful weapon.

“It’s like something from the Middle Ages,” Jennifer said quietly. “The peasants gathering against the lords.”

“Aye, except that it’s today, and they’re gathering against us, and people like us.” Mendick tried to push forward, listening to the slow snarl of the wheels as the brougham lost speed among the myriads of marching men.

The Chartists were congregating on a patch of rising moorland to the right of the road, group after group forming together until the torches formed an array that stretched far into the dark. Mendick eased to a halt as a column crossed in front of him then cracked his whip so the horse increased speed to a moderate crawl.

“Hey!” Somebody held up his torch so the light illuminated the coach. “Is that not Josiah’s coach?”

More torches were raised aloft and somebody set up a cheer, which hesitated and died as Eccles hurried up.

“That’s not Mr Armstrong! That’s the Sergeant!”

The news spread, passing from man to man and group to group. “That’s the fellow in the poster! Over there! It’s James Mendick, an enemy of the Charter!”

“Whip up, James!” Rather than revealing fear, Jennifer sounded excited as she grabbed hold of his arm. “I don’t think we should be here!”

Cracking the whip, Mendick pushed the coach through the crowd, watching the bravest men stand in front of the horse only to leap away when it became obvious that he was not going to deviate from his course. Men cursed or yelled and some threw their torches, the flames flickering in the air as the missiles rose, curved and descended rapidly toward the coach. One landed on the coach seat, and Jennifer snatched it up and threw it back.

"Come on, James! Use the whip!"

Glancing at her, Mendick nodded and stood up to spiral the eight-foot lash in the air before he swept it down on the Chartists surrounding the coach. He caught one man a resounding cut across the shoulders, heard him yell and slashed again, sideways, aiming at faces and bodies indiscriminately as he allowed the horse to trot uncontrolled along the road.

"Take the reins, Jennifer!"

Shifting his stance, he hefted the whip like a weapon, trying to ignore the barrage of missiles now hurtling towards him. He knew how difficult it was to face a speeding horse or stop a rolling coach, but should any of these stones or torches hit him, he would fall among the Chartists, who would kick him to pieces. He winced as a stone bounced off his arm and swore as he saw his hat topple from his head to be crushed to a shapeless mass by the rear wheels of the coach.

"You'll pay for that," he promised and swung the lash, grinning as it cracked across the back of a man's knees and brought him yelling to the ground.

"James! Clear a space in front!"

In a line two deep across the road, a dozen Chartists were frantically loading their muskets. Mendick watched and shook his head. Even the best regiments in the army could not load and fire in less than fifteen seconds, and these Chartists had nothing like their level of experience. However good they had been in training, he doubted they would stand against a rapidly advancing brougham.

The Chartists worked in unison, spitting the lead ball down the long barrel and ramming it in place.

"Come on, James!"

Folding his whip, he eased himself down from the seat onto the footboard and looked forward where the horse was moving at a spanking pace, its head tossing to and fro as Jennifer sawed at the reins.

The Chartists hefted their muskets, slamming them against their right shoulder.

"James!" Jennifer screamed, and Mendick balanced on the coachman's step and eased onto the wooden thill, the shaft to which the horse was attached.

The Chartists aimed, twelve muskets pointing at the advancing coach. Each muzzle was three quarters of an inch in diameter but appeared as wide as a six-pounder cannon when the Chartists cocked and aimed.

Taking a deep breath, Mendick rose again, balanced for a second then jumped onto the back of the horse. He landed with a painful thump and grabbed the horse's mane for support. He saw the Chartists altering their aim until every musket was pointing directly at him as he shouted and swung the whip.

"That's the way!" Jennifer yelled, snapping the reins. "That's the way, James!"

Mendick heard the order to fire, but before a single finger squeezed the trigger, the frantic horse had scattered the

Chartist ranks. Only three men stood their ground, one falling beneath the horse's hooves and another yelling as the whip sliced across his forehead. The third fired, but the ball zoomed harmlessly skyward.

"James!" Jennifer screamed. "I can't keep control!"

The brougham was rocking from side to side, the horse pulling desperately right and left as Jennifer fought the reins.

"Hold on!" Mendick backed from the horse and reached the driver's seat, hauling himself over to Jennifer's side. Dropping the whip, he grabbed hold of the reins.

"James! Watch out!"

A fresh group of Chartists had appeared in front, raising crude weapons and shouting threats.

"Oh, sweet Lord!" Mendick ducked, and a fist-sized stone missed his head by an inch.

"My turn." Jennifer lifted the whip. She balanced for a second; half rose, then straightened up and flicked out the lash. "Get out of the way! Move you blackguards!" Suddenly she was screaming, unleashing her fury at the Chartists, slashing at legs and bodies and arms.

"You!" Pulling back her arm, she unleashed a vicious blow that cracked across the buttocks of a tall Chartist, making him caper and yell.

"That's for Nathaniel! Now, get out of my way!" Her whip knocked a second man off his feet, opened a gaping cut in another's face, and then they were through, and the road stretched clear before them.

Jennifer collapsed back on the seat, allowing the whip to fall from her fingers. She began to sob, dragging the back of her sleeve across her eyes and shaking her head.

"Well, Jennifer, you certainly were not useless there!" Mendick tried to jolly her along, but when he realised she was shaking with reaction, he reached across and touched her lightly on the arm. "You're a spunky little yahoo, Jennifer, a regular trump."

She lifted her head. "Bar that, James. Anyway, you didn't do too badly yourself." For a moment they grinned at each other in complete accord, then they came to a tight bend that took all Mendick's skill to negotiate.

"Thank God this is a brougham," he said. "It's got the best turning circle of any coach ever made."

Jennifer's laugh rose wildly as the coach balanced at a precariously angle. "We showed them, didn't we, James? Did you see that man jump when I caught him right across his . . . unmentionables? Delicious! We showed them!"

"We certainly did." Mendick eased the speed a little, and they crashed back onto all four wheels. "My volunteers did well though, didn't they? They stood their ground until the last moment." He grinned across to her. "Those were some of my boys, you know. I trained them myself."

"You did a good job," Jennifer said solemnly. "They were as good as real soldiers."

The words sobered him enough to contemplate the Chartist actions with a more professional eye.

"They were keen enough," he said. "I did not see any drunkenness or any squabbling amongst them. Indeed, they seem to be better disciplined than many regular regiments, and I cannot fault their courage, but I doubt they'd stand against the Army."

"Why not?" Jennifer had been watching the array of torches, and she indicated the impressively silent swarm that spread over the moorland, becoming ever more visible as the dawn light strengthened. “There are plenty of them.”

“Yes, but they’ve only got infantry,” Mendick said. “The cannon would pound them from a distance, and then the cavalry would come in from the flanks and finish them off. They don’t have any artillery, and there’s not a single horseman amongst them.”

“Yes, there is,” Jennifer contradicted. “I saw two, one on a grey and the other on a great white stallion.”

“A white horse?” Mendick looked at her, momentarily ignoring the road ahead. “Are you sure?”

“I know what a white horse looks like! The rider was leading a whole host of men.”

Mendick swore as the coach rumbled on to the banking beside the road. He laid the whip across the rump of the horse so it straightened up and increased its speed. Holding the reins tight, he guided them around a deep hole, with Jennifer grabbing hold of her hat and ducking as a low branch flicked at them.

“What are you doing? You’ll have us over next!”

“The white horse! Rachel Scott and Trafford were always talking about a white horse; that must be the leader! They said they’d kill somebody called Drina, and then there was something about a white horse getting into its own stable.”

Jennifer shrieked softly when Mendick misjudged the next corner and the carriage veered alarmingly to one side. For a moment he thought they would overturn, but the brougham righted itself, and they pulled on, with Jennifer staring at him.

“Slow down, James! And tell me that again! They said what? They’d kill Drina?”

“Something like that,” he agreed.

Jennifer shook her head. "They can't do that! You can't let them do that!" She grabbed hold of his arm, shaking it until he looked at her. "You must stop them, James!"

"I'll try," he said, "but who's Drina? I don't know who Drina is!"

"What?" Jennifer looked at him. "Drina is the Queen's pet name! Queen Victoria! They're going to murder the Queen!"

CHAPTER THIRTEEN

London: April 1848

The sun finally broke through a misty horizon as Mendick stared at Jennifer, his mouth open while the full impact of her words sunk in.

"Are you sure? How can Drina be the Queen?"

Jennifer tutted, shaking her head.

"It's a short version of her name, James. Her full name is Alexandrina Victoria, and her family always called her Drina."

"Drina."

Mendick looked over the enclosed fields of the Midlands, the tall chimneys of a distant factory smearing foul smoke across the sky and a shepherd wearing a smock staring at them as he guided his sheep into their spring pasture. The mix of ancient pastoral England and modern industrialisation was a reminder of the oxymoronic nature of the times in which they lived. Only the monarchy had seemed a fixed star in an ever-altering firmament, but now even that was under threat.

"God in heaven! They're going to murder the Queen."

Planning to murder the Queen seemed more shocking than the Chartists' plan to wage rebellion on the country, perhaps because it was such a personal thing. It was also foolish. Queen Victoria was not responsible for the condition of the people in Manchester or for the excesses of the industrial age even though her lifestyle did provide an example of the stark contrast between the privileged and the poor. Mendick shook his head.

"Why would anybody want to murder the Queen?" Perhaps because he had lived all his adult life in a disciplined and loyal service, Mendick could not comprehend such an idea.

"Listen." Jennifer calmed herself with a deep breath. "Maybe that's the other part of the Chartist plan; kill the Queen and form a Chartist republic? We can't let that happen, James."

"It wasn't the Chartists who said that," Mendick explained. "It was Sir Robert Trafford and Rachel Scott. They were planning to use the Chartists as cover for the murder."

As the coach careened over the appalling road, he told her everything he had heard. Jennifer listened, her eyes nervous and her hands twisting together.

"The Queen and Germans and a white horse?" She shook her head. "What can that mean, James?"

"I wish I knew," Mendick said, "but whatever it is, Sir Robert Trafford is in it up to his neck. He and somebody called Ernie, or Uncle Ernest."

Jennifer started back in her seat and stared at him. "Ernie? Are you sure it was *Ernie* and a white horse?"

"Yes! Maybe the man you saw back there!" Mendick jerked his thumb behind him. "Maybe this Ernest fellow plans to take over when the Chartists have toppled the government."

"I'll wager that he does, although he won't be riding any white horse at the head of a Chartist rising, that's for certain." Jennifer was suddenly very calm.

Mendick frowned. "Do you know who he is?"

“Oh yes.” Jennifer was quiet again. “I know who Ernie is and where the white horse comes into it, and so do you, if you would only think about it for a moment and forget about the Chartists.”

“I don’t know any Ernie,” Mendick said.

“You do. Ernest Augustus, the Duke of Cumberland?” Jennifer’s voice rose in exasperation as it became obvious that Mendick did not recognise the name. “You must know him; he’s the Queen’s cousin, and he became the King of Hanover a few years ago? The white horse is their royal symbol, and he was nearly our king!”

At last Mendick understood. “Oh, him . . .”

“Exactly,” Jennifer said meaningfully. “Him.”

“But I don’t see what he’s got to do with the Chartists.” Mendick stared at her as he finally grasped the terrible possibility. “Sweet God. Do you think that the King of Hanover is planning to murder the Queen?”

There was a few moments silence before Jennifer replied.

“It sounds like it; he wanted the throne before Victoria was crowned, and he’s a queer chum, a bad man; remember the death of his servant Joseph Sellis? They tried to say it was suicide, but everybody knows that Ernest murdered him. Now he’s King of Hanover, but Great Britain is far bigger, and far wealthier.”

Mendick whistled. As a police officer in London he was used to dealing with all the darker walks of crime. He had seen house-breakers and pickpockets, confidence tricksters and drunkards, prostitutes, pimps and blaggards, and the overwhelming majority had come from the lowest possible level of society. Like everybody else, he knew that the upper classes had their own strange lives, but they were so separate from him he had never taken any interest. Now he had to consider the possibility that one of the highest in the land, a man of royal blood, a king in his own right and a cousin of the Queen, might be planning regicide. The thought was frightening for a newly created detective constable, but the few facts that he knew all seemed to point to the same conclusion.

Ernest Augustus, the Duke of Cumberland, was known to be an unpleasant man. At one time only his cousin Victoria stood between him and the British crown, and it was no secret that he hoped for power. It was also no secret that scandal clung to Ernest like a second shadow, with sadism haunting his army career, rumours of incest tainting his personal life and accusations that he murdered his valet, Joseph Sellis. If he had already committed one murder, another, and one that would bring him great advantage, was certainly not impossible.

The coincidence of the name, Ernest, and the repeated mention of the white horse, the symbol of Hanover, was too marked to ignore. Mendick ducked as a low branch nearly swept him from his perch.

"So where does Sir Robert fit in? Why should he help a German king murder the Queen?"

Jennifer sighed. "Don't you know anything about the people that rule us? Don't you take any interest in the nobility and how they operate?"

"None at all," Mendick admitted frankly.

"Well, Sir Robert is mucked; he's a gambling man and has been cleaned out; the bailiff's men are hammering at his noble door. That's no secret."

"God yes! I've seen the papers! A London firm called Dobson and Bryce is acting for his creditors . . ."

"Well, there you go then," Jennifer said. "Everybody knew he was short of readies when he discarded half his staff. He even let me go." She glanced at him. "I worked in the kitchen there once." She shrugged. "But that was in a different life."

"Even so, what has Trafford's financial position got to do with Hanover?" Mendick tried to recall everything he had heard in Trafford Hall. "When I first overheard Rachel Scott and Trafford, she was speaking in some foreign language, and then she mentioned something about the Germans pulling him out of a hole. She said that if he did what Uncle Ernie wanted, everything would be fine. All he had to do was focus on the money."

Jennifer nodded. "That's clear enough, then. Sir Robert needs the blunt to pay off his creditors, Ernest has money but wants the British crown, so they've done a deal of some sort.' She ducked as another low branch brushed the roof of the coach. 'I would say there is no doubt Sir Robert is helping Ernest to murder the Queen."

"Sweet Lord," Mendick said.

Having seen the deprivation in the industrial north, and having met men of the calibre of Armstrong and Monaghan, he could understand the demands of the Chartists. They had reasons and some validation for their actions, but there was no justification for a gentleman to ally himself with a foreign monarch to assassinate the Queen. Such an action was treason – purely selfish and diabolical.

Only a few moments ago he had assumed that the darker walks of crime encompassed thieving, murder and prostitution, but Sir Robert Trafford's regicidal intentions eclipsed the worst of them. Sir Robert was following the darkest walk of all.

"I thought that Armstrong was an evil man," Mendick said slowly, "but his actions are small beer compared to this titled gentleman. Trafford and Ernest are pretending to befriend the Chartists while they use them to create trouble and unsettle the nation. They are using the Chartists to create a diversion, and when the army and the Chartists are battling it out on the streets of London, they will send somebody to Buckingham Palace to kill the Queen." He was astonished at the enormity of Trafford's corruption.

"He is creating the possibility of civil war, thousands, perhaps tens of thousands of deaths and enormous suffering, so he can pay his *gambling* debts."

"He is a perfect and inveterate scoundrel," Jennifer agreed. "And whatever happens, the Chartists still lose," she sighed. "After all their efforts, after all these years, the common people are still unheeded, only pawns in the hands of the rulers." She looked up. "It would be sad, if we did not know how unpleasant the Chartists can be."

Remembering the sensation of acceptance in the back room of the Beehive and again at the Christmas festivities in Chartertown, Mendick looked away.

"Only some of the leaders are unpleasant," he said quietly. "I believe the majority are hard-working, respectable people desperate to create a better world for their families. I think they are far better people than Sir Robert or Ernest, King of Hanover will ever be."

"Perhaps that is the reason why they will always be exploited." Jennifer was equally quiet. "Perhaps the meek inherit the earth, but first they must suffer." She sighed. "Your decent people will suffer most, James, if this civil war occurs."

He nodded. "That's for certain. And if we have a murderer as king then God help the Chartists. He was a martinet when he commanded the 15th Hussars, flogging and picketing without mercy. God only knows what he would do to perceived rebels; he would destroy them, root and branch, once they have done their work."

"He would devastate the industrial areas of Britain," Jennifer agreed. "Like William the Conqueror did to the north or Ernest's own namesake, the Duke of Cumberland, did to the Scottish Highlands."

They were quiet for a minute, picturing the English Midlands and North under the brutal regime of a Hanoverian tyrant, with military law imposed, Chartists hanging in their own doorways and dragoons swinging their sabres against unarmed Radicals.

"We cannot allow that to happen," Mendick said.

"Whip up, James, and let's get moving." Jennifer sat forward on the seat. "We have to get to London."

The roads became busier the further south they travelled, slowing the brougham to a crawl. Shaking his whip at the cart in front, Mendick demanded passage, but the men who sat amidst its heaped up straw only smiled slowly and waved to him.

"We're going to London," they shouted, "to get the vote!"

"What?"

"We're going to get the vote," the man repeated. "Mr O'Connor said so."

It seemed like half of Britain was travelling south. They were blocking the highways, tramping the roads and even crossing the neatly enclosed fields in their desperation to join O'Connor's rally at Kennington Common.

Mendick recognised some of the banners, the hopeful beehives on the calico Chartist flags. He saw an embroidered harp, gold on green, in recognition of the Irish connection, while other banners carried brave, defiant words. He saw a disciplined group of men with the distinctive broad shoulders and small stature of miners marching southward to London to demand democracy from a reluctant government.

"How many people are involved in this movement?" He jerked his chin to indicate the long column of vehicles inching southward, the determined men marching, the drays and carts and carriages that jolted onwards with their mixed cargo of Chartists and dreams. "Maybe even Ernest has underestimated the dragon he has unleashed."

"A dragon of expectation." Jennifer sounded sober. "The people of the nation are trying to speak in the only way they know how. God, don't they understand that they don't matter a damn? Nobody cares for their hopes and aspirations! They are here to pay their taxes and work for their rulers. *That's* their only function in life."

"Perhaps they do realise," Mendick said, "and that's why they are uniting in such anger. They are beginning to demand more."

"Well," Jennifer was frowning, "they've chosen a fine time to do it. Tell them we must get past or they'll probably all be killed."

"I doubt they'd listen to me," Mendick said, "but we'll have to get in front of them somehow."

"Let me try." Jennifer faced him, suddenly smiling. "I'm going to use your idea. What was the name of that woman again? Scott?"

"Rachel Scott," Mendick told her. "But why?"

There was a sudden flash of spirit in Jennifer's eyes. "You'll see, but I'll have to get back inside the carriage first." She hesitated for a second. "Do you trust me?"

"Of course," he said, "but . . ."

"But trust me then, and pull over for a moment." Her grin was pure mischief. "And this time, all you have to do is follow *my* lead!"

"As you wish."

He waited as Jennifer leaped from the seat and ducked back inside the coach. He regretted the time they would lose but knew that the horse would welcome the rest, for it was visibly flagging. She returned within five minutes and without as much as a by-your-leave folded a shaped piece of red material on his head.

"I wear a scarlet flannel petticoat," she confided. "It's a bit rough and ready, but it'll do from a distance."

"I don't understand," Mendick said, and Jennifer smiled.

"You said you would trust me.'

"I do," he began, "but . . ."

"Then but me no buts," Jennifer told him. 'Drive on slowly."

Very aware that half of Jennifer's petticoat decorated his head, Mendick flicked the reins, and the coach lumbered forward again. Beside him, Jennifer rose to her feet, with one hand holding onto the top of the coach for balance and the other instinctively clutching her bonnet. She raised her voice above the rumble of wheels and the slow padding of hooves.

"Can you hear me? Fellow Chartists! Can you hear me?"

One or two faces turned in her direction, and one man nodded.

"You may have heard of me; I am Rachel Scott, and this is Josiah Armstrong. You'll know him from the scarlet cap of liberty; *everybody* has heard of Josiah Armstrong!"

There was a small cheer, and one of the men waved.

"They're not sure, so tell them to sing."

Mendick pulled the makeshift cap further down to disguise his features. Armstrong was a much slighter man than he was, and the disfiguring scar across his mouth must be familiar to Chartists right across the country. "Tell them to sing my song."

He began Armstrong's favourite song, roaring so loudly that it hurt his throat:

"Spread, spread the Charter
Spread the Charter through the land
Let Britons bold and brave join heart and hand."

"Come on boys!" Jennifer waved her arms in the air, trying to attract as much attention as she could without overbalancing on the rocking coach. "Sing along and make way for us! We must reach London soon; we have a nation to save!"

More of the crowd began to turn, with one or two singing, and one tall man pointed his blackthorn staff. "That's Josiah Armstrong's carriage; that's the red-capped revolutionary, the Demonian come back to save us!"

The initial cheering spread, men raising fists or banners, but Jennifer shook her head and, cupping her hands to her mouth, shouted again: "Please let us through! We need to get through!"

Slowly but definitely, the crowd edged away to the verges of the road, creating a narrow corridor for the coach to squeeze through. Hoping that nobody had actually seen

Armstrong in person, Mendick drove as quickly as he could, keeping his head down and praying that the red cap would provide sufficient camouflage.

The words of the song bellowed around him. People were cheering, laughing, wishing him luck, but others were grimmer, and he saw gaunt exhaustion amidst the defiance, the hollow cheeks of hunger, the dazed, defeated eyes of men to whom the Charter offered a last forlorn hope.

He felt familiar pangs of guilt. He was cheating these men whose only crime was poverty, these men who sought only a better life for their families. As Jennifer had pointed out, they were just pawns, disregarded by everybody. Their march was pointless; they existed only to create wealth for others, and he was an agent of their oppressors. He knew that he was not their enemy, but he also knew that neither was he their friend.

He sighed; he was only one man, he could not solve the problems of the country, but he might be able to help prevent an ugly civil war and save the life of the Queen, and even of many of these deluded, desperate and dangerous men.

"Let me pass, please, boys," he whispered, hating himself as he drove his horse through the ranks. "Let me pass and I will deal with the creatures who are duping you, the men who promise what they cannot deliver and who are leading you to certain defeat."

There were gaps ahead, short stretches of the road free of Chartists, and whenever there was congestion, the magical names of Armstrong and Scott cleared a lane for them to push through. By the late afternoon Mendick was hoarse from singing his Chartist song, and his arm ached from waving to the hundreds of supporters who wished him God speed and success.

"It's working." Jennifer sounded triumphant. "So who is useless now, eh?"

"Not you," he reassured her. "Certainly not you."

They exchanged grins, but Jennifer looked quickly away as they eased into the first outlying houses of the London sprawl. The gentle April dusk made even this ardent city look benign as the brougham rolled through the outskirts, the road lined with new villas interspersed with patches of dense industrial housing and a few remaining market gardens.

"Rather than go directly to Scotland Yard, could we not just report to the first policeman we see?" Jennifer asked.

Tempted for a moment, Mendick shook his head.

"I'm not sure if we can trust them," he said simply. "I'd hate to come this far only to throw everything away. If the highest in the land is corrupt, how can we trust a bobby on a guinea a week?" He pulled at the reins as the horse began to falter. "Come on, boy."

"The horse cannot keep pulling," Jennifer said. "The poor thing's about dropping."

"It has to keep going." He plied the whip harder than he had ever done before. He felt sympathy for the beast, but the suffering of one animal was unimportant when compared to the safety of the country and the life of the Queen.

"We'll be in Whitehall in a couple of hours."

He looked ahead. Even here there were Chartists. There was a small group of men marching on the road, one man carrying a furled banner over his shoulder and the remainder walked with their heads bowed and tired legs dragging in the dirt.

“That horse will not last a couple of hours,” Jennifer told him simply. “Unless you allow it to rest, it will die, and you’ll never get to Scotland Yard.”

He knew she was correct. The horse was drooping in its harness, its head down and its hooves trailing. Without rest it would simply collapse and he would have to walk through the streets. While his duty demanded that he drive onward, common humanity dictated that he should stop.

“You’re right,” he admitted reluctantly, “we should find some stables and hire another; any old hack will do for the short distance we have left.” He looked around to check their location. “We’re not too far from Horatio Chantrell’s.”

“What?” Jennifer looked at him.

“We’re not far from Chantrell’s Great Northern Inn. It’s not the grandest inn, but it has one of the best tables in this part of the country.” He grinned suddenly. “Are you hungry?”

Jennifer nodded, suddenly animated. “Starved,” she admitted cheerfully. “When did we last eat?”

Mendick shrugged. They had breakfasted before they left the inn that morning and had long since finished off the last of the bread the ostler’s boy had brought them three days ago.

“Many hours since.” He looked across to her. “The Great Northern it is. Every lord and duke in creation stops there if they get the chance. Chantrell’s food is famous from Reading to the Romney Marsh.” He enjoyed the look of anticipation on Jennifer’s face. “We’ll be there inside the quarter hour.”

CHAPTER FOURTEEN

London: April 1848

At one time London had a dozen great coaching inns, but the advent of rail travel had ended that flamboyant era. Now there were few, but Horatio Chantrell's Great Northern continued the tradition, defiant in the teeth of progress. Chantrell stood in the cobbled courtyard to personally greet every one of his customers, his plump and jovial face a byword for hospitality. More important for Mendick, his establishment was equally celebrated for its stock of horses, hosting anything up to twenty at any one time and hiring them out to passing travellers.

He eased the brougham to a halt within the arched gate, dismounted stiffly and fondled the ears of the horse that had performed so splendidly in pulling them down half the length of England.

Chantrell stepped forward, a smile widening his already broad face. "A suitable horse, sir? Mr . . .?"

"Armstrong." By now Mendick was so used to using the name that he replied automatically, "Josiah Armstrong."

"Mr Armstrong, of course, sir." Chantrell carried his belly before him and his mutton chop side-whiskers wagged as he spoke, but he bowed as best he could and examined the coach with shrewd eyes. "You have been travelling far, I see, and your nag is weary."

"Far enough," Mendick agreed. "But not long to go now."

"I see, sir. It's always good to come to the end of a long journey. You'll have a bite to eat, of course," Chantrell said. "I have a fine table inside, and good company." He continued to look at the coach, narrowing his eyes as if confused.

"More than a bite," Jennifer said, "for we are both famished."

"Ah!" Chantrell gave a conspiratorial smile. "I like a lady who enjoys her food." He bowed in appreciation. "Then, while your horse rests and feeds, you can enjoy the pleasures of my table. How does steak and fried oysters sound?"

"It sounds wonderful, and thank you, we shall enjoy it," Jennifer answered for them both. "Come, Josiah."

"We cannot spare too much time." Mendick sensed that Jennifer would welcome a prolonged stay at the table of the Great Northern. "As soon as the horse is rested, or when Mr Chantrell can find us a suitable replacement, we should be moving on."

"Food," she commanded. "I refuse to go a single yard further until we have dined, and dined properly."

"The lady knows her own mind." Chantrell sounded amused. "How exactly like my own better half." He gave a throaty chuckle but glanced again at the brougham, as if hoping to confirm something.

Already regretting his weakness in halting there, Mendick bobbed briefly to Chantrell and followed Jennifer inside the inn.

The Great Northern had a common board, with travellers of all types sharing a single room where massive, smoke-darkened beams stretched across the ceiling and a fire crackled comfortingly within the hearth. After days cooped in the coach, the hubbub of noise seemed almost overpowering, but the conviviality was so enticing that Mendick felt himself relaxing, particularly as the clientele were a complete contrast to the poverty-pinched people of the north. Here were well-fed, affable men and their padded, red-faced wives, successful merchants and roaring members of the lesser gentry laughing and joking together in cheerful conversation.

In such a place, thoughts of Chartist insurrections and attempts on the life of the Queen seemed surreal. Mendick smiled; he was back in the London he understood, where rich and poor co-existed in different worlds; each happily prepared to accept the other as a potential victim, if nothing else.

He pulled back a chair for Jennifer and then eased down on his own. For a second he leaned back, nearly drifting into sleep in the friendly atmosphere and warmth, until Jennifer nudged him in the ribs.

"Is that not Armstrong?"

"What?" Mendick opened his eyes, peering through the smoky atmosphere. "Where?"

"There you are, sir." Chantrell was smiling down at them. "This is the gentleman. He not only shares your name, he also has a coach with the same colours as yours, which is quite the strangest of coincidences I ever saw. I wondered if you might be related? It would be quite a thing if two cousins arrived here at the same time and entirely by chance."

Standing to the left of Chantrell, Armstrong nodded once. The red cap he wore bobbed, but Mendick was on his feet before the hand came out. Pushing past Chantrell, he thumped his knee hard into the muscle of Armstrong's thigh and shouted to Jennifer.

"Run! Jennifer, run!"

She did not need a second warning. Without hesitation, she fell backward from the table, rolled on the floor and rose to her feet, glancing from side to side as she sought the best escape route.

About to follow her, Mendick was just a second too late; he swore as a great hand closed on his neck and held him close. He had not heard Peter approach, but now the prize-fighter was breathing in his ear and dragging him up from the chair. Mendick tried to jerk his head backward, flailing with heels and elbows.

"Run, Jennifer! Run!"

There was a sickening thump as his head made solid contact with something. Peter's grip loosened for an instant, and Mendick elbowed backward as hard as he could, feeling the thump as he smashed against Peter's ribcage. The prize-fighter grunted slightly, but tightened his grip on Mendick's neck with his left hand while wrapping an arm like a wire cable around his body.

"Peter, it's me, your friend. Let go, for God's sake."

"Keep quiet, James," Peter spoke softly, "and please let me carry you away."

"Take him outside." Armstrong's voice was strained, and Mendick hoped his thigh was painful. "I'll get the woman."

Mendick saw that Jennifer was hesitating, one hand gripping the table and the other held out as if she could restrain Peter by herself. He saw Armstrong move toward her and yelled again, as loud as he could,

"Run, Jennifer, for your life! Please!"

Moving quickly for a damaged man, Armstrong lunged forward, dodged between two diners and grabbed at Jennifer. His hand closed on her sleeve, but she turned quickly and landed a stinging slap against his scarred back. Gasping, Armstrong released her.

"Help!" Jennifer raised her voice in a high-pitched screech. "Help me, please!"

"Jennifer! Run!"

As the crowd in the room looked on in astonishment, Jennifer aimed a wild kick at Armstrong, missed by a yard and ran to escape, still screaming as she knocked down chairs and upset plates in her passage. She slipped, staggered and jumped for the door.

"Stop her!" Armstrong ordered, still with one hand holding his back. "She is a thief!" But instead the crowd closed ranks behind Jennifer.

"Shame!" somebody shouted. "Leave the lady alone."

"You leave her be," a countryman in a white smock ordered. Leaning back in his chair and not at all overawed by Armstrong's sinister appearance, he thrust out a stubborn chin. "She wasn't doing you no harm, and I won't have you do any to her."

Others in the crowd nodded, although when Peter danced across in support of Armstrong, dragging Mendick with him, most of them backed away. Peter's size was enough to intimidate even the bravest of men. Only the countryman rose from his seat, holding a blackthorn staff in front of him as he defiantly blocked Peter's path.

"You can't bully me, mister; I've faced bigger men. Put that fellow down and fight me fair and square!"

Still struggling in Peter's grip, Mendick roared encouragement until a large hand clamped over his mouth, crushing his lips against his teeth.

"You've to keep quiet, James, when you're told."

"We're leaving," Armstrong ordered, his voice desperate. "Peter, forget the baggage; she doesn't matter. Bring the spy."

Mendick tried to bite at Peter's hand, but his grip was too strong, so instead he lashed out with his hands and kicked wildly with his feet, occasionally landing on flesh that seemed as unyielding as granite.

"Now you keep still!" Peter admonished, holding him securely and barging through a crowd that had lost interest as soon as they realised Jennifer was safe. A group of ostlers looked up in astonishment as they stormed into the courtyard.

"What's all the commotion?"

"Never you mind," Armstrong snarled. "Just get out of my way."

Armstrong's coach had the familiar blue and yellow paintwork, but the horse was fresh, and the bodywork was not disfigured with scrapes and mud. Mendick presumed that Chantrell had ordered it should be cleaned as a further example of his service.

"Toss him inside, Peter, quickly now."

Peter threw Mendick face down onto the damp straw on the floor and pinned him with a knee in the small of his back as Armstrong tied him hand and foot.

"You lie still, you Peeler bastard, until I decide what to do with you." Armstrong pulled the cord so tight it bit into Mendick's wrists and re-awakened the raw burns on his ankles.

"You don't know what you're doing!" Mendick yelled. "Trafford is using you and all the other Chartists! Listen to me!"

"I've had enough listening to you." Armstrong's voice was a sinister hiss. "Quieten him down, Peter; gag the bastard!"

"No! Listen!" Mendick said desperately. "You're all being duped . . ." He grunted as Peter pulled a spotted handkerchief from his pocket, stuffed it in his mouth and tied it securely in place. He gagged, almost choking, and wriggled in impotent frustration.

"That's better. Drive on, Peter," Armstrong ordered. "Take us somewhere quiet." He viciously kicked Mendick's ribs, grunting with the effort. "Then we'll take care of this rubbish." Slamming the door shut, Armstrong eased himself down beside Peter on the driving seat.

Wriggling helplessly on the floor, Mendick felt the coach jerk forward, moving slowly as Peter negotiated the awkward gate into the Great Northern, and then it suddenly stopped. He heard Armstrong's sibilant voice followed by the sharper tones of a Londoner, and then the coach door jerked open and Jennifer was there, dragging him across the floor with his shins scraping sharply against the legs of the seat and his face rubbing through the straw.

"Help me then," she panted. "Kick with your feet or something!"

He found purchase against the seat and propelled himself awkwardly forward until he tumbled painfully on to the straw-strewn cobbles. Looking up, he saw that Peter had tried to leave just as another coach was entering, and both coaches were jammed in the entrance. Armstrong and the other driver were shouting at each other, and Chantrell was bustling over on fat legs to try and keep the peace.

"Come on! We haven't much time!" Jennifer spoke in a harsh whisper although the driver of the incoming coach was making so much noise it was unlikely anyone would have heard even if she had yelled at the top of her voice. She wielded a short knife, presumably lifted from the inn, and sawed desperately at the cords.

"This blade is dull," Jennifer complained, hacking away furiously and making little impression on the tight cord. "It couldn't cut butter."

Mendick grunted, trying to hold his legs as still as possible to make her task easier. He looked up, aware that Armstrong was only a few yards away, and if he should happen to glance down, he could not fail to see him lying helpless on the ground. He widened his eyes, trying to urge Jennifer to greater speed. Twice her hands slipped and the blade rasped painfully against his ankle, but finally the cord snapped, and he stood up.

Perhaps it was the sudden movement that alerted Armstrong, but he looked downward at just that second.

"Peter!" Armstrong jerked a thumb backward. "The peeler's free!" He clambered down from the seat and reached inside his jacket.

"Run!" Grabbing hold of Mendick, Jennifer pulled him across the courtyard, stumbling over uneven cobbles. "Come on!"

Mendick followed, still with his hands tied behind his back and the foul gag in his mouth. A groom looked up in surprise and held a currycomb in front of him like some makeshift weapon.

"Is there a door? Another way out?" Jennifer demanded.

The groom pointed the comb at the furthest and darkest corner of the building, his mouth open in an adenoidal gape and his eyes questioning the tied and gagged man Jennifer dragged behind her.

Without pausing for a thank you, Jennifer lifted her skirt clear of the filthy ground and ran for the corner. Mendick joined her; he heard Armstrong's feet clattering across the cobbles. He heard Armstrong shout, and then Jennifer pushed him through an amazingly small door.

They emerged into a street bustling with activity. Two women were peering into the window of a shop, an omnibus rattled past and a group of workmen were busily building next year's slum. Everything seemed so normal that Mendick hesitated.

"James! Don't look back! Just run!"

Unable to speak, he nodded and lengthened his stride, following Jennifer as she disappeared into a side street that delved crookedly into the heart of London. People watched from low doorways and broken windows, throwing the occasional raucous insult as they passed.

Despite Jennifer's words, Mendick glanced over his shoulder, only to see Peter padding soft-footed behind them, his fists closed and his face creased in concentration.

"I told you not to look back," Jennifer reminded him. "Keep going and I'll untie your hands when it's safe."

A stranger in this part of London, Mendick glanced around, seeing wooden-fronted barns which had obviously once belonged to a rural community, an ancient thatched house with multi-paned windows and, standing in a muddy triangle that might once have been the village green, a gathering of men under a drooping calico banner. Unable to speak, he ran toward the group.

"What! No! They're Chartists!" Jennifer pulled at his arm, but he tore free, running to the clustered men. One stepped towards him, face concerned, and the others followed until Mendick and Jennifer were surrounded by a knot of men gesticulating and asking questions.

"What is it?" Somebody gently removed his gag, and a red-haired man produced a curved knife and carefully cut free the cords that tied his wrists.

"I'm a Chartist," Mendick spoke quickly, hoping that Peter did not whisper up before he had made his very hastily prepared speech. "My card is inside my coat." He hauled out the forged membership card Foster had given him, fumbling so desperately that he nearly dropped it. "That man works for the peelers!" He pointed to Peter, who was slowly advancing towards them.

The red-haired man glanced at the card. "Signed by McDouall himself," he said. "And that peeler tied you up, did he?"

"And my wife." Mendick indicated Jennifer. "They want to . . ."

"They can want all they like," the red haired man said, "but they'll not get, by Christ." He raised his voice. "Go it, boys!"

Peter looked at Mendick in disbelief as some thirty Chartists advanced on him. He pushed aside the first man without any effort, punched at the next then staggered as three men jumped on him simultaneously.

"I'm a Chartist too," Peter wailed, "fellow Chartists all. Tell them, James!"

Mendick hesitated, wondering whether he should become involved in the trouble he had started, but Jennifer nudged him.

"Run," she said. "Run, and leave the fighting to others for a change."

They ran side by side through the streets, the traffic steadily increasing and the buildings crowding increasingly close together. They ran until the breath burned in their chests and their legs trembled with fatigue. They ran until they reached Bethnal Green, a stone's throw from the sanctuary of Mendick's house, and fatigue forced them to stop, gasping with pain and holding on to each other for support.

"That was quick thinking with the Chartists," Jennifer said, whooping for breath.

"You saved my life back there," he countered, and they looked at each other, too exhausted to smile.

"I had to do something. After all, it was me who insisted we stop in the first place." Jennifer seemed to be expecting his condemnation, but he shook his head.

"I've never seen a braver act," he said and saw slow pleasure gradually replacing the worry in her eyes.

"It wasn't brave," she denied, but Mendick had learned when to say nothing. He looked up and swore as the blue and yellow coach eased to a halt a few yards away. Peter was sitting on the driver's seat, and the door was already opening.

"I thought you would run home." Armstrong emerged with his pistol in his hand and his eyes as venomous as ever.

"How in God's name do you know where I live?" But the answer did not matter; they were trapped.

"Goodbye, Mendick."

Armstrong levelled his pistol and pulled the trigger, and Mendick reacted without thinking; he ducked beneath the level of the barrel to jab straight-fingered into Armstrong's ribs. He saw Armstrong crumple, grabbed Jennifer's arm and began to run again, feeling his legs trembling beneath him. Jennifer gasped in protest,

"I can't go any further."

"We must." He pulled her on, following the street. He knew that Constable Williamson should be on duty here, but there was no friendly blue uniform, no swallowtail coat and top hat to provide succour. "Where are the police when we want them?"

"Probably watching the Chartists." Jennifer stumbled with sheer exhaustion. "Oh no, James! They're coming!"

Peter hardly had to flick the reins to catch up, and the blue coach grumbled over the cobbled road, the hooves of the horse drumming rhythmically.

"James!" Jennifer pushed him just as he heard the high-pitched crack of the pistol shot. For an instant he saw the black line of the shot the ball flattened against the wall at his shoulder. He noticed the blue streak the ball left on the red brickwork even as he straightened up.

"Jennifer! Run!"

He pushed her in front of him on the long straight street. There was no shelter, only closed doors and ochre walls, but if they could reach the western end there was a tangle of narrow lanes around Samuel Street. If they could not . . .

Faces began to appear at the windows as people wondered what was causing all the noise.

"You can't get away, you bastard!" Armstrong sounded strained. "And the more you run, the slower you'll get, and the softer shot I'll have."

When the coach drew level, Peter kept the horse at an easy walk, and Armstrong aimed his pistol. Mendick grabbed hold of Jennifer.

"Change direction! Now!" He pulled her so they were running back down the street, and Peter had to turn the brougham completely around, losing distance.

"Where are we going?" Jennifer stared around. There were side streets and openings, but none provided cover. Armstrong would have a clear shot. "There's nowhere to hide!"

Waiting until Peter had turned the coach, Mendick shouted, "Change direction again! And cross the road."

They ran in front of the brougham, but this time Mendick kept Jennifer moving, tacking from side to side until he pushed her into Abbey Street, which ran at right angles to Bethnal Green Road.

"Peter! Get after them!" The coach turned in their wake, the large rear wheels grinding on the cobbles.

The pistol cracked again, the ball smashed uselessly against the corner of a house, and then Mendick put down his head and ran, dragging Jennifer by the sleeve of her coat. He heard Armstrong's coach rumbling somewhere behind him, glanced around and saw a red-faced Peter lashing on the horse. As the coach closed in on them, Mendick chose another opening and gained distance, only to lose it on the straight.

"Where are we now?" Jennifer was drooping with the effort of running in a long skirt and tight shoes. She glanced behind her. "Oh God, James, he's still there."

Mendick nodded. "We're in the Ratcliffe Highway," he said, "and the people here don't fear God, the devil or Josiah Armstrong."

Mendick knew the bustling Highway well, with its transient population of seamen, bobtails and trolls, confidence tricksters and petty thieves. Until today, it was probably one of the last places he would have expected to seek sanctuary, but he had little choice. He paused outside Wilton's Music Hall, where a group of bare-headed sailors' women were gossiping. One adjusted her provocatively low-cut dress and thrust out her leg so her pink-stockinged calf was shockingly visible.

"Here! Ain't I good enough for you?" She clicked her brass heel on the ground as Mendick hurried past. "What are you running for? Are the bluebottles after you?"

"Keep going!" Jennifer pushed him on. "Here he comes again."

"He won't chase us here," Mendick said. "There are too many witnesses." He turned around, expecting to see the coach turn away, but instead Armstrong pulled himself on to the seat beside Peter.

"Oh God! Keep moving, Jennifer!"

They ran on, past bright-windowed shops displaying cheap and trashy trinkets, marine goods and drink of every variety. They passed respectable-looking dance-halls with large men at the door, and seedy dram-shops whose fronts were painted with pictures of sailors dancing with buxom women whose painted sisters waited outside to catch the eye and wallet of the passing clientele.

All the time, the coach kept easy pace a few yards behind. Reeling from exhaustion, Mendick pulled Jennifer close, leaned against the corner of the White Swan public house and looked back down the Highway. Amidst the scores of women and their maritime companions, the brougham looked an obvious interloper. Peter pulled it up and dismounted, helping Armstrong down to the street.

"That man," Armstrong pointed an accusing finger, "is a police spy! Don't let him escape!"

While most of the denizens of the Highway completely ignored his words, some began to watch, and a few even supported Armstrong, either by shouting insults or by moving towards Mendick.

"We'll have to split up," Mendick decided quickly. "Armstrong's not interested in you; it's me he wants. Get to Scotland Yard." He backed against the wall of the pub.

"Which way?" Jennifer glanced around the Highway. "Which way do I go?"

"That way." He gave her a gentle push. "Run, Jennifer, and warn them. Somebody's got to."

After a few seconds hesitation, Jennifer nodded. She looked utterly wearied, with sweat having drawn great scores down her dust-smeared face, her hat hanging by its pin and her feet dragging on the ground.

"You run too."

"Go!" Mendick ordered. "I'll slow them down."

Armstrong advanced toward him, Peter a giant shadow at his back. Jennifer began to move, slowly at first, but as she realised there was no pursuit, she hitched up her skirt and ran, hardly glancing over her shoulder.

"Well, Josiah, it's just you, me and Peter."

Mendick glanced around for a weapon but found nothing. Keeping his back to the wall, he slid his left foot forward and prepared to fight. He knew he could take Armstrong without much difficulty, but Peter was far too powerful for him. Nevertheless, he had to try. If he delayed them for even two minutes, Jennifer had a chance to warn Inspector Field. And himself? He hid his shrug; Emma would be waiting for him.

"Come on, you bastard!" He beckoned Armstrong closer. "You're too stupid to realise that Trafford is just using you, Monaghan and the whole Chartist network!" He raised his voice, taunting Armstrong into losing his temper so he might rush forward to easy destruction. “Don’t you realise that he’s teamed up with Rachel Scott in an attempt to murder the Queen?”

Armstrong frowned and reached inside his pocket for the pistol. “What the hell are you talking about, Peeler? You’re a bloody liar!”

“No lies, Armstrong, just God’s own truth that killing me won’t cure.” Mendick noticed that an appreciable crowd was gathering, some listening, others already discussing his words.

“Your friend Scott’s betraying you from Sunday to Christmas, pounding the mattress with Trafford and planning to put some tin-pot Hanoverian on the throne. She’s a traitor, Armstrong, and you’re a bloody fool to listen to her!”

“You lying bastard!”

Pulling back the hammer of his pistol, Armstrong aimed directly at his face. Mendick had expected this and rolled forward under the muzzle, kicking out with his right heel. He felt the satisfying thrill of contact and straightened up, weaving to avoid Peter's inevitable counterattack.

Armstrong’s arm was down, the gun pointing to the ground as he clutched his knee, but the acid returned to his eyes as he adjusted his aim. Mendick saw the flare from the right muzzle and felt the scalding wind from the shot hiss past his ribs. He dropped down, twisted, swivelled on his hip to sweep his right leg in a half circle and kicked at the back of Armstrong’s knees.

Armstrong fell at once, roaring away his agony as he landed on his damaged back. Rising quickly, Mendick smashed his heel onto the Chartist’s wrist, hearing the bone crack as he twisted his foot hard.

“That’s for Sergeant Ogden!” He dived for the pistol, just as Peter’s massive foot clamped down on it.

"Peter!"

The giant looked up and then gave a sudden yell and grabbed at his leg, lifting his foot high in the air.

"Thanks, Peter." That was Jennifer's voice. She scooped up the pistol and tossed it to Mendick. "Here, James. Back, you!" She jabbed at Peter with her hatpin for a second time.

Mendick scrabbled for the pistol. "I told you to run!" he shouted.

"You've no right to tell me to do anything!" she responded. Mendick realised that Peter had recovered and was moving toward him. He lifted the pistol grateful it had twin barrels though wishing it was his pepperpot revolver. One ball might not be enough for a man the size of Peter.

"James . . ." Peter had his arms extended, hands open. "Don't shoot me! Fellow Chartists all?"

"Fellow Chartists all," Mendick confirmed, grateful Peter had not destroyed him when he was busy with Armstrong.

He noticed the Ratcliff crowd was still watching, but not a single person had moved when the pistol had fired. Murder was part and parcel of the day's entertainment along the Highway, and the identity of the victim was immaterial.

"Is he dead?" Peter looked down at Armstrong, who was writhing on the ground, nursing the agony of his injured back and wrist.

Mendick shook his head. "Would you want him dead?"

"Yes," Peter said, "then he could not put me in the black hole again." He looked up, his eyes narrow and a frown of intense concentration on his face. "I could kill him now."

"You don't have to kill him, Peter," Jennifer said, "but you don't have to do his bidding either. Why don't you just run away and get a different job? This is London. There is plenty of work here."

Peter screwed up his face as if he were considering such a novel idea. "I'm going to run away," he decided, and the frown disappeared in a smile. "I'm going to run away from Mr Armstrong and find a different job."

He glanced at Mendick, as if for approval, held out his hand, appeared to change his mind and turned aside. Peter stepped over Armstrong, then moved off, his initial short, hesitant strides quickly altering to a light, loping stride.

"Good luck, Peter," Mendick called, amazed how the situation had changed in a few seconds. He knelt down beside Armstrong. "Listen, Josiah. You're a murdering savage, but I honestly believe there is still some good within you. I think that you do care for the working people. Get on your feet."

When Armstrong shook his head, Mendick hauled him upright, ignoring his protests.

"For Christ's sake, you can't send me back to Van Diemen's Land!"

"I certainly can't leave you alone to raise rebellion. You're under arrest, Armstrong."

There was no weight in the man, and not a single person tried to stop Mendick as he dragged Armstrong along. After being chased half the length of England, it felt good to be back in charge.

"We'll drop him off at Scotland Yard," he told Jennifer, "and Scotland Yard is exactly where you should be now, rather than endangering yourself along the Highway."

Jennifer gave a sweet smile as she replaced her hatpin in her hair. "You're welcome."

"You're a spunky little thing, aren't you," Mendick said sourly. "That's twice you've saved my life."

"I knew this hatpin would come in handy," Jennifer told him, "but I thought I would be sticking it in you, not some great ox of a Chartist."

"Speaking of such," Mendick reminded her, "we'd better disguise our companion. Somebody might recognise him." He removed his coat and threw it over Armstrong's head before he continued dragging him along.

There were more Chartists in the streets, some gathering beneath their green banners, others spilling out from gin palaces or beer shops, singing stirring songs and eyeing the uniformed policemen with obvious dislike. A few carried makeshift pikes, while one smallish man wore an iron breastplate, as if expecting an attack by Cavaliers rather than the metropolitan constabulary. The tension from the industrial north had been transported south; London would be the cockpit of the struggle when decades of repression came to a bloody head amidst the ancient streets and graceful squares of the capital.

"Not far now." Mendick looked at Jennifer as they turned the corner into Whitehall. She was weary and travel-stained, her dress splashed from the stable. "But I think we should have cleaned up before we meet Inspector Field."

It was strange that he included her in his plans. He had always kept his private life and his duty apart before but now . . . he shook his head; Jennifer was part of his duty. He knew her only because of her husband, and once this situation was resolved, he would never see her again. Yet, paradoxically, he felt close to her at that moment, as if their adventures in the brougham had created a bond between them.

"Cleaned up?" Jennifer asked. "Why?" Her face was red with exertion, her hair a tumbled net across her face.

When she smiled at, him he realised she had a dimple in her left cheek that had no match on her right; the lopsided effect was strangely appealing, as if she was composed of two halves that had not quite been correctly matched.

"We don't exactly look like the most respectable people in the country," he told her. "I doubt the inspector will be too impressed by our appearance. We should get back to my house and tidy up. There is a mirror there . . ." he stopped himself from offering Jennifer some of Emma's clothes.

"Is there?" Something in her tone warned him that he had said the wrong thing. Jennifer stepped away from him, the dimple fading as quickly as her smile. "No, James, I don't think that I will be going to your house, even if you do possess a mirror. Indeed, I think it would be best that we part now."

He frowned at this rapid alteration in her mood. "I don't understand; are you not coming with me to Scotland Yard?" Stepping toward her, he took hold of her arm. Suddenly he wanted her solid common sense when he spoke with Inspector Field and the penetrating Mr Smith. "You must come, Jennifer, it's your duty."

She shook off his hand. "There is no *must* about it, and I no longer owe a duty to anybody." Her eyes narrowed in genuine anger. "I've already told you that you cannot order me around, James. Nobody can order me around."

"I'm not trying to order you around, Jennifer . . ." Mendick began, but she had stopped, placed both hands on her hips and leaned toward him.

"We needed each other to get here, and we've worked well enough together, but now that we have arrived, I will follow my own life, and so should you. I'm sure you will manage just fine without me."

Fuelled by the tension of the past weeks and the strains of the last few hours, anger replaced Mendick's caution.

"Well, Jennifer, before I came along you were a frightened little woman cowed by her husband and afraid of being useless." He shrugged and turned his back. "Return to that if you will; if you can't find anywhere else, there might be a place for you along the Highway."

Dragging Armstrong with him, Mendick began to stride away, already regretting his final insult. Perhaps her experiences had made Jennifer temperamental, but she was good at heart and had proved a steady friend in time of need; she did not deserve such treatment. Cursing his temper, he turned to apologise, but Jennifer was also hurrying away with one hand holding her skirt clear of the ground and marching like a guardsman.

"Jennifer!"

She quickened her step slightly.

"Jennifer! I didn't mean that!"

Without looking back, she turned a corner and disappeared from view. About to follow, Mendick shook his head; she obviously neither desired nor needed his help. His duty was clear and Ogden's widow could not distract him.

"Come on, Josiah. Let's get you tucked up nice and quiet in your cell."

CHAPTER FIFTEEN

London: April 1848

It felt strange to be back in the room where it all started, with the same traffic noises intruding from Whitehall and the same brass chandelier swinging slowly above his head. There was a new grandmother clock in one corner, the hidden pendulum softly ticking away each passing second and the brass face engraved with the maker's name and the words *Tempus Fugit*. Mendick stood at attention, knowing he was unshaven and extremely untidy and that Inspector Field was examining him through those quizzical, knowing eyes, shaking his head slowly and very disapprovingly. He wished he had taken his own advice and spent an hour at home polishing and brushing before reporting to Scotland Yard, but he had considered his duty more important than his appearance. Perhaps he had been wrong.

Closing his eyes for an instant, Mendick's mind was swamped with images of Chartists marching under green banners, of volunteers drilling with new Brown Bess muskets, of the Chartist roadblock in the Midlands and of acrid smoke rasping in his lungs as he struggled in that hellish chimney.

"Are you all right?"

He nodded, wondering if he saw concern in Inspector Field's eyes rather than disapproval.

"You look terrible." Field held up a podgy hand as the door opened. "Ah! Here comes Mr Smith now, so you can make your report."

"Constable." Smith did not waste time in a preamble. He strode into the room, acknowledging Mendick with a terse nod of his head. "We had heard that you were killed."

"No, sir, I'm still alive. It was Ogden who was killed."

"Ah." Smith swept back the tails of his frock coat before carefully positioning himself on a seat by the fire. He looked strained; his mouth was set tighter than before. "That might explain things. I'm delighted that you're alive but sorry to hear about Ogden; he was a good man."

"He was a good police officer, sir," Mendick agreed. After hearing Jennifer's tales, he was no longer sure that Ogden had been a good man.

With his duty to Ogden's memory completed, Smith could move on.

"We heard nothing from you during your absence; pray tell me everything that happened in the north."

Mendick could hear the ticking of the grandmother clock as he began, and then he was caught up in his own story, speaking first of the plot to murder Queen Victoria, and then recounting the intended Chartist uprising. His audience listened intently, scribbling notes or raising their eyebrows in astonishment.

"Entire cases of muskets? Extraordinary!"

"Sir Robert Trafford? Unbelievable!"

When he mentioned Josiah Armstrong's name, Mendick noticed Field's face tauten, and the inspector wrote furiously for a few moments before returning his attention to what was being said.

The clock seemed even more audible when Mendick ended, and a piece of coal settled with a perceptible sigh.

"Well now."

For the duration of Mendick's report Smith had not moved from his position in front of the fire, but now he paced the few steps to the window, twirling one of the tails of his coat in his right hand.

"Well now, Constable. You seem to have had yourself quite the adventure, haven't you? And you have certainly opened a large can of worms."

He looked out of the window for a few minutes while one hand continued to work busily at his coat tail and the fingers of the other tapped a tattoo on his thigh.

"You have informed us of two separate threats to the stability of the realm. The first threat, of which we were already aware, comes from the Chartists. According to you, these radicals have become highly organised and have an unknown number of trained detachments ready to rise in rebellion." Turning swiftly, he raised his eyebrows. "Is that correct?"

"It is, sir," Mendick agreed.

"All bad so far," Smith said, "except for your single-handed capture of Armstrong, of course. That was a notable piece of work. Quite extraordinary, I would say. We all hoped that Armstrong would die quietly in Van Diemen's Land, but now it seems he will be hanged instead."

"I agree the man will be none the worse for a good hanging," Field said, "but in doing so, we may create a martyr for the Chartists."

When Smith looked up, the steel in his face matched anything that Mendick had seen from Armstrong.

"By the time I have finished, Inspector, there will be no Chartists." He nodded grimly. "And as for William Monaghan, I intend to have him transported shortly also."

Mendick nodded, remembering Ogden's screams and the horror of that flue.

"Yes, sir. However, not all the Chartists are of the same stamp. Monaghan is certainly a dangerous man, but the group of delegates who meet in the Beehive Inn seem to be sincere in their attempts to help the working people . . ."

Smith stopped his flow with an upraised hand.

"All of which is well and good, Constable, but certainly no concern of yours. Pray allow the politicians to take care of politics while you attend to your own duty."

"Yes, sir." Mendick realised Inspector Field was also frowning at him. "But if I may be permitted . . ."

"You may not, Constable. You have made your verbal report; now please remain silent unless I ask you a direct question." Smith stepped back from the window. "So, to continue; these Physical Force Chartists are coming to London in the train of O'Connor's circus, and if Parliament does not agree to all their demands, they will attempt a revolution either here or in the north." He paused, still twisting his coat tail in his hand. "Is that correct?"

"It is, sir," Mendick agreed.

"All right." Smith nodded to Inspector Field. "Then we shall take measures to counter this intended insurrection." He hesitated for a second. "I presume there is no doubt about any of this intelligence, Constable?"

"None whatsoever, sir," Mendick said. "As I mentioned, I was present at some of the meetings with Monaghan and Armstrong," he paused, "and Rachel Scott. I saw the gathering of volunteers in the Midlands, sir, hundreds, possibly thousands of men, some with muskets, collecting in a very disciplined manner."

"It is the discipline that worries me most," Smith admitted. "The army is quite capable of dealing with any size of mob, but a disciplined and trained force is a horse of an entirely different colour." He looked up. "White, perhaps?" He gave a brief laugh at his own joke but stopped abruptly when nobody else joined in.

Inspector Field left his seat to pile more coal on the fire, looking over his shoulder to Mendick as he did so.

"You were involved in the actual training of these militant Chartists, Constable. How do they shape up?"

"Very well," Mendick said. "They are fine material."

Smith nodded, frowning.

"Aye, well, I think the less said about the training the better. Some people could construe such actions as treason. Rachel Scott, however, interests me. I have not come across her name before, and her description is equally unfamiliar, yet you tell me she is heavily involved in both the Chartist plot and this alleged assassination attempt."

"Rachel Scott is an interesting person, sir," Mendick said, "but I am also unclear about her role in either affair. She is friendly with Monaghan as well as Trafford, but she is a chameleon; she alters to suit her surroundings." He shook his head. "And she has a connection with the man she calls Uncle Ernie."

The tail-twirling stopped as Smith again resorted to his notebook, leaning on the desk and writing non-stop for a full two minutes before he looked up.

"I would be obliged if you kept that information within these walls, Constable. Much of what you say is conjecture and speculation, and there is enough trouble in Europe without this country becoming engaged in an ugly diplomatic quarrel."

Mendick nodded. "Of course, sir. I was merely doing my duty in bringing these matters to your attention."

"Indeed," Smith said. "You have certainly done that, Constable. I believe you have acted with commendable zeal and some bravery, although, your interpretation of events may not be infallible."

Mendick said nothing; he knew that if he was correct, his superiors would accept the credit, but if he were wrong the blame would fall squarely on him. In that respect the police force was no different from the army.

"I am not at all sure about your alleged conspiracy involving Cumberland, or the King of Hanover as he is now, particularly as Sir Robert Trafford is known to me personally." Smith raised his eyebrows as if waiting for Mendick to comment. "On the other hand, it would be foolish to take any chances, and Her Majesty may well be under threat from the Chartists, so I shall advise that she leaves London for a time."

Mendick nodded. It seemed that Mr Smith was covering his options; nobody could blame him for advising the Queen to leave London in the face of massed radicals, and in doing so he was not completely dismissing the intelligence about the assassination attempt.

"And as for these Chartists . . ." Smith took a deep breath, "We shall swamp the streets with special constables, and we will use every uniformed officer we can scrape up. If the Chartists march down with ten thousand, I will have ten times ten thousand." He glanced down at his notes.

“I will ask the Duke of Wellington to take charge of the defence of London. He may be eighty years old, but he is still the best in the business.”

Mendick nodded. The thirty years since Waterloo had not dimmed Wellington’s military star.

Smith continued, “The Guards are on hand, of course, and we have yeomanry and line regiments within a day’s march. We will cover the bridges with artillery and have cavalry ready to break up the mobs.”

“My men are prepared,” Inspector Field said, “and we have already called up thousands of specials.” He looked at Mendick. “Your intelligence will ensure we are not caught unprepared, Constable.”

Again Mendick said nothing although he was impressed at the speed in which decisions were being made. With Smith and Field in charge of arrangements and Wellington commanding the military, it seemed that Monaghan would have to whistle for his utopia.

“You said the Chartists had infiltrated the telegraph system, Constable.” Smith ticked off another of the notes that he had made. “We will commandeer the system and, if necessary, we will take control of every railway line in Britain. By God, sir, we’ll show these Radicals.”

“Yes, sir, but remember not all the Chartists are set on destruction, sir. Most just want a decent standard of living . . .”

“Then let them work for it, Constable, let them work for it.” There was no sympathy in Smith’s face. “You, sir, have done your duty well. Rest assured that I intend to do no less. I will sew up London so tight that not even a Chartist mouse can enter, and to keep you happy, I will ask Her Majesty to retire to a safer place.” He nodded to Mendick. “Inspector Field will ensure you are present on that occasion, but for now, Constable," he held out his hand, "you have the thanks of the country."

Guessing that Smith was awarding him a great honour, Mendick took the hand. There would be no more reward for a man who was merely performing his duty.

"Right, Constable." Inspector Field resumed his authoritarian tone. "You had better get yourself cleaned up. You look more like somebody fit for the cells than one of the guardians of law and order. Report for duty as normal tomorrow. That will be all."

Pulling himself to attention, Mendick saluted. This seemed to be the end of his adventure in the north. There would be neither fanfare nor effusive praise. Inspector Field had reminded him that he was nothing more than a very small cog in a disciplined machine.

CHAPTER SIXTEEN

London: April 1848

Something was wrong. Perhaps it was an instinct developed through years of police work, but Mendick felt the tingle of apprehension the second he stepped into Hart's Lane, the street in which he lived. Ignoring the burning sensation in his legs, he increased his speed and stopped just outside the brick building with its narrow windows and sagging roof.

"Oh, good God in heaven!" His front door was swinging drunkenly on its single remaining hinge. Belatedly he remembered the Chartists had already paid his home a visit. Swearing, he pushed inside and looked around at the wreckage of what had once been his home.

Somebody had gone through the house systematically destroying everything that could be destroyed, either for the sheer love of destruction or in a calculated attack on his life and memories. Leaning against the wall, he took a deep breath.

The rocking chair on which he had spent so much time and labour had been broken; its curved runners were splintered, the back shattered and the seat with its carefully sewn cushions hacked to pieces. Worse, much worse, was the mirror, in front of which he always imagined Emma. Now the frame was destroyed and thrown to the four corners of the room and the glass scattered in a thousand reflective shards. The legs had been hacked from the table, his chair lay charred in the fireplace and the bed, his marriage bed, was smashed beyond repair. Feathers from the mattress were strewn all around the room and the fabric ripped by a sharp knife.

"Oh, sweet Lord," Mendick said. Possessions had never meant much to him, but everything in his house attached him to Emma.

"Somebody's been busy." Jennifer looked through the open door. She spoke quietly, hiding any emotion.

Mendick felt too sick to be surprised at her presence. "I thought you had gone on to manage your own life."

"I changed my mind." Jennifer hesitated, one foot inside the room. "May I come in?"

"Of course you can come in." Mendick extended a hand. "Mind you wipe your feet first, though; Emma was very house-proud."

He crunched over the broken glass to the far wall. Emma's silhouette had been torn down and was now scattered around the floor in a hundred ragged pieces. Ignoring Jennifer, he began to gather together the scraps of paper. He felt numb, as if he was looking from above as someone else knelt on the shattered glass, retrieving fragments of Emma's picture from the ground.

"What is it?" Lifting her skirt from the knee, Jennifer joined him. "What are we doing?"

"It's my wife's picture," he explained, and she nodded, scrabbling on the floor. After a few moments he warned her, "Watch your fingers for the broken glass."

"Only if you watch yours," she retorted. "I'm not completely useless, you know." Then she glanced at his face and looked hurriedly away. "I'm sorry; I should not have said that."

The portrait had been torn in half, then quartered, and then torn again, but with Jennifer's help Mendick managed to gather most of the pieces. He held them helplessly, unsure what to do next, until Jennifer reached out.

"Let me take care of them," she said, quietly.

"No."

For much of the time in the north he had clung to Emma's memories as a safe haven in a world gone mad. Now these shredded remains were the only tangible reminder he had, and he could not let go.

"Trust me," Jennifer pleaded, and her eyes were as sympathetic as he had ever seen them.

His nod was reluctant, and she reached over and gently took control.

"It will be all right, James. I promise."

He looked at the shambles of what had once made Emma proud and remembered Rachel Scott producing the document that Scotland Yard had sent to him. Perhaps it had been she who had ripped his life apart, but more likely she had sent a minion.

"Hell mend them," he said, hearing the break in his voice. "Hell mend whoever did this to my wife."

Suddenly any sympathy he had for Armstrong and the Chartists disappeared and with it his last reserves of strength. He began to shake, and he did not object when Jennifer put her arms around him.

"What's it all about, Emma? Tell me, what's it all about?"

“I’m sure I don’t know,” Jennifer told him, her eyes equally shadowed with memories.

For the first time since Emma’s funeral he gave way to his tears.

*

“Come along there, clear the way.” Back in uniform for the occasion, Mendick pushed along the platform of Nine Elms Station using his staff to ease away the crowd. In common with most railway stations in Britain, Nine Elms was used as a meeting spot for lovers and a haven for loungers, gazers and pickpockets as well as being a place for respectable travellers. None were pleased when the Metropolitan police arrived to clear them out of the way. There were protests, angry words and the occasional scuffle as young men pushed back and respectable ladies lifted parasols in self-defence, but eventually the police achieved a platform that was empty except for themselves and a few trusted railwaymen.

“Good work, gentlemen.” Inspector Field dabbed at the sweat that coursed down his round face. He glanced at Mendick. “We can only hope that all this effort is not wasted, Constable.”

“Let’s hope not, sir.” He tugged at the all-too-familiar stock which seemed already to be wearing a groove in his neck

With the travellers and loafers dispersed, a column of special constables marched through the neo-classical entrance. Mendick had imagined Smith would send a score of men, but hundreds streamed in to the station to ensure that no Chartists dared to enter. They took up position at every doorway and along every platform, standing sentinel with their staves held across beefy middle class chests and with disapproving frowns on faces more used to surveying balance sheets and poring over ledgers than braving the outdoors.

At around ten in the morning a dark green train chuffed into view, excess steam hissing from its boiler and proudly displaying the gold-painted name *Elk* on its side. The royal banner and decorative gingerbread work made it obvious for whom the three carriages were intended, and the open sided luggage van seemed like a scolded servant as it sulked in the rear.

"You stay close, Constable." Inspector Field had remained to ensure the operation proceeded smoothly. "You are the only person who knows what these alleged assassins look like, so I want you at my side."

"Yes, sir."

Mendick watched as the driver clamped his pipe between his teeth and reversed against the platform. Despite the importance of his charge he looked as excited as a marble statue. In contrast, the smaller of the two firemen stopped working to stare at the ranked police while his giant companion kept his back turned and continued to shovel coal.

The specials formed a cordon around the train, standing with their staves held ready and their faces impassive. For a moment Mendick wondered what sort of mess Eccles and his Volunteers would make of their immaculate ranks but pushed the thought aside.

"I can't imagine anybody would get through this lot, sir."

"That's the general idea, Constable."

At ten twenty there was a stir, and the men sprang to attention. The laconic engine driver stiffened in anticipation as a small convoy of coaches halted just outside the station and the passengers filed out in an orderly and colourful procession.

"It's Her Majesty," somebody whispered, and every eye swivelled to watch Queen Victoria cross the platform.

It was the first time Mendick had seen the Queen in person, and he was surprised at her youth and lack of size. He knew she was a small woman, but although she walked as proudly erect as any seven-foot guardsman, Queen Victoria was only five feet tall. Her entourage followed respectfully a few steps behind, headed by the elegant, moustached figure of Prince Albert and most of the royal children. A nursemaid carried Louise, the youngest of Victoria's brood.

A troop of superior ladies' maids came next, with two ladies-in-waiting in case Her Majesty should grow bored on the short trip south. Finally there was a gaggle of nurses and a group of dark-clothed equerries, valets and servants.

There was one other man there, and Mendick realised that despite his apparent cynicism, Inspector Field was not taking any chances. Foster, the veteran detective from Scotland Yard, was also with the royal family. Although he posed as one of the servants, he looked the very opposite of servile as he stared into the face of every special constable he passed and examined the engine driver as if he were some sort of personal enemy.

"Is the royal train expected to stop en route, sir?" Mendick wondered, but Field shook his head.

"Not even once, Constable. Her Majesty will travel directly for Gosport, where she will be conveyed to Osborne House in the Isle of Wight. And in case you think Hanover might attempt some rash attack in the Solent, Admiral Ogle has a squadron of the Royal Navy standing by."

"You seem to have thought of everything," Mendick said.

"Aye, but it was your intelligence that brought Her Majesty's possible danger to our attention," Field graciously admitted. "And we've spent a great deal of money and inconvenienced a great many people in humouring your allegations."

Appearing as relaxed as if she were out for a stroll in Windsor Great Park, the Queen passed along the platform, with the parade of specials stiffening to attention and the uniformed officers saluting. Only Foster and one of the dark clothed servants looked elsewhere as they scanned the station and everybody inside.

"Who's that, sir?" Mendick nodded toward the inquisitive servant. "I seem to recognise the face, although I am damned if I remember from where."

"How the hell should I know who he is? He looks like one of Her Majesty's footmen, or maybe an equerry, a cousin of the blood or similar." Inspector Field was having difficulty keeping his spreading stomach under control as he stood to attention. "Keep saluting and don't ask damn-fool questions."

Prince Albert held the door open for the Queen to board, and then the royal children swarmed aboard. While the nurses curtsied to the railway official who helped them into the rearmost carriage, the ladies-in-waiting were too imperious to even acknowledge his existence.

"How many servants does she need for one train trip?" Mendick wondered but quickly closed his mouth when Field glared at him.

There was a flurry of petticoats, skirts and bonnets as the female servants boarded. The third stumbled, giggling, so that Foster had to help her up, but most kept their heads down and their dignity intact. The male servants were next, separated from their female counterparts by the royal carriage, and finally Foster slipped aboard, taking a last long stare over the platform before he closed the door.

"So that's that then; all safe and serene," Field said. "Duty done, Constable, and we can get back to our proper business of defending the city against these Chartist friends of yours."

"James!"

The voice was so unexpected that Mendick started. He turned to see Jennifer waving through the assembled top hats of the specials.

"Who in God's name is that?" Inspector Field pulled at his whiskers.

"Jennifer Ogden," Mendick said. "She wouldn't come here without a good reason." He raised his voice. "Stand aside there. Let her through!"

The ranks opened, and Jennifer bustled up.

"How did you get past the specials?" Field sounded more intrigued than annoyed.

"I said I was your daughter," Jennifer told him quickly. "But watch that man." She pointed to the closed door of the male servants' carriage, now partially concealed as the engine ejected surplus steam. "You can't let him go with the Queen!"

"What man?" Mendick asked. "They're all royal servants."

"Maybe they are, but I've seen him before. When I worked at Trafford Hall, I saw him visit Sir Robert."

"That doesn't mean anything," Field told her. "Maybe he worked there too."

"He wasn't dressed as a servant then." Ignoring Field, Jennifer nudged Mendick. "Are you going to take the chance, James? You're here to make sure that Sir Robert Trafford does not murder the Queen; you can't allow a friend of his to travel with her."

"That bloody servant!" Mendick swore. "I knew there was something wrong about him."

He began to move forward, easing through the uniformed ranks and barging aside the specials. He had brought the information about the intended assassination in an attempt to save the Queen, but instead he had persuaded her to travel on a closed train with her killer. All his efforts had only managed to put the Queen in even greater danger.

"Constable! What are you going to do?" Field was only a step behind.

"I'm going to save her Majesty's life," Mendick shouted over his shoulder.

The train was moving, pulling slowly through clouds of hissing steam and shrouding the assembled specials in smuts of black smoke.

"I'll telegraph Gosport to warn Foster!" Inspector Field tried to shout above the engine. "What's the man's name? I said, what's the man's name?"

As he strained to board the van, Mendick grabbed at the handle of the leading carriage, missed, and stumbled onto the platform. He fought to recover his balance and tried again as the central and then the final carriage thundered past. Lunging forward, he clutched hold of the wooden struts, gasping at the sudden strain on his arm.

"James!" That was Jennifer's voice, hoarse with anxiety.

Swearing, he clutched at the struts as the train rattled through the station, building up speed for the run down to the south coast.

Aware of the gaping faces of the specials, he clung on desperately, with his feet scraping along the platform and the wood rough under his fingers. He felt the top hat flick off his head and for an instant saw it suspended in the air before it vanished in the wake of the train. If he slipped, he would go the same way; there would be a second of apprehension and then a dragging, agonising plunge along the track.

He had to get on board before his strength failed.

As he stretched, Mendick felt the scab over his burns split, but he fought the pain and slid onto the wooden floor of the van, probing for purchase with his foot. He slipped, yelled, and then a brawny hand grabbed his arm and hauled him inside.

"What in God's name are you doing, Mr Policeman?" The guard was around forty, with oiled whiskers and large blue eyes that seemed about to burst from his face. His dark uniform was immaculate, the red trimming echoing the buffer beams of the train. "People normally buy a ticket if they want to go by rail." He grinned hugely at his own joke.

"Thanks."

Mendick took deep breaths to regain his strength. The train increased speed, whirling out of Nine Elms Station with its royal passengers sitting comfortably inside and a probable assassin loose in one of the carriages. There was a sudden nerve-rending screech and a blast of steam clouded the full length of the train.

"Right, Mr Policeman." The guard helped him upright. "Are you all right? Suppose you tell me why you're here?"

"There's a plot to assassinate the Queen," Mendick explained quickly and saw instant comprehension in the guard's face.

“So that’s why she’s leaving the city!” The man’s whiskers bounced as he nodded. “But that doesn’t explain why you are on my train?”

“You don’t understand,” Mendick spoke rapidly. “The assassin is here! He’s on this train!”

The guard stared, open mouthed. ‘My God! Where? Can you stop him?’

“If I can get to the front carriage . . .”

“The carriages are all independent saloons,” the guard interrupted. “You can’t get through from one to the other.”

“Is there not a way around the side? How do you retrieve the luggage?”

“This is a royal train.” The guard controlled his obvious anxiety. “The passengers board at one station and leave at the destination. You cannot move from one carriage to another.” He thought for a moment. “Unless you go over the top.”

For a moment Mendick contemplated the swaying carriages rattling through London at over twenty miles an hour.

“So that’s what I will do.”

It was a simple task for an ex-climbing boy to hoist himself onto the roof of the rearmost carriage, but not so easy to walk forward through the sooty smuts. The carriages were only thirty feet long, the roofs had an easy camber and the ornate railings ensured he could not fall, but when Mendick stretched across to the royal carriage, he blanched. The couplings jolted eight feet beneath him, and the streets of London whirled past at what seemed to be breakneck speed.

Taking a deep breath, he intoned Restiaux' favourite mantra:

“Lord, I shall be very busy these next few minutes; I may forget thee, but do not forget me.”

He tensed himself, but just before he jumped, the train eased into a bend and he saw directly inside the royal carriage. It was a picture of luxury more intense than he had ever imagined, with a red and white Axminster carpet on the floor, padded white walls to match the upholstery on the chairs, frilled curtains on the windows and a marble table complete with flowers. Even the ceiling was elaborately decorated. For a second Mendick compared the splendour of this temporary carriage with the squalor of the Holy Land or the endless brick terraces of Manchester.

The stark contrast wrenched at his stomach with its reminder of the essential decency of the Chartists and the simple justice of their demands. Why should some people have a surfeit of indulgence while others struggled to merely eat? Maybe he had been on the wrong side all along? He glanced again, studying the woman who ruled over such inequality and injustice.

Draped in a long dark dress that failed to disguise her somewhat dumpy figure, the Queen was listening as Prince Albert read from a book. Mendick imagined it to be one of the novels of Walter Scott that Her Majesty loved so much. She lay on her couch smiling up at him, and Mendick recognised the expression in her eyes. Emma had looked like that when he had worked on her profile.

The train straightened from the bend and his view into paradise ended, but he knew what he must do. He could not allow Trafford and Hanover to plunge the country into civil war. Any other thoughts were worse than madness; they were treason. It was duty that had kept him sane when Emma had died; he had no other option.

Stepping over the gingerbread work, he balanced for a second and then jumped the gap. He hung suspended over that rattling, moving space for a long, heart-stopping second then landed heavily on all fours. Exhaling noisily, he padded towards the third and foremost carriage. Foster was in there, as was the servant that Jennifer had identified. He watched for a moment, hoping for another fortuitous bend so he could look inside, but the line stretched straight ahead.

Taking a deep breath, Mendick leaped over the final gap, landing as softly as possible so as not to alarm the occupants. There was a door at either end of the carriage, and he poised himself above the nearest, gripped the rail running along the roof and allowed his body to drop until he hung downward with the wind battering his body.

Peering in the window, he glimpsed Foster's cynical face, released his left hand and grabbed for the door handle just as the train hurtled around a curve. Coughing in a sudden gust of smoke, he tried to twist the handle open, but his palm slithered on the polished brass.

"Foster!" He bellowed, pitching his voice above the thunder of the engine. "It's me! Open up!"

As the train tilted at an astonishing angle Mendick felt the muscles of his right arm scream in protest. There was a sudden screech and a blast of steam as the handle shifted in his hand and the door swung open, smashing him backward against the body of the carriage.

"Sweet God in heaven!"

He released the handle and clutched the roof bar trying to ease his legs around the madly oscillating door and wishing that he was as supple as he had been as a boy.

"Foster!"

Mendick struggled around, probing for the interior with his feet, but as the train curved into a straight, the door slammed shut on to his thigh. He yelled and writhed as the heavy metal bit into his burned legs, and it took all his will power to release the roof bar and thrust himself inside the carriage where he landed heavily with his legs protesting in pain and the breath rasping in his chest.

"Mendick!" Foster hauled him upright. "Are you all right? What in hell's name are you up to?"

"I'm doing your job for you." He did not like Foster, but it was immensely reassuring to have that misanthropic face glowering into his and those hard, wary eyes examining him. "You already know about the plot to assassinate the Queen?"

"Of course; that's why I am here."

"I think that one of the servants is the assassin," Mendick explained hurriedly. "Trafford must have ordered him on board as soon as he learned we intended to send the Queen to safety."

"It's all under control." Foster was almost smiling as he shook his head. "I already know exactly what is happening in this train, and it is not as you imagine."

Mendick glanced into the carriage, seeing a mass of anonymous faces, none of which merited a second look.

"We have to save the Queen!"

Foster put a reassuring hand on his shoulder.

"It's all under control. Just do as I say." He faced the servants again, his voice quiet but carrying an unmistakable authority. "Gentlemen, you cannot leave this carriage, so do not try. We suspect that there is an assassin on this train, so if anybody does try to follow us, rest assured that I will blow his head clean off." He left the threat hanging in the air. "Now, Constable, just follow me."

It was only then that Mendick realised that the carriage was split in two, with the servants confined to the rearmost two-thirds and a heavy door separating them from the forward section.

"Should we not be guarding the Queen?"

"Relax, Constable. I know what I am doing." Reaching inside his frockcoat, Foster produced a double-barrelled pistol and checked the percussion lock. He replaced it in his pocket, slid his blackjack down his sleeve and tapped its lead-weighted end on his hand. His smile was not pleasant. "Now we are ready for any trouble."

In contrast to the remainder of the train, the front section of the carriage was little more than an ordinary van, with a neat pile of bundles and boxes that were probably indispensable to the royals. The second of the carriage's external doors was firmly closed.

Mendick glanced around, feeling his tension drain away at Foster's quiet assurance.

"What's happening?"

"We're happening."

The servant who had followed them was so nondescript he would be unnoticeable in a crowd of three, but as soon as he spoke, Mendick he realised where he had seen him before.

"You were the barman in the Beehive!"

He reached for the truncheon in the tail of his coat as a pepperpot pistol appeared in the barman's hand, propelled from his sleeve by some spring device. Mendick weaved sideways, grabbing at the barman's arm, but Foster smashed his blackjack on his shoulder so he yelled, staggering backward.

“Close the connecting door,” Foster ordered, and the barman leaped to obey, slotting home a steel locking bar for extra security.

“Foster!” Mendick yelled. “What the hell . . .?”

“What do you think?” Foster asked and swung his blackjack again.

The blow was aimed at the point of Mendick’s jaw, and he blocked with difficulty, feeling the flaring pain as the sausage of sand and lead smashed against his right arm. He swore and staggered as the barman hooked a leg behind his knees. One push from Foster and he was lying flat down on the floor, staring upward.

“What in God’s name . . .?”

He tried to roll away, but Foster was waiting, blackjack raised ready to crash down on his head. Trained in a score of barrack room brawls, Mendick reared upward, butting his forehead hard into Foster’s chest and following up with a straight-fingered jab to his throat.

But Foster was also an experienced street fighter and turned sideways so Mendick’s fingers jarred against his shoulder instead. The barman landed a roundhouse punch that bounced pointlessly from Mendick’s side. It was obvious the barman was no warrior, so Mendick ignored him to press home his attack on Foster.

With his right arm virtually useless after the blow from the blackjack, he had to use his weaker left, feinting for Foster’s eyes before trying to ram his doubled knee into his groin. Foster jerked back, but as Mendick was about to press his advantage, the barman smashed something hard and heavy over his head, sending him crashing to the floor once more.

This time Foster made sure. He lifted his boot and stamped hard on Mendick's chest, driving the air from his lungs before landing a backhand that crashed his head against the side of the carriage. Mendick lay stunned, unable to move as Foster glared down at him.

"Open the door," Foster ordered, "and we'll throw the bastard out."

"Why go to all that bother?" The barman shrugged. "If we leave him here, he'll die with the others."

"Very poetic," Foster said. "The gallant police officer dying to protect the Queen who does not even know his name." He kicked Mendick again. "You don't understand what this is all about, do you?" He leaned closer. "You have no idea how stupid you are, do you? Do you remember who recommended that you work in the north?"

Mendick glared his hatred.

"I recommended you, because then I would know exactly who was up there, a Johnny Raw who knew nothing and did not have the sense to work it out."

Mendick struggled to rise, but Foster put his instep against his throat and pushed him back down.

"Stay still, you bastard."

"It was you!" When it came, the realisation made him wonder at his own stupidity. "You told the Chartists who I was, you told them my address, and you provided the book with the pictures of every Scotland Yard officer."

"Well done, Mendick." Foster was grinning now. "You're correct, but far too slow."

"But why? Why betray me? And why work with this man? He is going to assassinate the Queen!" Again Mendick struggled to rise, but Foster thrust down with his boot, grinding the heel against his throat.

"You're still a fool, Mendick. He's not going to assassinate the Queen; I am."

"Why? You're a Scotland Yard officer!"

"I know exactly what I am. I was one of Bobby Peel's original bluebottles. I have put my life on the line every day since 1829, and what do I have to show for it? Enough blunt to fill the arse of a very small mouse and a future of poverty and the workhouse. Sir Robert Trafford has offered me a fortune, Mendick, so think of that in your last few minutes alive."

"You're a murdering hound, Foster! At least the Chartists have a genuine grievance for their rebellion, but you," Mendick grabbed at Foster's ankle and tried to wrestle it away, "you're the worst sort of traitor."

Foster laughed. "A traitor is only somebody who supported the loser, Mendick. Once King Ernest is on the throne, the history books will write me as a hero of the real dynasty. You'll be the traitor, Mendick, the man who tried to prevent history from taking its natural course."

"I'm a loyal officer . . ."

"You're an impoverished fool. I've seen your home, remember, with its pathetic sticks of furniture. Broken furniture now. Is that just reward for your years of service?"

"It was you." Mendick wriggled beneath Foster's foot, feeling the terrible agony of frustration. "You smashed my mirror! You ripped up Emma's picture!"

"You smashed my mirror!" Foster mocked, bending close. "You ripped up my picture! Listen to yourself, bleating about nothings while we're altering the destiny of a dynasty."

Mendick felt his hatred mount, replacing the frustration and sorrow and loss. He looked away, aware that his feelings must be transparent and unwilling that Foster should know exactly how much he hurt. For the first time in his life he wanted to kill somebody, not just because it was his duty, but out of sheer loathing.

"Foster," he said, "I'll be coming for you."

Foster kicked him again, taking time to put real force behind the blow. "How will you do that, Mendick, when you're dead?"

Taking a silver hunter from his waistcoat, the barman squinted at it. "We'd better hurry, Mr Foster, or we'll be caught in the crash . . ." He looked away when Foster glowered at him.

Mendick forced a mocking laugh.

"A train crash! Is that the best you can think of? The most powerful monarchy in the world and you're going to destroy it by crashing a train. How utterly unimaginative!"

He grunted as Foster kicked him again, the hard boot thudding against already painful ribs, but he began to think furiously. The authorities would keep the line clear, so there was no possibility of a train coming toward them; by crash, Foster could only mean a derailment. He ran his mind over the route: Farnborough, Winchfield, Basingstoke, Andover Road, Winchester and finally Gosport.

The line was fairly straightforward, a quiet run over a pastoral landscape, except for one spot near the ancient market town of Godalhurst, where the train would have to climb up the Downs and then negotiate a bend onto a narrow viaduct. That would be his choice for a train crash, but how would he do it? Easy – plant explosives on the viaduct and jump clear when the train slowed for the climb.

"That would be the trap you set at Godalhurst, then?" Mendick enjoyed the momentary surprise on Foster's face. "We know all about that one, Foster, and there are men waiting for you at the viaduct."

"How do you know?" The barman stepped back. "How does he know, Mr Foster?"

"He doesn't," Foster said. "He's bluffing. I would know if he knew."

"You'll soon find out, won't you?" Mendick grunted as Foster pressed his foot hard against his chest. "They hang traitors, Foster, and your pal there will enjoy spending the remainder of his life in Van Diemen's Land."

The shriek of the whistle startled both assailants, and Mendick used the distraction to grab hold of Foster's foot and push it from his chest, ramming the detective hard against the barman so both crashed against the side of the carriage. He rolled free of the tangled bodies and stamped on Foster's hand, relishing the sensation of breaking bones as he twisted his heel.

"You wrecked my house, Foster." Lifting his foot, he smashed it down against Foster's chest. "You destroyed my wife's rocking chair, Foster." He kicked out, catching the Scotland Yard man under the chin and throwing him against the side of the carriage. "I'm going to kill you, Foster!"

"You flash your gab too much, bluebottle bastard!" The barman thrust his pepperpot revolver against the base of Mendick's skull.

Lashing back with his fist, Mendick was surprised when the barman ducked away. The return blow cracked against his temple, momentarily unbalancing him, and then the barman brought down the pistol in a short but effective chop against his head.

The steel floor of the carriage seemed to rise toward him as he fell, and then Foster was taking revenge for his smashed hand by kicking madly into his body.

"Mr Foster!" The barman restrained him. "We haven't time for that. We've things to do before we reach Godalhurst."

After landing a final kick, Foster pulled a silver watch from his pocket. "Aye, it's about time. Let's get to work."

"What about him?" The barman jerked a thumb toward Mendick.

Foster grunted. "Tie him and leave him; he's in no condition to do anything."

Mendick groaned. His ribs were on fire, and the burn blisters on his legs had opened up, weeping yellow moisture through his trousers and onto the floor. He watched, unable to move as Foster opened the door and swung himself outside.

The barman ripped a cord from one of the royal packages and looped it around Mendick's ankles before attaching his wrists to a strut on the inside of the carriage.

"Lie quiet now," the barman mocked and followed Foster outside, leaving Mendick alone.

For a long minute Mendick nursed his pain then forced himself to move. Foster had betrayed him to the Chartists, Foster had played him for a fool ever since that day in the Holy Land, Foster had destroyed Emma's picture.

Pain stabbed at his chest as he shifted sideways, toward the metal strut running the length of the carriage wall. He had hoped he might unravel the knot with his teeth, but the barman had done a good job. He swore, jerking at the cord in frustration. If he did not escape, Foster would crash the train, the Queen would die, and a new Hanoverian dynasty would rule the country. Despite all that, it was the memory of Emma's ripped picture that made him fight the pain.

He tried again, pulling at the cord until it began to slide, oh-so-slowly, along the metal strut. He tugged, ignoring the warm blood that dribbled down his wrists as he sawed the cord against the metal, biting away the pain as he thought of Foster tearing at Emma's picture.

One by one the strands of the cord frayed and parted until a final agonised effort wrenched it apart. Gasping, Mendick hugged his wrists to him until the initial torture faded and he could untie his ankles and plan his next move.

He hauled himself upright, wincing, but the memory of Emma encouraged him. She was urging him to move, to save his life and that of the Queen. Holding onto the spars for support, he staggered as the train swayed around a great curve. Foster had gone outside, so he had to follow. He had to endure the pain as Emma had suffered the agony of childbirth. Edging onwards, he wrestled with the iron catch on the external door and thrust it open.

The blast of fresh air and soot-smuts nearly tore him from the tiny metal step, and he looked forward, across the tender and on to the engine. The driver was standing very stiffly, with Foster's pistol pressed against the back of his neck. The barman leaned back negligently, pointing the pepperpot at the firemen.

The railway line ran on into the distance, twin steel arrows that should mark security for the Queen and stability for the nation. The lovely Surrey countryside spread on either side, a picture of perfection leading to the stiff climb of the Downs where, far in the distance, tall stone arches marked the fateful Godalhurst viaduct.

Mendick swore; the tender was rattling ahead of him, with the nearest two thirds securely covered, but a haze of black dust above the loose coal that slid and slithered next to the engine. Beyond the tender the engine footplate was open to the elements but crowded with the three railwaymen and two potential murderers. The only way to stop Foster was to clamber forwards.

Gasping at the pain from his ribs, he hauled himself to the front of the carriage, braced himself and stretched across the couplings and onto the coal tender. The covered part was easy enough, but the final third was treacherous. One irregular coal lump shifted beneath his feet, and he fell heavily, landing agonizingly on his injured ribs.

Biting away the pain, he rose, very aware that the ground was a moving blur on each side and hoping that Foster was too preoccupied with the driver to turn around. The firemen were still working hard, ignoring him as they shovelled coal into the furnace.

"What the Hell are they doing?" Mendick mumbled to himself as he negotiated the treacherous coal, one hand pressed to his ribs and the other scrabbling for a hold on the edge of the truck. He saw the driver grasp one of the levers that worked the engine, but Foster pushed him back, gesticulating with his pistol.

Mendick had no interest in steam engines, but he knew that the fire heated the boiler, which supplied steam to power the engine. If the driver did not regulate the pressure, the boiler could burst, with calamitous consequences. Only then did Mendick decipher Foster's plan. By having the firemen constantly add fuel, he was increasing the pressure inside the boiler, so all he had to do was prevent the driver from releasing excess steam until the whole thing exploded. Naturally Foster and the barman would have already left the train when it was travelling slowly up the incline of the Downs.

If the Queen and her family were not killed outright, Foster and the barman would be on hand to finish them off. It would seem as if the exploding boiler had caused the crash. Nobody would suspect King Ernest; he would step on to the throne, and the white horse of Hanover would be back in its British stable. The plot was so simple that for a second Mendick admired its audacity. He then thought of the innocent victims: the maids and nannies and cooks and could only despise its inherent evil.

The train was climbing now, producing more smoke as it struggled with the incline of the Downs, and the driver was shouting at Foster and pointing toward his levers and dials.

Wiping sweat from his forehead, the nearer and smaller of the firemen stopped shovelling for a second, but the barman rammed his pistol against the man's back and pushed him forward. The fireman staggered and would have fallen into the furnace if his giant companion had not extended a hand to catch him.

The train was slowing by the second, tilting to one side so that Mendick could pick out villages and cottages spread out like a spring green map at the foot of the Downs. He sensed the driver's confusion as the steam pressure mounted. The driver pointed to one of the dials, where a hand was edging steadily into the red, and lunged toward one of the levers. With his broken left hand awkward within his jacket, Foster slashed him with the pistol.

"Stop!"

Mendick jumped forward, landing on the very edge of the footplate and tottering as the train rattled onto the top of the incline. He swore, clutching at his chest as his ribs screamed protest.

"Shoot the driver!" The barman shouted above the noise of the engine. "He's done his job. Look!" He pointed to the dial where the hand indicated the farthest edge of the red danger zone.

"It's going to blow!" the driver yelled, high-pitched. "It's going to bloody *blow!*"

They were cresting the Downs: the ridge falling away on both sides and the tall stone arches of the Godalhurst viaduct striding across the gap a hundred yards ahead. As the firemen continued to shovel coal into the furnace the wheels altered their rhythm and the train began to pick up speed again. Mendick marvelled at the timing involved.

If Foster and the barman jumped now, they would be safe, but the train would roll on to the viaduct, pick up speed and explode. The lucky would die at once, the survivors would plunge onto the ground far below. If, by chance, the Queen or any of her children were still alive, Foster or the barman could finish them off.

"You can die with the rest." Foster aimed at Mendick, his face totally devoid of expression.

Mendick threw himself forward, knocking the barman aside as he grabbed at Foster, but the Scotland Yard detective was equally as agile and more experienced. Turning his injured arm away, he raised his right elbow and caught Mendick a glancing blow to the eye, not enough to damage but sufficient to deflect his rush. Mendick fell sideways, put out his hand for balance and yelled as he touched hot metal. The pain forced him back, and Foster was in control.

The muzzle of the pistol looked huge as it focused on Mendick's forehead, and the sneering face behind the weapon seemed far away and out of focus. Mendick saw Foster's finger whiten as he increased pressure on the trigger and the hammer rose to its apex. Within half a second it would begin the rapid descent that would end when it made contact with the percussion cap, sending a half-inch thick lead ball crashing into his skull.

He had failed. Foster would win, Ernest of Hanover would take the throne, and the future of Britain would change forever. But Emma was waiting for him, smiling just beyond a dim veil, and her hand was stretching toward him in welcome.

"Hey!"

The deep voice was shockingly familiar as the large fireman moved up. In the excitement, nobody had paid him any attention, but now he danced forward, one huge arm sweeping Foster aside as if he were a featherweight.

"It's me, Mr Mendick."

"Peter!" Mendick looked up in surprise as Peter grabbed Foster's hand and removed the pistol as easily as he would a rattle from an infant.

"I got myself a job, just like the lady said," Peter told him as he casually lifted Foster by the back of his neck. "What will I do with him?"

"Throw him overboard, please."

Peter obliged and tossed Foster out of the moving train. He hit the ground at the side of the railway and rolled rapidly four or five times before he lay still.

The barman was already locked in a desperate struggle with the driver, each man's hand clamped on the throat of the other; Mendick reached across and dragged the barman away until Peter was able to fetch him a single blow to the chin and push him after Foster.

Immediately he was free, the driver leaped frantically to his charge and pulled on a brass lever. There was a scream of escaping steam, and the hand wavered from the red mark.

"What in God's name was that all about?" he asked, checking the line ahead.

"We've just saved the Queen from an assassination attempt," Mendick explained and laughed until he fainted from the agony of his smashed ribs.

CHAPTER SEVENTEEN

London: May 1848

Mendick leaned back in his new chair at his new table in the otherwise empty room, scanning the pictures and desultorily reading the pages of the *Illustrated London News*. He read about the 'monster meeting' of the Chartists at Kennington Common on the twelfth of April and the presentation of the petition to the House of Commons. Apparently Feargus O'Connor had been extremely polite to the authorities. Thanks partly to Mendick's warning, the government had been prepared for great violence, with pickets of the Foot Guards at the park gates, detachments of yeomanry hidden around the capital, artillery ready to hold the bridges over the Thames and armed men waiting at every public building.

In the event, there was hardly even a skirmish as the Chartists returned home peacefully. With O'Connor past his prime and Josiah Armstrong under arrest, they lacked conviction. Without his chief supporter William Monaghan had proved a disappointment. He was a fine orator but not noted for being in the forefront of any physical action and had hardly protested when the police arrested him. Mendick nodded sourly; things were as they ought to be, he had helped prevent a bloody outbreak in London and should be pleased.

He read on, learning that the Chartists had grossly exaggerated the numbers of those who signed the petition, and many of the signatures proved to be forgeries. He smiled sourly when he learned that the Duke of Wellington had apparently signed the Charter on numerous occasions, and the final signatory had been Queen Victoria herself. Not surprisingly, the House of Commons once again rejected the petition.

"So things have not improved for the working classes," he murmured. "After all that effort, all that planning, all their hopes, they are as neglected as they ever were.'

Jennifer looked over her shoulder at him and nodded.

"Some things never change," she said. "But others do. You'll have heard about Sir Robert Trafford?"

Mendick shook his head, folding the newspaper neatly.

"Not a word."

"The bailiffs got him; he tried to run abroad, but they stopped him as he boarded the ship, and he's locked away in the Queen's Bench Prison while they sell everything he once owned. For him, that's worse than being hanged."

Mendick nodded. "That sounds like justice," he agreed. "Where did you read about it?"

"In the scandal pages, of course," Jennifer grinned to him. "That's where you find the juicy bits."

"Let's have a look."

He took her paper and she pointed to the page. Most of the names in the columns dealing with society balls and marriages meant nothing to him, but one small piece interested him. Tucked away between an advertisement proclaiming that Monsieur Meyer had a large selection of *corsets perfectionnés* and another announcing that James Lough, chimney sweep, was ready to execute all orders with which he may be entrusted were four significant lines:

Miss Rachel Scott, natural daughter of Sir Henry Scott of Southerby House and first cousin to Sir Robert Trafford of Trafford Hall, has been found drowned off Heligoland. It was supposed that Miss Scott had been swimming with some friends from Hanover, but they have proved elusive in giving intelligence of her recent activities. On her mother's side, Miss Scott was a distant relative of Ernest, King of Hanover.

"So Uncle Ernest was not pleased," Mendick said.

"It could have been an accident," Jennifer pointed out. Turning around, she placed a picture on the wall and stood back, hands on her hips. "There now, that is back where it belongs." She stepped aside so that Mendick could see.

Emma's silhouette had returned. Jennifer had taken some backing paper and glued all the torn fragments of the picture on top, fitting them together like a jigsaw, but so cleverly that Mendick could hardly see the tears. Rising from the chair, he stepped closer, touching the familiar image.

"Welcome home, Emma," he said, and the bittersweet memories crowded back. "Welcome home." He smiled to Jennifer. "I cannot thank you enough for that," he said.

"That's what friends are for," Jennifer told him.

They held each others' eyes for a few minutes, and then Jennifer sighed and reached for her coat.

"Well, James, I think I should be getting along. I cannot spend all my day making your house more comfortable, you know."

Mendick shook his head, holding out his hand. "You don't have to," he said. "You are always welcome to stay here . . ."

"As what?"

The words were too quick to be casual. Jennifer held his gaze and then allowed her eyes to drift over to the silhouette of Emma.

"As a substitute? Or as a friend?" There was no bitterness in her smile. "We both know that I would not accept the former, and the etiquette of respectability dictates that I could not remain here as the latter."

"Stay," Mendick asked. "I don't know as what, but stay."

She shook her head and then bent to kiss him softly on the mouth. "It would not work, James."

He helped her on with her coat, handed over her battered bonnet and watched as she fixed it in place with the wickedly long hatpin. Giving him one last smile, she stepped outside and softly closed the door. A piece of coal fell from the grate, and sighing, Mendick lifted the tongs and replaced it in the fire.

HISTORICAL NOTE

Chartism arose after the 1832 Reform Act, which granted a limited franchise to the male middle classes and nothing to the workers. The Chartists created a demand for parliamentary reform, based on the famous six points:

Equal electoral districts
Universal male suffrage
Payments for MPs
Annual parliaments
Vote by secret ballot
Abolition of the property qualification for Members of Parliament

The Kennington Park Chartist rally took place on April 12th 1848. Feargus O'Connor, the fiery leader of the Chartists, had threatened dire action if the government did not accept the Chartist petition and agree to their points. In the event, he handed the petition to the House of Commons, but there was no major trouble. Parliament did not bother to debate any of the Six Points.

Chartism was arguably the largest working class movement of the nineteenth century and is still the subject of much historical debate. By the 1840s it had split into two groups, Moral Force and Physical Force Chartism. While the Moral Force Chartists hoped to persuade the government to adopt their demands, the devotees of physical force preferred a more muscular approach. It is possible that this split in the Chartist aims contributed to their eventual demise.

The 1848 rally created great consternation in London, and Queen Victoria was hustled away to the Isle of Wight by special train. However, there was no attempt on her life during the journey. The other details of her journey to Gosport are also fictitious, including the existence of the Godalhurst viaduct.

The 1848 petition was the last surge of Chartism, which faded away with the more prosperous years of the 1850s and the death of O'Connor, but the ideas remained. Although none of the six points were achieved during the lifetime of the Chartist movement, all save annual parliaments have since been incorporated into the British electoral system.

Ernest Augustus, King of Hanover and Duke of Cumberland, and the fifth son of King George III, was indeed near to the British throne, and he was rumoured to have murdered his valet. His cruelty in the army is well attested. He was involved with the Orange Order and was suspected of having a son after an incestuous relationship with his sister. Although there were rumours that Ernest desired the British throne, there is no record of Ernest Augustus attempting to murder Queen Victoria in 1848. However, although the amended Treason Act of that year was apparently intended to curb the Chartists, it would also have been useful against any attempt to suborn the monarchy by a foreign potentate.

Malcolm Archibald was born in Edinburgh and holds a history degree from Dundee University. He has also just completed a Masters in Urban History at Dundee University. Malcolm has worked as a lecturer and in historical research as well as in a variety of other jobs. He writes mainly historical fiction with the occasional venture into folklore and believes that history should be accessible to everyone. A winner of The Dundee Book Prize 2005, he has published several novels with us. Among the most notable are *Powerstone* and *Mother Law.* Malcolm lives in Moray with his wife Cathy.

Other Books by Malcolm Archibald

www.malcolmarchibald.com

Bridges, Islands and Villages of the Forth: Lang Syne Press, 1990
Scottish Battles: Chambers, 1990
Scottish Myths and Legends: Chambers, 1992
Scottish Animal and Bird Folklore: St Andrew Press, 1996
Across the Pond: Chapters from the Atlantic: Whittles, 2001
Soldier of the Queen: Fledgling Press, 2003
Whalehunters, Dundee and the Arctic Whalers: Mercat, 2004
*Whales for the Wizard:*Polygon Press, 2005,
Dundee Book Prize 2005
Horseman of the Veldt: Fledgling Press, 2005
Selkirk of the Fethan: Fledgling Press, 2005
Aspects of the Boer War: Fledgling Press, 2005
Mother Law: a parchment for Dundee: Fledgling Press, 2006
Pryde's Rock: Severn House, 2007
Powerstone: Fledgling Press, 2008